What was wrong with her?

No guy had ever had this effect on her. Maddie rubbed her hand along her arm where the rough stubble of Haki's jaw and the warmth of his breath had inadvertently caressed her skin. Even the vibrations of his rich voice, when he'd gotten permission to touch her, had made all the hairs along her skin sway and dance.

She wanted this feeling to go away. It was overpowering. It was dangerous. It betrayed Pippa.

Maddie set her fork down and took a drink of water. Maybe she needed a shower or maybe she was still jet-lagged. That had to be it.

"I know what's on your mind, Maddie," Pippa called out from the far end of the long wood table.

Maddie's stomach churned. "You do?"

Dear Reader,

After I wrote *The Promise of Rain*, many of you asked me if spunky little Pippa would ever have her own story. Pippa was only four at the time! Still, there was something about her and her friend Haki that I couldn't let go of and, after the children in the following books, including introverted Maddie in *After the Silence*, endured the impossible and stole my heart, I simply couldn't quiet their stories.

Every Serengeti Sunrise takes readers back to the wilds of Kenya about fifteen years after the third book, *Through the Storm*. I never imagined sweet little Pippa's future involving a love triangle, but both love and a writer's imagination work in mysterious ways. I also felt guilty writing this story because Maddie, Haki and Pippa are good, kind souls who deserve to find true love. It made me wonder about the many different kinds of love and the complexity of relationships. Love is priceless, but it opens the door to pain. Would you turn down the chance to grow old with your soul mate if it meant hurting someone else you loved? Is being true to your heart selfish? Or is it *always* the right thing to do?

The Kenyan Wildlife Service is a real organization dedicated to protecting Kenya's unique and extraordinary wildlife. Its teams are on the front lines, fighting poaching and providing emergency veterinary care to wildlife, including elephants. Their conservation efforts, along with those of the smaller rescue and rehab groups they cooperate with, are critical in the fight against poaching.

My door is open at www.rulasinara.com, where you can sign up for my newsletter, get information on all of my books and find links to my social media hangouts.

Wishing you love, peace and courage in life,

Rula Sinara

HEARTWARMING

Every Serengeti Sunrise

───

USA TODAY Bestselling Author

Rula Sinara

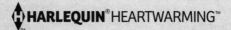

Recycling programs
for this product may
not exist in your area.

ISBN-13: 978-0-373-36864-8

Every Serengeti Sunrise

Copyright © 2017 by Rula Sinara

This edition published by arrangement with Harlequin Books S.A.

For questions and comments about the quality of this book, please contact us at CustomerService@Harlequin.com.

Printed in U.S.A.

Award-winning and *USA TODAY* bestselling author **Rula Sinara** lives in rural Virginia with her family and crazy but endearing pets. She loves organic gardening, attracting wildlife to her yard, planting trees, raising backyard chickens and drinking more coffee than she'll ever admit to. Rula's writing has earned her a National Readers' Choice Award and a Holt Medallion Award of Merit, among other honors. Her door is always open at www.rulasinara.com, where you can sign up for her newsletter, learn about her latest books and find links to her social media hangouts.

Books by Rula Sinara

Harlequin Heartwarming

The Promise of Rain
After the Silence
Through the Storm

To Jeannie Watt for your wisdom, kindness and friendship, and for writing books that make every anticipated release a special gift for the reader in me...and to Victoria Curran for your guidance, for believing in me and for buying my first book, *The Promise of Rain*. Jeannie, I'll never forget how you urged me to pitch that story and, Victoria, I'll never be able to thank you enough for seeing that book as the first in a series that would take readers on a (literally) wild and romantic journey to Africa. I owe the birth of my From Kenya, with Love series to you both, and will be forever grateful.

Acknowledgments

To Claire Caldwell for her patience, incredible editorial insight and for always helping me bring out the best in a story. You're one of the smartest and most talented people I know. I'm so lucky to have you with me on this journey and am beyond grateful for all you do.

CHAPTER ONE

HAKI ODABA'S FUTURE was written in the stones: a few goats, plenty of elephants and a wife who would light up his days like the Serengeti's blinding sun. He grumbled, slid farther behind the brush that camouflaged his jeep and peered through his binoculars. *There* she was. Tracked and spotted. A beautiful sight for the worried and weary. He lowered his binoculars and rubbed the heel of his palm against his throbbing temple. God help him. According to locals, the stones never lied—at least not when thrown by the tribal elder. The local Masai's *Laibon* had certainly earned his role as healer and wise man over the years, but it didn't take a rocket scientist or a tribal oracle to know who was destined to be Haki's "blinding sun."

The sunrise backlit Pippa Harper's unruly, corkscrew curls like a fiery beacon glistening against an emerald backdrop of tree canopies in the distance. Her focus on Malik, a beloved, old male African rhino deep in a courtship ritual with several females, didn't waver.

Not good.

How many times had Haki warned her about being aware of *all* her surroundings at all times? The heart of Kenya's savannah beat with the rhythm of life and death…predator and prey. She hadn't even noticed his presence, and he wasn't being particularly stealthy. What if Haki was a stalking cheetah or lion?

He pinched the bridge of his nose. As if that wasn't dangerous enough, predators around here didn't only come on four legs. What was she thinking? She might as well have radioed her coordinates to the poachers that the Kenyan Wildlife Service were tracking in the area. The KWS had informed Haki and his colleagues at the Busara Elephant Research and Rescue Camp of their presence early that morning, and everyone knew to be on the lookout. Given that her parents, along with Haki's, ran Busara, one of Kenya's most reputable elephant rescue camps, Pippa would make quite the prize if she got cornered by ruthless poachers.

Forget being destined to marry. At this rate, Haki would die from exasperation first.

The male rhino's grunt rippled through the air. Pippa pushed her auburn hair out of her face, peered through her camera lens and began taking shots like her life depended on it.

Raised here or not, she either didn't fully comprehend the danger she was putting herself in...or she didn't care. Heaven help him. Haki had faced death before. The scar on his left thigh proved it. Working with wildlife, which included treating five-thousand-pound pachyderms in the field with fanged predators around, was risky business, but there was only one thing Haki truly feared, and that was Pippa's fearlessness.

Haki put away his binoculars, grabbed his rifle out of the jeep and slung the strap over his shoulder as he made his way toward Pippa. He needed to get her back to Busara and convince her to stay put until they had confirmation that the poachers had been caught or were at least out of the immediate area. He seriously hoped that crash of rhinos Pippa was observing wasn't what those poachers were after. They'd make a killing off rhino horn. Medicinal powder. Murder for money. It was all too sick and infuriating.

Fifteen meters and closing in, and Pippa hadn't even turned around. The breeze whispered a soft, luring melody as it caressed the dry savannah grasses and urged each slender blade to stretch and claw at his hands like seductive sirens. Mesmerizing…and full of hidden dangers.

Pippa shifted her knees against the crusty soil and leaned her shoulder against the outcropping of boulders to her left, edging into its shade as the sun crested over it. She readjusted her camera angle and took another shot.

"Come on, girl. Show him your big, beautiful behind already. You're such a tease," she muttered as the female rhino stepped away from the restless bull. Two more females in heat joined the group.

"*Crash*ing the party, are we?" Pippa chuckled.

Haki shook his head. *That isn't remotely funny, Pip.* She'd been out here *way* too long and she was lucky her voice hadn't carried toward the animals. He resisted calling out to her. A few more steps and he'd be able to keep his voice low enough not to startle the rhinos.

Malik, intent on his first choice, didn't seem to notice the onlookers—two-footed or four. Much like Pippa hadn't noticed Haki, now five meters away.

A young clump of elephant grass to her right swayed as a traitorous breeze lifted her curls away from her forehead.

The wind shifted.

She seemed to tense, then lowered her camera just as Haki stopped in his tracks.

Rhinos had terrible eyesight, but a keen sense of smell. They both knew it, too.

Malik grunted.

"Pip. Time to go."

Pippa jerked around at the deep timbre of Haki's voice and bumped her head against the rocky outcropping.

"Ouch! Get down before you get us both impaled." She pressed her hand against the back of her head.

"We're leaving right now. Get up and hope that he's too distracted by his girl to charge."

"Don't give me orders like that. I have everything under control and my jeep's not far," she said. She rose to her feet and gave the dust on her khakis a brisk swat.

Haki glanced toward the battered jeep she'd driven from Busara. It was parked in the shade of an acacia tree less than twenty-five meters east of the rhinos. Not a safe spot at the moment. He looked at her pointedly.

"They weren't there when I parked it," she said.

"Of course not. Now back away slowly." The bull raised his head and snorted, as if irritated by the putrid scent of man in the air.

Pippa steadied her camera with one hand as it hung from her neck strap and backed away from the rock. Knowing Pippa, she'd take a bruise to the head any day if it meant protecting that camera from damage. It was the same camera her father, geneticist Dr. Jack Harper, had been given by his adoptive parents during his troubled teen years. It was also the same one he'd brought with him on his first trip to Kenya. Pippa had been four, and prior to that trip, Jack had been unaware that he had a daughter, let alone one being raised in the wilds of Africa.

Haki waited until Pippa was at his side, then nudged her safely behind him as they retreated toward his jeep.

"I appreciate the lift, but I would have been

fine," Pippa said, climbing onto the front passenger seat.

"Fine? You didn't even hear me walking up. What if it hadn't been me?" Haki secured his rifle in the back, then got behind the wheel. They'd have to return for her jeep when the situation was safer. He churned the ignition and it choked several times before the engine roared to life. Malik raised his horn in their direction, but Haki left a screen of dust in their wake.

"I knew it was you all along. I saw your reflection in my camera lens when I held it away from my face," Pippa called out over the engine noise.

Haki's glower was met with a cheeky grin.

"You were ignoring me."

"You were stalking me," Pippa countered.

"Sta— I wasn't stalking. There were poachers in the vicinity and your mother asked me to track you down when you didn't answer her radio call. Ignoring is not okay."

"I wasn't ignoring *her*. I was going to radio in as soon as I got the shots I needed for the Busara website. I didn't want to miss the moment."

The Busara Elephant Research and Rescue Camp had come a long way over the past fifteen years. Its website was run and edited by one of the Harpers' closest family friends, Tessa Walker. Everyone in the family contributed posts and updates, and Pippa was responsible for most of the photographs.

After marrying their "uncle" Mac, Tessa had begun building the site, which was dedicated to educating the public on just how precious and fragile their wildlife and the ecosystem were. It highlighted both Camp Jamba Walker and the work done to rescue elephants at Camp Busara. Mac Walker wasn't blood-related to anyone at Busara, but he was everyone's uncle Mac nonetheless. He was a bush pilot who'd spent years helping KWS and wildlife research groups in tracking both animals and poachers. He'd become friends with Pippa's mother back when she first established Busara. So Uncle Mac had known both Pippa and Haki since they were babies and, as far as anyone was concerned, was their honorary uncle. Just as Tessa was an auntie to them all and the nephew she and Mac had raised together after his parents' death, Nick Walker, was like a cousin.

"You know our safety rules."

Pippa squeezed fistfuls of her hair before letting the wind have its way.

"How many times do I have to tell you all that I don't need protecting? I'm twenty-two and you only have a year on me and we *both* grew up here. I know how to survive here as well as you do. Being a woman doesn't make me stupid or less prepared."

Her cactus-colored shirt and sun-kissed hair upped the intensity of her green eyes. Pippa was anything but stupid. Sometimes a bit reckless and sensitive. Always fearless, stubborn and headstrong, but not stupid. She'd even graduated with top grades from her geology program, back when the two of them attended university together in Nairobi. He'd learned about living things and earned his veterinary degree; she'd studied the nonliving. She knew all there was to know about the earth beneath their feet. If only she'd learned how to ground all that energy of hers enough to do something with that education. He reached over and gave her hand a squeeze.

"Of course it doesn't, but it can make you more of a target or tasty morsel. I may have only a year on you, but I'm also bigger. Not to mention the intense, military-style training I endured alongside KWS. Do I need to remind you who my supervisor was?"

Pippa closed her eyes and slumped back against the seat. She tilted her chin up and let the sun warm her face. Haki put his hand back on the wheel and scanned their surroundings as he made his way toward Busara. She knew full well that, training aside, physical strength and fitness were crucial in his line of work. Even at his peak, his strength didn't come close to the brute force some of the larger animals he treated or rescued were capable of. Plus, he'd trained under her uncle Ben.

"Fine. You win," she said.

He glanced over at her and couldn't resist smiling. Everyone knew that anyone training under her uncle deserved a medal. Ben Corallis had been in the US Marine Corps before losing his wife—Jack Harper's sister—to a traumatic accident about seventeen years ago. His youngest son had been a newborn at the time—way out of Ben's comfort zone. Plus, he'd had a hyperactive four-year-old on his hands and his only daughter, Maddie, Pippa's then ten-year-old cousin. To make matters worse, Maddie had retreated into a shell of silence after the loss of her mother. It wasn't until Dr. Hope Alwanga, the sister of a family friend in Nairobi, had entered their lives, that they'd begun healing. And that healing had led to Ben and Hope falling in love. Ben later began using his marine experience to help train Kenyan Wildlife Service rangers in their battle against illegal poaching.

Haki had learned from the best, even if he had only worked as a ranger for a year before quitting so that he could go to vet school. Now, working as a field vet for Busara, often in areas where poachers had been spotted, that training was priceless.

"I don't want to win. I want you safe." Haki leaned over, keeping one hand on the wheel, and kissed her cheek. Pippa smiled but kept her eyes closed.

She really was beautiful. Haki couldn't ask for anyone with a kinder heart. The trumpeting of elephants reverberated through the air and he straightened in his seat as he rounded an outcropping and merged onto the worn dirt road that led into camp. Pippa sat up and took a shot of the view ahead. The same photograph she'd taken a thousand times. Busara. The one place that would always be their sanctuary and home.

"I'm sure Aunt Tessa will appreciate those photographs, but until we find whoever was involved in the killing yesterday, maybe you could help out with the orphan we rescued from the scene. I heard she hasn't taken a bottle yet and you know if she's too depressed to eat, she won't make it. I'm betting a little attention from you might help."

Pippa could never resist a baby elephant, and since her mother, Dr. Bekker, was known as Mama Tembo, or mother elephant, the keepers had nicknamed Pippa "Mini-Mama" long ago. In fact, the vast majority of photographs she took in her spare time were of baby animals. Helping their latest orphan would keep her safely at camp. At least for a little while.

"The poor thing. Of course I'll check in on her, but don't think I'm not onto what you're doing. I've known you long enough to read your mind."

"I'm not that easily read," Haki scoffed.

"Is that so? Don't worry. I won't go walking into a lion's den. Besides, my jeep is still out there."

"Good."

"Oh, I'm not done reading you. You're extra upset right now because you think the poachers had help. Or maybe this wasn't the work of poachers at all. It irks you even more when good people succumb to the dark side."

Haki took a deep breath and tightened his grip on the wheel as they hit a rut on the dirt road.

"I'll give you that. This baby should have been with her herd. Or if the herd had witnessed the murder, one would think the other mothers would have taken the little one into their protection. Unless, because of the drought and the baby's age, the herd decided they had to move on and leave it to die. Maybe the situation was still too dangerous to keep the others around. As in, they sensed the human threat was still nearby."

Female elephants were highly maternal and protective. They wouldn't have abandoned one of their own, especially not a calf, unless circumstances were extenuating. Unfortunately, with reports of nearby crop destruction by elephants, he didn't doubt some of the Masai farmers had taken to deadly means to protect their land. Pippa understood the dilemma as well as he did. Man's indigenous rights versus the elephants'. And all the other wildlife. She touched his shoulder.

"You did your best. You rescued the calf. You're a good man." Pippa sighed and put the protective cover back on her camera lens. "How is that legislative proposal coming along? Any progress?"

Haki shook his head. That proposal had been keeping him up at night.

"*Still* waiting on cabinet approval. Apparently, it has raised the hackles of a human rights organization. No word on if that will slow things down or not."

He'd helped a group of wildlife advocates draft the proposal aimed at increasing the punishment and/or penalty against individuals from indigenous tribes, like the Masai, who killed elephants in retaliation for crop damages. The killing had to stop. Hopefully, before the extinction of the species. This proposal was a step in the right direction, but the notion that anyone would want to block it made his skin burn. A very slow burn, considering how long it was taking for it to go through.

"Don't give up hope. Maybe Uncle Ben can ask Maddie if she has any connections to lawyers who can help. Did you hear that she's planning to visit? I'm so excited. I can't wait to see her again."

Maddie was coming to Kenya? Pippa had a knack for switching subjects as quickly as a cheetah on caffeine. He was used to it, but the mention of Maddie's visit nearly gave him whiplash.

His thumb pricked against the rough patch where his steering wheel had been gnawed by something wild and nocturnal. He shifted his grip. It had been two years since he'd last seen her and even then, they'd barely had a chance to catch up. Usually, her family returned to the States during the holidays and the few times she'd visited her parents and brothers in Nairobi, she'd cut her trips short for some reason and Haki had never managed to see her. The last time she came around he was out in the field for several days with KWS teams and never made it into Nairobi. She'd had no real reason to fly out to Busara, since Pippa and her parents had gone to see her instead. Apparently, getting to see him hadn't been reason enough.

"Is she coming out here or are you going to Nairobi?"

It didn't really matter, did it? Haki had clued in long ago that spending time at Busara no longer held the attraction for Maddie it once had. When her family first moved to Kenya, she was only ten and had just regained her ability to speak. She used to beg Hope and Ben to let her spend the night out here so that she, Pippa and Haki could sit around a campfire surrounded by nothing but stars and the call of the wild. Maddie loved animals back then and had always wanted to visit Africa. Being out here had helped her heal after the loss of her biological mother.

Of course, they'd been within the safe boundaries of Busara and their parents were nearby, but those nights had been exhilarating just the same. The kind of experiences that childhood memories were made of. He and Pippa had loved having a new friend around and the three of them had formed what seemed like an unbreakable bond. At least Pippa and Maddie were still close. He still wasn't sure why things had gotten awkward and distant between him and Maddie. Sometimes he wondered if he'd done something or said something to offend her. Her visits to Busara had slowly fizzled out, and once she took off for college in the US, it was as though they'd both gotten too busy with their lives to bother with one another.

"I honestly have no idea if she's coming out here or how long she's staying," Pippa said. "She was a bit vague in her email, which is strange. I know law school wiped her out, so maybe with this new job in Philadelphia, she just needs a break." Pippa sat up bone-straight and her eyes brightened. "Oh, my gosh! I bet she met someone. She'd want to tell me in person, especially if it's serious. Think about it. She's twenty-six, out of school and working at a firm that's probably full of handsome, eligible bachelor lawyers. Her nerves must be fried right now. With brothers like hers…and Uncle Ben… I can't blame her for not introducing any guys to them yet. This one would have to be worth it. But I can't believe she hasn't mentioned him to me. I wouldn't have said anything. Well, maybe to you, but not to anyone else."

Trust. Life was nothing without it. Trust meant a sense of peace, honesty and truth. It meant feeling safe. A person could be themselves around those they trusted. He was honored that Pippa would confide in him…but Maddie? Getting married?

Something faint and indefinable pinched at his chest. The young Maddie he'd known had loved wearing jeans, feeding baby animals and camping. The last Maddie he'd seen had looked more like a big-city office type: hose, heels and tied-up hair. Maybe the real Maddie was the one who'd be happy spending her life with a man in a suit. They could carpool to court the way he and Pippa liked to floor a jeep across the savannah. He lowered his chin briefly to release a cramp at the back of his neck. It was none of his business anyway. There was no reason why any of it should bother him.

"Maybe you should just wait and see before making up stories," Haki said, pulling up next to three other Busara jeeps parked just far enough from the camp's wooden pens so as not to disturb the baby elephants. They were all recovering from injuries incurred when their mothers were killed in the name of ivory. A keeper stood feeding a ravenous calf with a milk bottle in a small grassy clearing to the left of the pens. Dr. Bekker—Auntie Anna, as Haki called her—glanced over her shoulder and gave them a relieved thumbs-up when Pippa hopped out of the jeep. She shook her head at her daughter, then ducked into their small vet clinic.

Judging from the absence of their rescue vehicles, Haki's father and his crew had already been called off on mission. Dr. Kamau Odaba was a field veterinarian who'd been working at Busara from the start…and who'd fallen in love with Haki's mother, Niara Juma, and had taken them both under his wing when Haki was five. He was the only father Haki had ever known, and the only one he ever wanted to. He and his mother had taken Kam's last name after the marriage and his legal adoption. Since his father was Dr. Odaba, their staff avoided confusion by calling him Dr. Haki.

"Maybe I'm right," Pippa said as she came around the jeep and leaned on the rim of Haki's open window. "Maddie will need us as backup if she tells Uncle Ben she's getting engaged. If you thought training with her dad was tough, can you imagine the vetting he'd put this poor guy through?"

"Good. He should."

"Haki, have a heart."

"Me?" He couldn't help but chuckle. "You spent too much time hanging upside down from trees as a child. You haven't even met this man who—I might add—is a figment of your overactive imagination, yet you're already defending him. But *say* he does exist. What if he's not good for her? What if you end up hating him?"

"I won't because I trust Maddie's judgment. I'm sure I'd adore any man worthy of her love."

Haki rubbed his forehead, then restarted

the jeep. Mosi, a small vervet monkey, squealed at them before scampering down a nearby fig tree and eyeing Pippa for food.

"My hands are empty, Mosi."

The little guy was the only child of the late Ambosi, a three-legged vervet who'd been rescued by Dr. Bekker when Pippa and Haki were infants and who'd spent his life hanging around Busara for treats…or because of the amusing crush he seemed to have had on Dr. Bekker. He'd gotten quite jealous when Pippa's father, Jack, had shown up at Busara. It was no secret that Pippa missed Ambosi. Everyone did.

"I have to get back to work, Pip."

"I know. It's just…" She wrinkled her nose and shrugged. "Never mind."

"What is it?"

"Nothing. It was a totally selfish thought. Best to keep it in my head."

"There's not a selfish bone in your body. An uncontrollably wild imagination, yes. But not selfishness. Out with it."

Pippa sighed and looked at Mosi, then gazed wistfully at the house that her and Haki's parents had built after they'd married. It had been built for both families so they could live more comfortably at Busara. Both of their younger siblings had been born in that home. Maddie had played in that home.

"It hit me that I hardly get to see her as it is. Once she's married or has children, she'll be even busier. I want her to be happy, the way you and I are, but a part of me is afraid of losing her. See? Rotten selfishness. Don't you dare repeat anything I just said."

Haki grabbed one of her hands and pressed her knuckles to his lips.

"First, you're going to freak Maddie out when she finds out you've planned her wedding with a man she's never met. Second, you'll always have me. And third, you'll never lose her. She's your cousin. She's family."

Pippa gave him a small smile.

"Okay. You're the best, you know? Now, go save some animals or help catch some bad guys." She ducked her head in the window and gave him a quick peck. "Be safe."

"You, too," he warned, then backed out. He pulled his sunglasses out of the glove compartment and slipped them on.

You'll never lose her. She's family. But he knew Maddie was more than just Pippa's cousin. They were best friends the way Haki's mother, Niara, and Anna were. Pippa was right about a woman's strength. Their mothers had raised them both at Busara when the remote camp consisted of nothing more than a few tents and a water well. They'd had no amenities. No extravagances. Just each other. Pippa hadn't had a lot of other girls around growing up out here.

That's why he hated that Maddie didn't seem to understand how much Pippa missed her. It was also why Pippa wasn't just any girl to Haki. He'd known her all his life. They'd been through every growing pain together, from infancy to toddlerhood to the troublesome teens. Maddie had been around during their teens, too. But he and Pippa had a future together. Not because Haki put faith in the *Laibon*'s divination methods—that silliness was Pippa's thing, along with reading her horoscope every now and then. No, Haki knew she was the one because their lives had become so intertwined he couldn't see them ever being apart.

They were perfect for each other. The whole family saw it and often dropped hints about what their wedding would be like. Something small at Busara surrounded by family and the baby elephant orphans they both loved so much…or something more elegant at one of Amboseli National Park's lodges? It didn't really matter to Haki. He just wanted life as they knew it to carry on. As long as they both continued their work to save the elephants and he could take care of her and their family... As long as Pippa was happy, he'd be happy.

Maybe asking Maddie for insight on their legislative proposal wasn't a bad idea. It would give him the chance to talk to her and to nudge her into spending some time at Busara. Like the good old days.

For Pippa's sake.

Static buzzed over Haki's radio and he grabbed it just as the call came through. The air rushing through the jeep's windows went from refreshing to thick and heavy with the burden of death.

He made a sharp left around a dense mass of Red Grass and aimed for the coordinates coming through. Coordinates that were all too familiar.

He wiped his face against his sleeve and stepped on the gas.

The poachers KWS had been hunting down had been apprehended about a kilometer west of where Haki had found Pippa photographing the rhinos. The poachers had tracked the rhinos and were intercepted while heading toward the Kenya-Tanzania border with their tusks.

The old bull, Malik, was dead.

CHAPTER TWO

MADDIE CORALLIS'S PALM STUNG as she caught herself against the bathroom door at the law offices of Levy, Hatterson & Palomas. Every door in the restored historic building in Philadelphia was the original oak—as solid as nature had intended. She balanced her laptop and a stack of documents in her left hand and gave her right wrist a quick turn to ease her cramped joint.

Higher heels boost confidence and make a girl look more dignified, huh? That was the last time she'd listen to the women in the break room at lunch. No, they had not specifically told her to run out and buy new shoes, nor had they suggested an eye-catching dark red, but she'd overheard them emphasizing that women who— Darnit. Maddie gritted her teeth. They'd wanted her to overhear them. *You gullible idiot.*

She righted her brand-new pumps using her toes and shoved her foot back in, then glanced around the firm's loft-style top floor in the hopes that no one had witnessed her klutziness. Patrick Cole, the other junior lawyer, quickly turned back to whatever he was feeding the fax machine, but he made no effort to hide his smirk. *Of all the stuck-up—*

She pulled back her shoulders, entered the bathroom and locked the door behind her.

"Oh, for heaven's sake. Of all people," she muttered. She set down her pile on the shimmery, black granite counter by the sink, inspected her reflection and took a deep breath. "Keep your eyes on the goal. They won't be laughing when you make partner. Now get yourself together and get back out there."

The concealer she'd dabbed under her eyes was holding up. Her hair wasn't. Her long, wavy locks were annoyingly thick and silky, always slipping out of any band or clip she used to keep them in place. No wonder her first mother, Zoe, had finally cropped hers short after Maddie's little brother, Ryan, was born. It had no doubt made her routine with three little kids around a lot easier. Maddie tried that once during her first year in law school. She had it all chopped off and the resulting dark brown bob looked just like her mama's did in an old photo. Only instead of looking pretty and chic on Maddie, it made her look boyish and even more pale.

She pinched her cheeks, pulled her bun loose and flipped her head upside down. The three silver bangles she never took off her wrist tinkled like wind chimes as she finger-combed her hair and twisted it back up in a tighter knot. Her second mom had given her those bracelets when Maddie was only ten years old. They'd belonged to Hope's grandmother...or Maddie's step-great-grandmother. Hope hadn't been married to Maddie's father at the time, but she'd already become an important part of the family. She'd helped Maddie cope after the death of her birth mother and those bracelets meant more to Maddie than anything. Three silver rings, one for each of the three of them—Maddie, her mama, as she used to call Zoe, and Hope, her mom. Her bracelets held memories...and a magical bond. They were a reminder that life went on, and their soft, bell-like music always gave her courage.

She'd make it through this meeting with her boss, the toughest of the partners at Levy, Hatterson & Palomas. She'd presented her work to the senior lawyers before and had survived any criticism thrown her way, but the memo requesting that Patrick be there, too, had her a little rattled. What did presenting her case research have to do with him?

She smoothed her brown tweed pencil skirt and matching blazer, grabbed her pile of folders and headed toward the conference room, this time careful not to catch her heel on an uneven floorboard.

"Good morning, Mr. Levy." Maddie aimed for pleasantness, without the smile. Being serious, both in expression and looks, was part of her strategy for climbing the ranks. She'd noticed early on that if a guy smiled around here, he was being congenial, but if a woman did, it somehow diluted her brainpower and made her flirty. If she had to play borderline cold, she would.

This office was a man's world, and Maddie was desperate to move on from being a junior lawyer. The position was synonymous with grunt worker, and a year into the job, the grunt was already getting old. While the seniors got to spend their evenings dining clients at four-star restaurants, she and the other glorified minions in the office burned the midnight oil researching cases, or making sure dates and other details were in order. Being a junior lawyer was beginning to make her wonder why she'd gone to law school to begin with. No hearings. No appearing before judges. No showing what she was made of.

Showing her family—particularly her father—what she was made of was why she'd worked so hard. She wanted to prove she could be strong and successful on her own. And after all those years in law school, here she was getting bossed around and doing work for others. For stern, older men just like her military dad. She scratched her wrist below her bracelets as her boss shuffled through papers.

"Good morning." Mr. Levy hit Send on what she assumed was a text, then set his smartphone on the polished cherry-wood conference table. "Have a seat. Where's Patrick?"

"I saw him at the fax. I'm sure he'll be in any minute. Oh, here are the files on the Clear Lake housing developments you needed." She set the pile—all but her laptop—next to him, then went to the opposite end of the table to sit. "It includes signed affidavits from tenants who've been discriminated against, as well as some who've tried contracting new builds. Incident specifics are there, as well, including emails and text messages between defendants and the builder."

"Excellent." Mr. Levy began scanning pages. "Good work. Ah, Patrick," he said, as Patrick waltzed in. He stuck out his hand, which Mr. Levy didn't hesitate to shake. "Have a seat."

The brownnoser sat in a chair right next to Levy, without greeting Maddie. Maddie fiddled with her bracelets under the table. Man's world, much? She'd known coming into this practice—which was a huge honor in and of itself—that competition for senior partnership years down the road would be high, but the subtle animosity and jealous streaks among the juniors was worse than she'd expected. Downright ugly, in her opinion. This place redefined competitive.

You grew up surrounded by brothers and a hard-nosed dad. Remember, Patrick is nothing but a twerp, and your boss is a teddy bear in disguise—on some plane of existence.

"I called you both in here to discuss the next two months. Ms. Corallis, we spoke briefly about you helping out temporarily at our office in Nairobi."

Patrick scooted his chair closer to the table

and scratched the side of his neck. A junior lawyer being sent to an exotic locale was a pretty big deal, although Kenya wasn't exactly exotic to her. At least not in the way it was for those who'd never lived there. Eight years of her childhood, plus regular visits since she began college in the US, made Kenya a second home to her. Not a vacation spot. Plus, traveling overseas and coming back a week later would be exhausting. She'd get jet lag whiplash. And since this was a work trip, she'd barely have time to see her family.

However, the color creeping up the back of Patrick's neck did remind her of a sunrise over the Serengeti, or better yet, the vibrant red dress of a warrior in the Masai Mara. She tipped her chin up ever so slightly.

"Yes, sir. The Native Watch Global case." The one she had yet to be fully briefed on. The one that, incidentally, had nothing to do with Patrick. Maybe he was being sent to their London office for something related?

"I had Helen book your tickets. I'm assuming you'll be able to stay with your family while there." Mr. Levy passed an envelope down to her via Patrick. "We need you to leave on Wednesday. I trust that all works for you?"

About a week sooner than expected, but did she have a choice?

"Of course," Maddie said as she opened the envelope. That wouldn't give her enough time to check on her grandparents a few hours west of Philadelphia. She'd call them. She also needed to drop by the store and get a slow-release vacation feeder for her Betta fish. She pulled the ticket out of the envelope.

"Patrick," Mr. Levy continued, "I'll need you to take over this Clear Lake discrimination case in her absence."

Everything registered in the same second. The dates on the ticket. Mr. Levy turning her stack of blood, sweat and tears over to the enemy. Maddie's feet went cold.

"Sir. I think there's a mistake with the tickets. These have me gone a month. I was only supposed to be in Nairobi for a week. I think I've given you everything you need for now on the Clear Lake case, but I'll have my computer with me if you need anything else."

It had better be a mistake. She didn't care if she sounded territorial; she couldn't lose that discrimination case to Patrick. It had high-profile written all over it. If she helped propel her seniors to victory on it, it would build their confidence in her and, in turn, increase her chances of eventually making partner. Handing all her work over to the twerp was worse than a slap in the face. The corner of Patrick's mouth curved up as he flipped through her files.

"I'm afraid we need you overseas longer than we previously thought," Mr. Levy said. "Patrick, I'd like you to familiarize yourself with that paperwork, then return it to me after lunch. *Today.* I want you on the same track we've been on with it. This won't add too much to your workload, given the Kline-versus-Boone case is over. I must say, I love a victory."

"Absolutely, sir. I won't disappoint with this one, either."

You won't disappoint because I did all the work.

She wanted to scream. She folded her hands on the table in as poised a manner as possible, crossed her legs and let her dangling foot buzz back and forth like a hovering hornet, itching to sting someone. Patrick sat back, all smug, in his chair.

"Feel free to get started on that right now, Mr. Cole." Mr. Levy gave him a raised brow.

Patrick jumped up and gathered his—no, *her*—assignment.

"Of course. Thank you for the opportunity, Mr. Levy. I'll have this back to you today." He hesitated briefly on his way out of the conference room. "Have a safe trip, Maddie. Say hello to your family for me."

Maddie's foot kicked up speed, but she managed to keep her lips sealed shut and her look composed from the waist up. What a phenomenal jerk. He didn't know or care one iota about her family. He just wanted to emphasize to Mr. Levy that he'd be working hard while she'd probably waste time in Kenya lounging around with her siblings. Having younger brothers had helped her develop a certain level of immunity to button-pushing, but this kind of insidious workplace manipulation just irked the—

Her shoe flung off her foot and hit…something…with a thud.

Oh, God. Please, not Mr. Levy's leg. Anything but the leg.

Mr. Levy frowned at her. Maddie smiled back, big and bright. She was toast.

She ducked her head under the table. *Oh, thank you, thank you, thank you.* Her heart eased back into its normal position. Her shoe had only knocked the table's Federal-style leg. Hopefully the grooves would hide any nicks. She stretched her leg and managed to get her foot back in the pump, hands-free.

"Sorry about that. Umm…new shoes. They, uh, don't fit well."

He nodded as if that all made perfect sense. Then again, he *was* married. She'd seen the boutique heels his wife paraded around in whenever she dropped by the office. Shoes Maddie could never afford. Maybe it *did* make sense to him. She curled her toes in the knockoffs that were doing absolutely nothing for her confidence.

"Better take a more sensible pair to Kenya. You won't be walking in the city," he said.

"About that. With all due respect, I *can* handle both cases. I'm the one who brought the Clear Lake discrimination situation to our attention. I did all that research. The people involved know my name and face and—"

"And you've done a remarkable job with it. That's in part why I personally recommended you for the Kenya case. Listen…" He folded his arms and sighed. "I understand your frustration. I was at your stage in my career once, more years ago than I care to mention. Everyone wants a high-profile case, or at least one that's bigger than the rest. The Native Watch Global case may or may not be big in terms of headline news, but it's significant in terms of humanitarian impact. When I interviewed you out of school, you made it clear you were interested in human-rights law."

"I am."

"Good. Because NWG is counting on us. What's happening with Kenya's native tribes—the Masai, in this case—is very similar to the type of land loss or encroachment our own Native Americans are still suffering. And on top of the tribe's desperation, a more recent proposal was submitted to increase punishment for defending their crops against destruction by wildlife. Our barristers at the Nairobi office are currently inundated with other cases. Of course, they'll still handle any actual court appearances with this one, as required by law there. However, they need the extra manpower in gathering firsthand research to counter this proposal before it goes to the Kenyan cabinet for approval."

Maddie placed her hands on her laptop and nodded. *Man*power. More of the same work, only overseas. It was like being a ghostwriter. A behind-the-scenes ghost lawyer. And they were getting off without paying for a hotel, to boot. She took a deep breath and was assaulted by the overuse of air freshener in the old building.

This case was absolutely a critical one. She couldn't argue with that. She understood the cause and loved Kenya and its people. She really did. But the difference between being a lowly junior lawyer in the US and being one in Kenya was that her family was over there. She loved her family, but an entire month under the same roof? She hadn't lived there since she was eighteen. A whole month under the watchful eye of her overprotective dad, her medical doctor mom…and her brothers.

Chad had made their dad proud by following in his footsteps and joining the marines. Ryan would be headed to college soon and said he wanted to study medicine like Hope. Maddie felt a bit sorry for Philip, Hope and Ben's only child together, whom Maddie adored. He was only fourteen, and she could tell from his emails that he was feeling the pressure of keeping up with everyone else. As for Maddie, on one level she knew her accomplishments were great. She'd worked hard because she always felt the need to prove herself. Success meant getting out from under her dad's umbrella. Sometimes his protectiveness and worry came off as critical no matter what she did. And now, he'd get to see firsthand how she was barely getting by as a lawyer, let alone excelling. She'd handled shorter holidays in the past with skillful maneuvering around certain topics of conversation. And those trips had been about kicking back. But a monthlong work trip was enough for everyone to catch on to the fact that she was basically a nobody. And then, heaven forbid, the career advice would start pouring in.

She shifted in her chair and put her hands in her lap, noticing belatedly that she'd left sweaty handprints on her matte laptop cover. Mr. Levy had probably noticed it, too. Could her day get any worse? She wiped her palms against the scratchy tweed of her skirt. The bottom line was that she'd been given her orders. Nine in the morning and she was already spent. She felt like a teenager all over again, getting told what she needed to do with her life. What she needed right now were her sweatpants, slippers and some ice cream.

"I understand, Mr. Levy. I'll do my best."

"I know you will. If there's one thing I've learned, it's that to win, you need to have the right person on the case. I'm not putting you on this one just because of your dual citizenship. I want you on this because you finished your undergraduate studies in three years, graduated law school at the top of your class and do everything meticulously—down to the way I've seen you water the ficus tree by the break room that everyone else forgets about—and you're fluent in four languages to boot."

"Three, sir. I only know a few words in Swahili. I wouldn't call myself fluent." She was fluent enough in French and Spanish, though not as comfortable with them as English.

"Well, that's a few words more than I know. More importantly, you have an understanding of the people and culture. Their needs. The cultural dynamic. We need someone to actually get out in the field. And, yes, you have family who can take you around to gather information, but if you need help with that, let us know. Visit some of the Masai villagers who are being essentially pushed off their land. Find out their views and concerns regarding potential new punishments imposed on them. Get to the heart of it all, but I don't want emotion—I want solid facts that'll stand up in court. You have a tendency to think outside the box. I like that about you. Let me put this bluntly—if we win this case, you'll be number one on our list the next time a promotion opens up."

A jolt akin to the one she got from the first sip of a hot, salted caramel mocha latte coursed through her. He'd actually taken note of her work and effort? Top of their list? Her cheeks warmed. She'd had no idea he had that level of confidence in her. Everything in her seemed to shift. This was it. This was her big break. She pushed back a lock of hair that had liberated itself from her bun.

"Thank you. Mr. Levy, that—that means a lot to me. I won't let you down."

"I hope not." He stood to leave. She followed suit, but gave her right hand another subtle wipe on her skirt, just in case he extended his. He didn't. "Helen should be emailing you some files for review on the case. Easier for travel. Other than that, there's only one thing left for you to do. Go home and pack."

"Yes, sir."

She gathered her things and walked out of the conference room. She could do this. The assignment, she could handle. If she felt too smothered at her parents' house, she'd go spend time at Busara. After all, she'd be out there anyway to visit tribal villages. And seeing Pippa again would be incredible. No doubt she'd see Haki, too. The last time she'd seen him he'd gotten so much taller and... older. He'd always been mature for his age, but there had been something different about him. She'd also noticed how his relationship with Pippa had changed, even before Pippa had confided that she and Haki had become more than friends. They were an item. A couple. It was a beautiful thing, it really was, but something about it unsettled her. Probably just fear of being a third wheel.

Maddie took a deep breath and let it out as she stepped onto the sidewalk outside the building. Yes. She could stay with Pippa if she needed a break from Nairobi and her father. Pippa, though she was almost five years younger than Maddie, had always been the spunkier one when they were kids. She never let anyone pick on Maddie back then. She still always had her back.

Maddie would always have hers, too.

CHAPTER THREE

IF THERE WAS EVER a prime example of man versus nature, the disaster Haki was witnessing was an arrow in the bull's-eye. Good thing there was no bull in sight—this time. Haki trekked through trampled earth and mutilated scraps of what had been rows of sorghum. Understanding Swahili and a few of the tribal dialects was an asset to his work, but all he could do right now was nod his head and let the Masai farmer continue to vent. He'd slip in peace talks at the right time. He was just relieved that the elephant bull hadn't been caught "red-handed."

He assumed it was a bull because one such bull had been reported missing that morning from a conservation area dedicated to transitioning teenage elephants into the wild. It was the same group that took on the orphans rescued at Busara once they were too old to stay there. KWS had been trying to locate that missing bull all day. Haki was hoping the elephant would be found alive.

Just a few weeks ago, another farm had suffered a raid by a hungry elephant in search of food. The farmer had killed it in retaliation. Had KWS not found the body in time, the farmer might have even tried selling the tusks to make up for income lost from crop destruction. And that would have fed into the illegal ivory market, which would in turn have encouraged more poaching, and the vicious cycle would go on. Late-summer droughts made everyone and everything, including vegetation and wildlife, desperate. And desperation had a way of pushing a person's moral boundaries.

Crops could be replanted. Fences could be mended. But driving a species to extinction—eradicating it because of either anger or greed—was an irreversible, unconscionable act.

Haki understood the plight of farmers in the region. He understood that they had children to feed. But killing was not the answer. If the tiny oxpecker bird could ride the back of a massive rhino in peace—trading the benefit of a bodyguard and free meal for keeping the beast's hide free of insects—then surely humans could figure out a way to live symbiotically with other species.

A group of women swathed in a geometrical-patterned fabric of oranges and reds, with equally colorful beads adorning their necks, stood watching expectantly. One held tight to a toddler. That had to be the farmer's young child. The one he said had been playing near their garden when the elephant came stomping through.

Haki wiped the sweat off his forehead with one khaki sleeve, then turned to two of his crew near their medical unit. They'd come out to assist, in case an injured animal was found, after a bush pilot spotted the damaged field and reported possible trouble in the area. Haki's team had been nearby and the KWS vet assigned to this area was on another emergency call. Luckily, the only casualties here were the crops—not that that didn't have an impact on the farmer.

"Let's help him repair his fence before we leave," Haki said. The fence wouldn't hold up if the elephant returned for another meal. Even the electric fences used to block off large areas of land reserved for farming weren't always enough to keep elephants from roaming in from the forests and reserves. But it was all he could do to temper the situation for now.

"We've been called out. Another aerial tip. A young elephant stuck in a mud pit. I have the coordinates. KWS still has their area vet unit working with a bull they had to dart. Infected hip wound. No time to build fences," his medical unit driver called out.

Mud pit. That was one of the repercussions of drought. Haki braced his hands on his belt and stared at his worn and weathered boots. No time. Ironic, given that the savannah was all about time...the cycle of life from dawn until dusk. Yet they were constantly running out of it in an attempt to save lives here, to stop the unique beauty of this place from disappearing.

"Okay. Let's go," he said, signaling the medical team to get a move on. He called over to Lempiris, the farmer, and his older sons, who were beginning to clean up their planting rows.

"I'll try to return to help you with the fence," he said, in Maa. He *would* try, on his own time. Good fences make good neighbors. Wasn't that the expression? Unfortunately, it didn't translate into elephant.

Lempiris squatted down and scooped up

a handful of soil near his sandaled feet without looking up. He probably didn't believe a man like Haki would care enough to return. Haki was the enemy. The one who only cared about the elephants. And Haki couldn't blame him, because in all honesty, if this man had killed his intruder, his family would be watching KWS arresting him at this very moment. Haki would have made sure of it.

MADDIE HOISTED THE STRAP of her laptop case higher on her shoulder and picked up her pace when she spotted her mom and brothers through the airport crowds. She waved until they saw her and waved back.

The twenty-hour flight, including a stopover in Zurich, had exhausted her, but seeing their faces gave her a second wind. At seventeen, Ryan towered over their mom and even Philip was an inch or so taller than the last time she'd seen him. And at fourteen, he still had some growing to do. Hope was a beautiful sight with her bright smile and kind eyes. She wore the orange, floral-print scarf that Maddie had sent her for her birthday, and dangling coral earrings to match. Hope wasn't blood-related, but she was their mother to the core, just as Philip was their brother. Blood had nothing to do with how much they loved each other or how family was defined.

"Mom, guys! It's so good to see you." Maddie collapsed into Hope's arms first. She clung on a few seconds longer and let herself feel welcome.

"Mmm, you smell so good," Maddie said. Hope hadn't changed her perfume for as long as she could remember and there was something so comforting about a mother's scent. Maddie and her brothers used to love it when Hope dabbed her perfume on their pillows at night if they were afraid of bad dreams. Somehow, it had helped lull them to sleep, a reminder that they were safe and being watched over.

"Maybe you're smelling *mandazi*. I asked Delila to make them as a special dessert tonight."

"Are you sure you weren't just using me as an excuse, Mom?" The donuts had been her mother's favorite treat since she was little. Delila, their housekeeper, had told Maddie so. She'd been the family housekeeper since Hope was a baby, born with a heart defect. Hope's parents—both doctors with demanding schedules—needed help at the time.

They'd also hired Delila's husband, Jamal, as the family driver. The two had been part of the family every since. After Hope married Ben and the entire family moved to Kenya, Hope's parents had insisted that it was time for Delila and Jamal to help the next generation. They began splitting their time between the two homes and were loved dearly by everyone.

"She made us come along out of fear that we'd eat them all before you guys got home," Philip said.

"You mean you didn't come because you missed me?" Maddie gave him a big hug and then reached up to hug Ryan.

"What have you been eating? I'm supposed to be your *big* sister."

Ryan grinned and patted the top of her head.

"Karma, for all the times you bossed me around."

"Right." Maddie chuckled. "I only have one suitcase and I'm ready to get out of here. I've had enough of airports. I was barely able to sleep on the flight over. Here, Mr. Karma. How about carrying the heavier one?"

He easily lifted the bag she'd broken her

back carrying and then grabbed the second one Philip was reaching for.

"Hey! I was taking that one," Philip said. "You're such a show-off."

"These, heavy? They feel empty," Ryan told Maddie, ignoring Philip's complaint.

"Here, Philip. Can you take this for me? My shoulder is aching."

She slipped her laptop case off of her shoulder and held it out. She could have handled carrying it, but having your ego bruised at his age wasn't fun. Philip took the bag from her and followed Ryan through the crowd.

"Let's go before those boys challenge each other to a duel," Hope said. "Jamal is waiting with the car."

"How's Chad?" Maddie asked as she and Hope followed the boys out.

"We heard from him last week. He's okay. Sounded tired, but okay." Hope put her arm around Maddie as they walked. "I worry. They have him in Afghanistan right now. I know your father is proud that his oldest son followed in his footsteps and joined the marines, but he worries, too. I'm more willing to say so out loud."

"When will he get to visit?"

"Not for months. And soon, Ryan will

be off to college and I'll only have Philip around."

"But you're busy seeing patients. You won't feel the empty nest."

"A mother always feels it when her nest is empty. I feel your absence, too, my dear." She gave Maddie a squeeze. "I'm so glad you're here. Your father will be home by the time we get there. He was called out for work."

"How's he doing?"

"Good. He's excited that you'll be here awhile."

A subtle pang of guilt made her stomach twinge. Here she was, nervous about staying in her parents' house for so long, while her dad was excited about it. She smiled rather than lying in agreement. Maddie hated lying.

"I expect I'll be pretty busy this trip. I'm supposed to stop by the law office tomorrow. I have the address. If Jamal is busy, I can always call a taxi."

"Nonsense. Jamal already plans to help you out as needed. I'd rather you not drive here. It has been too long since you last did."

Hope had never liked driving in Nairobi. It was nothing like driving in America and she'd always had Jamal take them to school or anywhere else they needed to go. Which wasn't to say that Maddie hadn't done it. Once, at sixteen, she'd taken the family car without permission. It hadn't ended well and Jamal had taken the blame for the fender bender, not wanting her to get in trouble. He'd also told her parents that he'd forgotten the time and had, thus, picked up her brothers from school late, when in fact, he'd found the car missing. Halfway through that night, Maddie had woken her parents up and confessed. The guilt alone had been keeping her awake. Truth and justice. Probably why she'd ended up in law.

Jamal stood waiting by the same old black sedan he'd been driving for years. His salt-and-pepper hair was more salt than the last time she'd seen him, but he looked as tall, dark and handsome as ever. He and Delila were like having extra grandparents around. His face creased with a wide grin.

"Maddie. You've brightened the skies over Kenya already."

Maddie gave him a big hug, then stood back as the guys loaded her bags into the car.

"I missed you, Jamal. How's Delila?"

"She can't wait to see you, but you'd think there were ten of you coming. She's cooking for an army. From the looks of you, you could use some home-cooked meals."

"Well, you know. I figure why bother eating if Delila hasn't cooked it," Maddie teased.

"I thought all that food was because we're having company," Philip said.

Ryan elbowed him and Hope scrunched her face.

"That was supposed to be a surprise," Ryan said.

"No one told me it—"

"It's all right, Philip. I forgot to remind you," Hope said.

"He forgets everything. No wonder you're not allowed to get a pet. Mom and Dad would have to remind you to feed it," Ryan said.

"That's not true." Philip scowled at his brother as they climbed into the car.

"Remember what happened to Mad's fish when she left for college?"

So that was how Barracuda died? Philip's face turned red.

"That was years ago. I was like…five… and you were supposed to help feed it."

"Boys," Hope warned. This was going to be a long ride.

"Who's coming over?" Maddie asked, trying to help break up the argument. Her first thought was Simba and Chuki. Her uncle Simba was Hope's brother. His actual name was Dr. David Alwanga, but Hope had always called him Simba, so when Maddie and her brothers moved to Kenya, they'd insisted on calling him Uncle Simba, too. It was so much more fun. "Dr. Alwanga" was a well-known scientist at the university and a good friend and colleague of Maddie's maternal uncle Jack, Pippa's father. Chuki, Hope's childhood friend and the last person anyone would have thought Dr. Alwanga would fall for, had ended up marrying him. It made sense that they'd stop by the house with their kids, since they lived in Nairobi.

"Simba and Chuki," Hope said. No surprise there.

"Pippa's coming up, too," Ryan said. He shrugged at Philip. "I figured I'd say so before you did."

"Go put your head in a—"

"Hey, you two. Stop it now." Hope gave them a look no kid would have challenged. Then again, these were Maddie's brothers. "That was your surprise. Pippa and your uncle Jack are already at the house waiting to see you."

Maddie grinned.

She couldn't wait to see Pippa. They had so much catching up to do. Plus, in all honesty, with everyone around, her dad would be less likely to ask about the case she was working on. At least for tonight.

As they departed, she looked out the window at the familiar buildings and scenery. The conversation in the car faded to the back of her mind. A horn blared at a man weaving a motorcycle-like *boda boda* through the traffic while transporting a daring passenger. No helmets for protection. A man stood at a small kiosk near the intersection up ahead selling freshly squeezed juice, while his goat ate peels on the ground next to him. A brand-new, rather stunning hotel, with beautifully manicured gardens at its entrance, stood across the street from the man and goat. The old and new. The familiar and unfamiliar.

The past, present and future always seemed to collide when Maddie came here. A trick of the mind. A side effect of memories. She was tired. It had to be why she suddenly felt down. She rubbed absent-mindedly at her stomach and barely heard someone say something about her being hungry. She wasn't, but she couldn't move her lips to explain. Her lids felt heavy and the hard glass of the window touched her temple as the world outside disappeared. She missed having good friends around. She wanted more than anything to see her cousin Pippa, but truth be told, she wished Haki was going to be there tonight, too.

CHAPTER FOUR

MADDIE SET HER hair clip next to her keepsake box and gave her scalp a quick rub. The wooden box carved with elephants had been a gift from her uncle Jack and auntie Anna. Hope had delivered it to Maddie when she'd visited College Town, Pennsylvania, for the first time, back when Maddie was ten. She pushed her hair over her shoulders and ran her fingertips along the carvings and the lid's seam. She wouldn't open it. Not right now, at least.

"Why isn't this cute guy on your bed in Philly?" Pippa plopped onto Maddie's bed and picked up the plush monkey—a lemur, to be specific—that had been her favorite doll when she was a kid. It had been a gift Pippa had given her shortly after they'd first met. Most kids under the age of five wouldn't have given up a new toy, but Pippa wasn't like most, not then and not now, and the moment she'd given Maddie that monkey, their friendship had been sealed.

"I can't take everything back with me." *You could if you wanted to.* She turned away from her dresser and collapsed onto the bed next to Pippa. "My place is small and every time I visit and pack to go back, I run out of room in my suitcase."

"You could mail yourself a box, you know." Pippa made the monkey's head nod and Maddie let a small laugh escape. What was it about hanging out with her that made Maddie feel like a kid again? Like she didn't always have to be serious or prove herself. There had been a point in her childhood, after her mother died, when she'd become painfully serious, but once Hope had entered their lives, Maddie had changed and promised herself she'd never go back to feeling that way again. What had happened? Growing up? She snatched the little lemur from Pippa.

"You want me to stick this poor guy in a box? You're so mean."

"I know. I'm terrible. Besides, I kind of like that you haven't totally vacated the place. It made it a lot more comfortable when I stayed here during university, for one thing. And it always felt reassuring. I could count on you coming back to visit. Not necessarily because you missed your family and friends, but because of this guy, of course." Pippa smirked at her. It *had* been a while since she'd seen her, but Maddie hadn't realized it actually bothered Pippa.

She reached over and twirled one of Pippa's corkscrew locks around her finger and gave it a tug.

"You know I miss all of you and would come here more if I had time."

Her stomach pinched. It wasn't exactly a lie. She did miss everyone, but staying away was less stressful. Even the pressure of proving herself to her boss wasn't as bad as trying to live up to her dad's expectations in real time.

"I know you're busy. Being a lawyer must keep you weighed down with things. I personally couldn't imagine having to work in an office all day. I think I'd lose my mind. You used to love the open spaces, too. Oh, the begging to get your dad to let you spend the weekend at Busara, over and over and over."

Maddie took a deep breath as she studied the fine crack that was making its way across her bedroom ceiling. How long had it been there? Did her parents know? Did it matter?

"Hey, you." Pippa sat up, so Maddie followed suit. "I can leave if you need to sleep."

"No, why? I'm good."

"You were daydreaming. I asked you if you ever adopted a cat. You said last time that you'd think about it. If the answer's no, then whoever this guy is who's allergic to them better be worth it."

"Gosh. No. To both. No boyfriend, and I don't have any pets except for a Betta fish. He's blue this time. My neighbor's kid is watching him for me, since I'm here so long."

She had kept a fish in a small tank ever since the first fish her well-intentioned dad had gotten her as a kid. She'd always loved animals and wanted a pet. In a moment of parental weakness—not a term that came to mind often with her dad—he'd succumbed to the idea. Rather, he'd decided to use bribery to get her to go to a therapy session. She'd expected a kitten or a puppy. He bought a fish. Not a big tank or a school of fish. Nope. A single, red Betta. Named Ben the Betta, after her dad. Funny how, though she'd been a bit disappointed with that first fish, she got hooked on him. When Ben the Betta died, she'd gotten another, then another after that. Each with a name beginning with the letter B. And when she left Barracuda with her brothers in Kenya and returned to Pennsylvania for college, she found herself at the shop buying another red one. She'd named this one Bilbo, and had decorated his bowl like a hobbit hole. It was sort of comforting having him around; plus, she liked feeding him.

"How do you do it? I mean, it just sounds so lonely over there. I have to admit, when you emailed and said you were coming, I thought something exciting was up. Like you were getting engaged and needed to plan a wedding and—"

"Oh, for heaven's sake, Pippa." She'd have to meet a decent guy for that to happen. The few she'd even looked twice at over the years were either the kind of guys who commanded respect but were also narcissistic jerks who didn't *get* her, or they were nice, decent guys…the kind that her father and brothers could flatten with one look. Not that that should matter, but there always seemed to be something lacking.

"I'm just so used to having everyone around—especially Haki, who, by the way, says hello."

Maddie smiled and hopped off the bed.

"How is he? Or should I ask how the *two* of you are?" Maddie peered out her window to the garden below. She watched as Delila lifted the hem of her vibrant wrap skirt, crossed the cool grass in her bare feet and began plucking figs from a tree overhanging a couple of wicker chairs. Maddie sat back down on the edge of the bed, took off her socks and wiggled her toes. Man, that felt good. Freeing.

"Haki is the same guy you last saw. Never changes." Pippa chuckled. "He was such a little man as a kid, he didn't have much to change. And I think we're getting closer. You know what I mean?"

No, she really didn't know. Or understand. The last time she'd seen Haki, she thought he'd changed a lot. Or maybe it seemed that way because she didn't see him all the time. Then again, Pippa knew him better.

"You *think* you're getting closer? Nothing official yet?" Maddie threw her socks in a woven-grass hamper and rummaged in the bottom drawer of her dresser for a pair of loose-fitting khakis. She stripped down to her bra and underwear and added her gray dress slacks and thin sweater to the laundry, then put on the khakis and a green T-shirt. She really needed to wear these on the flight home. So much more comfortable. Her dress slacks were the most casual thing in her closet back in Philly that were decent enough to leave her apartment in. She just didn't have much occasion to wear anything between business attire and pajamas.

"Like I said, when it comes to change, he tends to walk on eggs. Slow and cautious. I suppose there's a comfort in the status quo, but sooner or later, he'll get the nerve to make it official. I mean, it's no secret we're together and I seriously think our parents are wondering what he's waiting for."

"Hmm. Maybe since you both have practically lived together all your lives, he already feels like he's married." She opened the bottle of water on her dresser and took a swig.

"It's not like he's already milked the goat or anything," Pippa said. Maddie's water went down the wrong way, but she waved Pippa off when she jumped up at all the coughing.

"Pip, what I meant was that maybe he feels comfortable. He doesn't have to walk on eggshells. You know how he's all about safety and being in control. He's also a family kind of guy. Marriage to him probably means kids, and perhaps he's not ready for that. Or maybe he wants things to be perfect down to the last detail. You know, X amount of dollars in the bank, a life plan…predictable weather. Who knows."

"How much planning does he need? We have a place to live. He has a career and a job."

"If I were Haki, I wouldn't want to live at Busara with both families if I got married. Too many people. It's a rescue center, not a compound. So he'd need to be able to afford a place of his own. Maybe he's saving up and wants to surprise you."

Pippa frowned and picked at her cuticle.

"I guess, but it doesn't make sense to leave since he works there. We could just put up our own small house, possibly where the old tents used to be. Why have a commute when you don't have to? He already drives enough."

"Maybe you're right. Just give him time," Maddie said.

Pippa hopped off the bed and gave her a hug.

"It'll happen sooner than later, I'm sure, and when it does, you have to swear that even if you have the biggest case on your hands, you'll be here for the wedding. Promise?"

"Of course."

She meant it. She did. Pippa was like a little sister. Her happiness meant everything to Maddie. She took another sip of water and hoped it would wash away the bittersweet feeling that clung to her chest like morning dew on the branches of a weeping willow. She took a second sip to drown her guilt and to bury her secret as deep as the ocean she'd crossed to get here.

"Pippa, I wouldn't miss your wedding for the world."

THE SKY BEYOND the valley was deep scarlet this time. Yesterday, it had been streaked with bands of carnelian and amethyst. It was never the same. Each evening promised an unexpected blend of colors. Every sunset promised change. It was Haki's favorite time of day.

"Checkmate." Kamau leaned back in the rocker on the front porch of the Busara house and linked his hands behind his head. "You're losing your touch."

Haki scrutinized the board and retraced their last few moves. He really was losing his touch. His father hadn't beaten him in at least six months.

"I don't see it. What happened?"

"Your knight. Three moves ago," Kamau said, indicating how he'd created a weakness.

Haki had made one wrong choice and left himself vulnerable. He held his head in his hands for a moment, then scrubbed at the stubble on his jaw and sat back in defeat.

"I can't believe I did that." He picked up the wooden box that housed the chess-and-checkers set that Kamau had given him as a gift when he was only six, right after Haki found out that Kamau was going to marry his mother and become the father he never had. Kamau had taught him to play checkers even before that, but back then they used to sit on overturned buckets outside the tent that had served as the camp's kitchen and dining area. And Kamau used to let him win. He began putting away the pieces.

"Your mind wasn't here. I could tell I had a chance halfway through the game. Anything I can help with?"

Haki shook his head. "Just tired. Long day."

The camp had quieted; even the baby elephants were sound asleep in their pens with their keepers, but the ebb and flow of insects crying out for their mates rippled through the air like waves licking at the parched, hot sand. Nightfall masked the harsh effects of the drought. It masked a lot of things. But Haki's father had a way of seeing through veils, even in the dark.

"Perhaps you should have taken the day off and flown with them to Nairobi."

"No need," Haki said quickly. He closed the wooden case.

"I said nothing about need."

Haki smiled and stood.

"Are you going to try to checkmate me all evening? Don't let one win go to your head."

Kamau laughed and pushed back his chair.

"All right. Deflect, but you know I'm here if you need to talk, or gain insight into the minds of women…or for tips on how to win at chess," he added with a chuckle.

"Hey," Haki said, shaking his finger at him. "Tomorrow will be the start of my next winning streak. You've been warned."

Kamau left the screen door creaking to a close behind him and Haki caught a glimpse of his younger brother, Huru, sketching in the family room. At fifteen, an age when most kids wallowed in hormones and angst, Huru was as mellow as they came. Maybe he channeled it all into his artwork—there was no doubt he had a gift—but sometimes Haki had to wonder if names carried enough power to define a person, or if it was the emotional state of the mother at the time of naming and rearing the child that made all the difference. Huru had always had a carefree way about him. *Free*, just as his name meant in Swahili, or perhaps how their mother felt at his birth: married, happy and loved, unlike how she'd been when Haki was conceived in an act of violence. Haki meant *justice*. And there had never been a time when he didn't find himself wanting it. Wanting those who caused pain and harm to be held accountable, wanting to be sure he'd always be the kind of honorable man Kamau was…and not like the criminal whose blood he shared.

MADDIE CLOSED HER room door gently and tiptoed downstairs. Everyone but Simba and Chuki, who lived nearby, had opted to stay the night, rather than fly out of Nairobi in the dark. Her uncles had crashed in Chad's empty room and Pippa was hogging most of her bed. Not that it mattered, given that Maddie couldn't sleep. It was almost midnight, but for her it felt like midafternoon.

She turned on the kitchen light and squinted until her eyes adjusted. Maybe some chamomile tea would help her get sleepy. What she really needed was to force herself not to nap during the day. The one she'd taken on the way home from the airport had given her a second wind.

She set her laptop on the kitchen butcher block and went to put a kettle of water on the gas stove. If sleep wasn't happening then work was. She needed to be prepared for tomorrow. The last thing she wanted was for the lawyers overseeing the case to call up Levy and ask him why he'd sent them someone clueless. She pulled up a stool and flipped open her computer.

"A bit late for work."

She startled but immediately relaxed when her dad put his hands on her shoulders and pressed a kiss to the top of her head. She closed her eyes briefly and took it in. Moments like this, his love felt unconditional. Earlier, he'd wrapped her in a bear hug that she never wanted to leave. There was no mistaking he loved her. But that only made it more hurtful when he was critical. She closed her laptop. Maybe just tonight, this first night, she could avoid a serious conversation with him.

"Couldn't sleep," she said. "But you should be. I hope I didn't make too much noise."

"Nah." He padded over to the fridge and pulled out a wrapped sandwich. He held it up for her to see, then unwrapped it. "I tell you, I'm spoiled. Made and waiting for me."

"A sandwich at this hour?"

"Peanut butter and honey. My go-to late-night snack. You want one? It'll help you sleep. I can't sleep if I'm hungry."

"No, thanks. I ate so much at dinner. Hunger isn't my problem."

As much as he'd eaten, she couldn't imagine why he'd be hungry, but then again, his work was quite physical.

"You look great, Mads." He took a bite. "Tired, but great. They treating you well at that firm? Good health-care coverage? They're not bumming off their worst cases on you, are they?"

So much for the warm fuzzies.

"I'm happy there, Dad, and yes, I'm covered. I did read the fine print when I signed on with them. It's a habit they teach in law school." The kettle began whistling and she hurried to turn off the stove so it wouldn't wake anyone.

"I don't doubt it. Good habit, too. So is carrying pepper spray, or better yet, not leaving work alone after dark."

"Dad, I'm twenty-six. I can take care of myself. You don't have to worry."

"You work in Philadelphia. Big cities have crime problems. Predators lurk in parking lots after dark. If you leave the building every night at the same time, they'll catch on to your pattern."

"I know. You went over every safety tactic when I left for college, and I haven't forgotten the self-defense moves you taught me, either. Luckily, I haven't had to use them. Do you want a mug of tea with that?" she asked as she poured water on some loose chamomile, dried from the garden.

"No, I'll grab some milk in a sec."

"I'll get it for you."

"Thanks. Did you hear that Chad got promoted? Lance corporal."

"Mom didn't mention that. Just that he was okay."

"Yep. He's okay. More than okay. He's working his way up."

"That's good." Chad had always wanted

to follow in his father's footsteps. No doubt he'd command a unit someday. Obviously, their dad was proud.

"Ryan and Philip are both at the top of their classes, too. Smart boys."

"It's so good to see them. I can't get over how tall they are."

"So what's this case you're here for? If I have any contacts who can help, let me know."

He had to ask. She set a glass of milk next to him, then cradled her mug of tea as she sat down. Might as well put it out there and deal with the backlash.

"I'll be stopping by our sister office tomorrow to meet with the barristers, but I'll also need to spend time in some of the villages. I'm thinking of staying at Busara or Camp Jamba Walker and taking day trips to talk to the village elders and leaders. I'll be looking into the hardships some of the farmers are experiencing and getting testimony in their defense."

"Defense of what?" Ben took his last bite of sandwich and brushed the crumbs off his hands.

"A proposal was submitted that calls for harsher punishments against Masai farmers who kill elephants. We intend to have it thrown out."

His brow furrowed and he cocked his head.

"On what grounds?"

"On the grounds that they're already enduring hardship and the fines proposed are beyond anything they could afford. The prison terms would prevent families from being able to keep up with their farms or generate income to feed their children and survive."

"What are you doing, Mads?" He got up, shaking his head, and dumped the last sip of his milk in the sink. "Of all cases, why would you take this on?"

"What do you mean? Why would I fight for human rights? That seems like a no-brainer to me."

"What about animal rights? You know what goes on out there. Half of your family works to fight poaching. You lived here. You know this. That proposal is needed to discourage native tribes from aiding and abetting. Busara is about elephant rescue. You plan to stay there and expect them to take you around so you can fight this?"

"This isn't about poachers. We're not trying to encourage elephant killing. You know

I wouldn't do that. This is about protecting the only land the tribes have left. It's about protecting their livelihood."

Ben pinched the bridge of his nose, then rubbed the back of his neck. This was going about as well as she'd expected. Every ounce of confidence she'd been mustering up for tomorrow sank to her feet. Why did conversations with him always leave her feeling confused and plain bad? She put down her steaming mug and gathered her laptop. Even if she didn't sleep, lying in bed and staring at the ceiling would be better than arguing.

"Maddie, you need to tell them you can't work on this case."

"I can't do that and you don't get to make that call. My future depends on me helping to win this. This is what I do."

"What about conflict of interest?"

"I don't understand. There's no conflict of interest, especially not if we win." *The only conflict is between the two of us right now.*

"Maddie. I've personally seen that proposal, and I support it. It was submitted by a wildlife advocacy group and has the backing of Busara and other rescue groups around the national parks. I have no doubt it'll get passed."

"How can you be so sure?"

"Because Haki helped put it together. He, of all men, won't stand by and watch you tear it apart."

CHAPTER FIVE

MADDIE ARRANGED IT so she could fly out west to Camp Busara with Pippa, Jack and Mac midday, after reporting to the law office that morning. Her dad had promised to stay out of it and not call Haki with a briefing. She wanted the chance to talk to him in person. If he'd worked on the proposal, then all she had to do was get through to him. Haki was a listener. He'd hear her out.

The aerial view of Busara, nestled on a plateau with the river valley to one side and grasslands to the other, was nothing short of spectacular. A lone acacia tree shaded a small observation platform Dr. Bekker used when watching the herds passing through the valley. Lush groves of wild fruit trees flanked the camp, giving it the appearance of an oasis. She could even spot several keepers in rimmed hats leading the baby elephants in their care out for some sun and socializing. A cloud of dust trailed along the road beneath Mac's helicopter and turned into the camp ahead.

"Haki just got back," Pippa said into the mic of her headpiece. She pointed at the man shielding his eyes and looking up.

A flutter of excitement mixed with apprehension swirled in Maddie's stomach. She nodded to let Pippa know she saw him.

Mac began his descent into a clearing just far enough from the camp to keep the draft from kicking up a dirt storm. She waited for the all clear, then removed her headgear, hoisted her backpack onto one shoulder and managed to climb out of the chopper without stumbling. Pippa grabbed her hand and tugged her at a jogging pace toward the jeep.

"Look who's here, Haki!" She ran to his side, then stretched out her arms and made a show of presenting Maddie. Sometimes the pep in Pippa was too much.

Haki stood there, his strong jawline softened with a few days' worth of stubble that looked disconcertingly good on him. His shoulders seemed broader, too, unless it was the dark green shirt he wore with his khakis and the way his hands rested on his hips. He'd put on a few pounds of muscle for sure.

The corner of his mouth lifted and he let his gaze rest on her for a few seconds.

"Maddie-girl. Finally here."

She ducked her head and smiled. Why did she suddenly feel shy?

"It has been a while, Haki. Pippa says you're becoming quite the hero around here."

He shot Pippa an annoyed glance and let his hands fall to his sides.

"No. Nothing I've done comes close to what others do here. But I hear you're on your way to becoming a world-famous lawyer."

"Not even close. Pippa," she admonished. Was he being sarcastic? Had someone already told him what she was here for?

"We could use good counsel around here," he said.

So he didn't know.

"Both of you are much too humble," Pippa said.

Haki put a hand to his shirt.

"I wanted to shower. I mean, I thought I'd make it back ahead of you—all of you—and have time to clean up."

Mac's chopper whirred as it lifted off. The air current pushed past them, and Maddie quickly pulled her arms back and wrapped them around her waist before anyone realized she almost went in for a hug.

"Hey, Dr. Hak-man, do you know if Anna is here or off in the field?" Jack asked, walking past them and giving him an air salute.

"I just got here. Last radio communication, my father was out, so she's probably in the clinic."

"I'll check. See you guys at dinner," he called back.

"Sounds good. I'm going to head in to wash up," Haki said, thumbing toward the house. "I'll see you two afterward."

No hug, then. Friends hugged, didn't they? Even if he'd been covered in mud from head to toe, it shouldn't have mattered. This all felt so anticlimactic, but what had she expected? They'd both been so busy the past few years that they hadn't seen much of each other even when she'd visited her parents. She hadn't made the effort. So why did it matter now? Because she was afraid he'd hate her by tomorrow?

Pippa looped her arm in Maddie's and they made their way to the house, purposefully lagging behind Haki. His long, focused strides made it easy.

"Dr. Hak-man? Really?"

"My dad is silly when he's in a good mood. He doesn't get that it annoys Haki. By the way, you have to find time for a reading while you're out here," Pippa said.

"No way. I don't need my fortune told. I have enough in my head without cluttering it with nonsense. Besides, it's kind of over-stepping. It's a tribal custom, not a tourist attraction."

"You're not a tourist and you'll be right there talking to the villagers and elders any-way. One reading wouldn't be disrespectful or overstepping. It would show that you re-spect their ways."

The aroma of freshly baked *chapati* wafted past them and Maddie inhaled deeply.

"Why is the mere smell of freshly baked bread like a drug? I don't need to eat any-thing else but that while I'm here."

"You're switching subjects."

"I'm not promising anything." She had to admit, Pippa had a point about respecting the Masai culture. It was all in fun, though, right? Or was it? The one reading she'd done, back when she was seventeen, had come so close to the truth it made her nervous. The *Laibon* had taken one look at his stones and told her she would go far away. *Journey far.*

Leave. Those had been his words. She hadn't yet told anyone that she'd been applying to colleges in the US, not even Haki or Pippa. She hadn't told anyone she'd desperately needed to get away. To escape. To live without parents or siblings constantly checking over her shoulder. The *Laibon* had known, though. Whether it had truly been the stones, or the old man had simply guessed it from her notoriously expressive face, he'd been right. And it had freaked her out a little.

"Fine, but at least think about it. For old time's sake. I miss having you around and doing things like henna tattoos and…ditching Haki. Oh, yes. Right now. Don't say no."

"No. I want to go in and say hi to Auntie Niara and the boys, then run by the pens to see Auntie Anna."

"Come on. Wearing a suit all day is really sucking the fun out of you. Leave your backpack on the porch steps. We won't go far. Just far enough to get his attention."

Haki's attention. As if Pippa didn't already get enough of it.

"WHAT DO YOU MEAN you haven't seen them?"

It had been at least an hour since Haki had showered. He'd stayed in the house to help

Noah and Huru with some homework problems they'd been assigned via their virtual classes and figured Maddie and Pip had gone to see the orphans and everyone at the clinic.

"We assumed they were here," Anna said. "I just finished logging treatments and Kam just got back from rounds. They're still restocking their jeep supplies for tomorrow. But none of us has seen them yet." She pulled her walkie-talkie off her belt, then set it back and flung her hand toward the unit sitting on the console by the door. "That's hers, isn't it?"

Haki flattened his lips. It was hers, all right. She hadn't taken it to Nairobi, naturally, but she also hadn't come by the house to grab it today.

"I'll go look for them. Huru, Noah, go check the old mess tent and the area behind it. Don't wander off. Just see if they're hanging out there. Tell them dinner is ready. Let me know if they're there. I'll check the lookout." The old mess tent and adjacent framed tents were original to the camp and where Haki and Pippa had spent their toddler years. They were used mostly for storage now, but Pippa still liked to go back by the old water well and sit in the hammock under the mango tree.

He had a gut feeling they weren't there right now, but with the sun setting and Pippa's recent carelessness, the more ground covered, the better.

"I'm sure they're close," Niara said, setting the last of the dishes on the long, wood dining table. His mother patted his back. "Pippa really knows how to push your buttons." She nodded toward the massive floor-to-ceiling window that overlooked the southwest side of camp and the valley beyond. Anna's acacia tree sprawled like a black mushroom silhouetted against a watermelon sky. A flash of blue on the lookout platform beneath the canopy caught his attention.

"I'll be back in a minute," he said. He couldn't help but wonder if wedding bands could be rigged with two-way mics or maybe even tracking devices. Not that he'd do that to Pippa, but what was up with her lately?

He made his way past the elephant pens and through the low-lying grasses that spanned the stretch to the tree.

"I see him coming. Took him longer than usual."

Pippa's voice drifted toward him. Always happy. Always energizing. His lips twisted into a smile. She made it impossible to stay upset or annoyed. He couldn't quite make out Maddie's response. Her voice had always been soft, even when she was younger. Especially when she was younger. But even now it had a mellow warmth to it, one that blended into the summer evening and disappeared before it could reach him. It made his mind spin with curiosity.

He stuffed his hands in his pockets and slowed his approach.

"We really should get back. I feel like I'm being rude, not having said hello to everyone yet."

"You're so much like Haki. So concerned with what others think, always busy worrying and following rules. No one will care. I'll take the blame if they say anything. Let yourself relax. I mean, look at that. A 360-degree view. Isn't it amazing?"

He could see Maddie's silhouette as she pulled up her knees and wrapped her arms around them.

"A part of me could sit here and watch the sun rise every morning and set every night and never tire of it. I remember reading books up here a time or two. I do miss how peaceful it is. Out here you can actually feel the day end," she said.

"I know what you mean. Whenever I stay in the city, I have trouble winding down. It's kind of true when they say cities never sleep. All that nightlife."

The idea of Pip never winding down was borderline scary. A chuckle escaped him. He was answered with soft laughter.

"Okay, you two. Game over." He climbed the weathered, wooden ladder and crossed his arms on the edge of the platform. "You left your radio behind again, Pip."

The last remnants of light reflected off her auburn curls, bringing out golden highlights. Every year, the sun seemed to make it lighter.

"I never really left camp, did I?" She gave him a cheeky grin. "Besides, I knew you'd come and rescue us. I can't climb down if you're on the ladder."

He backed down a few steps, then jumped to the ground. Pippa backed down fewer and jumped farther. He didn't comment. Maddie turned onto her knees, carefully found her footing and looked down at the rungs each time to be sure she didn't miss a step. He figured she wasn't planning on any jumps. She was almost there. Her hips were level with his shoulders. Pippa had jumped from much higher than that. Maddie stopped altogether and began tugging at her waist.

"Something wrong?" Haki moved to the side of the ladder.

"Nope. I'm fine. My pants snagged on something. Just give me a second." She sucked on her lower lip as she held on to the ladder with one hand and tried stretching and tugging at her waistband with the other. Her cheeks took on the colors of the sunset, but since the sky had darkened, he knew reflection had nothing to do with it.

He pulled a flashlight off the back of his belt and shone it at the rung in question. The wood had split and she'd managed to fish-hook a thick shard through the empty belt loop of her khakis.

"What is it?" Pippa asked.

"These rungs need to be replaced as soon as possible," he said. "Guess you'll have to stay here all night, Maddie-girl."

"I don't think so. Besides, you'd never leave me here. Unless you plan to sleep under me." Her face turned even redder. He kept a straight face. He knew what she meant. Her poor pride needed rescuing.

"I could cut you loose with my knife, but I don't think we have to ruin your clothes. Stay still a minute and move your hand. Hold on to the ladder with both."

The bottom of her shirt lifted just enough for the moonlight to touch her skin as she reached for the rung above her head and held on. He stepped behind her, put his hands around her waist and felt for the snag. Her shirt brushed against his cheek and the subtle scents of citrus and fresh soap filled his next breath. He closed his eyes just for a second. He needed to focus. He needed to visualize. He needed to be standing right where he was to keep her from falling backward.

"I'm going to break off the piece of wood at the base of where it splintered. I don't want it to hurt you, so I'm going to put my hand against your waist to protect your skin. Okay?"

"Should I hold a flashlight for you?" Pippa asked.

"Nah, I've got this." At Pippa's height, she'd be flashing the light up in his face and his hands would block most of it anyway.

"Do whatever you need to do. If it's too much work, just cut my pant loop," Maddie said.

He slipped his fingertips barely below the waistline of her pants and pressed his palm against her, so that the belt loop and jagged end of the piece of wood were against the back of his left hand. With his right, he broke off the shard in one quick move.

"All done. I've got you. Let go of the ladder." He held her by the waist, set her feet on the ground, then immediately let go and took several steps back.

"Thank you," she breathed. Her long hair shielded her face as she looked down, unhooked the piece of wood from her loop and tossed it into the grass. Pippa hurried to her side and put her arm around her.

"I told you he's a hero around here. You okay?"

Maddie pushed her hair behind her ears and smiled, but it didn't quite reach her eyes.

"Of course. I'm totally fine. Thank you again, Haki." She nodded one too many times.

"No big deal. Stuff like that happens pretty much every day around here," he said. And by "around here" he meant somewhere in the vast wilds of Kenya. Not that he'd witnessed it, but surely she wasn't the only woman in the region to hang from an observation platform by her belt loop. Maddie's color seemed to fade back to normal in the moonlight and her shoulders relaxed. Good. "We should go eat before Huru and Noah clear the table. And I don't mean the dishes. The appetite of teen boys—surpassed only by the appetite of teen elephant bulls." He motioned for them to walk ahead of him; then he curled his fingers into his palm and pressed against the stinging abrasion on the back of his hand.

He could handle the sting. In fact, he needed it right now. He deserved it. *Justice.* Pain for punishment. *You have a future, here, with Pippa. Where's your sense of honor?* He closed his eyes and took a grounding, cleansing breath of night air, and then another… but it failed to clear Maddie from his senses.

CHAPTER SIX

MADDIE WAS RELIEVED that she wasn't seated close to Haki and Pippa at dinner. She couldn't bring herself to look either of them in the eyes. God help her, she'd always been told she wore her emotions on her sleeve. One of her law professors had even warned her that she needed to work on a poker face if she ever hoped to catch a witness off guard on the stand. She projected with her face. She couldn't help it. She didn't do it consciously.

Her mom often reminded her that her facial expressions had been a key part of how she'd communicated back when she couldn't speak as a child and that she thought it was a beautiful part of her. That it showed honesty. But Hope had a way of finding the positive side of everything. At the moment, the last thing Maddie needed was honesty plastered all over her face. If Haki or Pippa could see what she was *honestly* feeling or thinking…she'd die. Plain and simple. It would destroy them.

She put another bite of mango in her mouth. Dinner had been a delicious, savory stew with homemade flatbread, and dessert was an array of fruits—so much healthier than *mandazi*—but she was full. The only reason she kept eating was so she could listen instead of talking. Talking when she still felt confused and guilty and couldn't focus… yeah, that wouldn't be good.

The conversation rolled from Jack's latest findings in his genetic research to the steady flow of donations coming in to help support the orphans, to how Huru and Noah were doing with their studies. Haki said something and his voice seemed to be the only one she keyed into.

She rubbed her hand along her arm where the rough stubble of his jaw and warmth of his breath had inadvertently caressed her skin earlier, at the tree. Even the vibration of his deep voice, when he'd gotten permission to touch her before unsnagging her, had made the hairs along her arms dance. And now… just listening to him… What was wrong with her? No guy had ever had this effect on her, and she wanted the feeling to go away. It was overpowering. It was dangerous. It betrayed Pippa.

She set down her fork and took a drink of water. Maybe she needed a shower or maybe she was still jet-lagged. That had to be it.

"I know what's on your mind, Maddie," Pippa called out from the far end of the table. Maddie's stomach churned.

"You do?"

"Tomorrow? You probably want to sleep because I know you didn't last night and we need to talk about what time you need to head out, who's taking you. You know. All that," she said.

"I'm sorry. You lost me. Out where? I thought you were just visiting," Niara said.

"I am, but I also have some work to do. For my law firm's sister office in Nairobi."

"Cool," Noah said. "Maybe I should go into law. You get paid for arguing."

"Well, that's not all there is to it." Maddie grinned. She had to give him credit for his unique take on the profession.

"But you get to stand up in court and try to win a case before a judge, right?"

"A lot of work goes into cases before anyone ever shows up in court," she said with a tactical maneuver her dad would appreciate.

"Do they really have artists drawing people in the courtroom?" Huru asked.

"Yes, sometimes."

"Ben told me you'll need to get out to some of the farms and villages. I promised him you'd be safe," Jack said. He hesitated, glanced up at her, then pushed his plate away. She got the distinct impression her dad had told him about the specifics of the case. "Mac was going to help you tomorrow, but they got unexpected guests at the camp and Mugi and Kesi need his chopper services. So we'd better figure out new plans."

Maddie frowned and sat up taller. He had her attention. Had Uncle Mac really backed out because of work, or because he didn't want any part in helping her counter the KWS proposal? She knew Mugi and Kesi, and they were good people. They were an older couple who'd taken Mac under their wing when he'd first come to Kenya from South Africa as a young man. Then about fifteen years ago, they'd helped him and Tessa out after she had escaped to Kenya with their nephew and needed a place to lie low while trying to find out if her husband was involved in an ivory-smuggling ring. Mac had ended up going into business with Mugi and Kesi, expanding their ecotourist camp in the Masai Mara, about a half day's drive north of Busara.

"I can take her," Pippa said. Pippa would volunteer no matter what Maddie was doing because she was that loyal. Maddie's chest pinched.

"I don't think so," Anna and Jack said almost simultaneously. Pippa gave them a look.

"Honey, I know you can get around here as well as anyone, but it's not safe for the two of you to go that far alone," Anna said. "In fact, depending on how much time you spend in the villages, if you're headed toward the river, then looping up closer to Narok and back into the Mara, you might not make it in a day." She turned to Maddie. "I saw your list of stops and am basing it on that. You'd better take some camping supplies just in case."

"And second, Pippa," Jack added, "Mugi and Kesi need you at their camp. They said you promised to teach a group of kids about some of the geological attractions in the area and why our soil is rich and red."

Maddie had meant to ask her what she was doing with the undergraduate geology degree she'd gotten. Teaching at a camp once in a while didn't seem like much of a use, though.

Oh, great. She was criticizing—judging—

just like her dad. Who was she to say anything? At least Pippa seemed happy with her
life. Despite looking irritated at the moment.

"I did tell them I'd do that. I just didn't
know it'd be tomorrow."

Maddie noticed Haki hadn't said anything.
He sat there making tracks through the con-
densation on his glass with his fingertip. The
muscle along his jaw twitched.

"I won't know if I can help, until morning,"
Kamau said. "If I'm needed for a rescue, I
have to put that life first. You understand."

"Absolutely," Maddie said. Pippa had assured her she'd made arrangements. Maddie
had been so tired that she hadn't double-
checked. She knew better. She'd learned early
on as a junior lawyer to do her own work if
she wanted it done right. Yet seniors dele-
gated all the time. That's why she was here in
the first place. She suddenly understood why
Mr. Levy had chosen her. What he'd meant
when he'd said all those nice things. She was
someone he could count on. But wasn't Maddie supposed to be able to count on family?
Her first day on the job and she was already
going to look incompetent. She'd assured her
law firm that she had a guide. After all, they
were lawyers and too smart to risk sending

her out in the field without safety measures. But regardless, traveling alone would be dangerous and not something she was experienced enough to do. "It's not an issue. I'll call the office in Nairobi first thing in the morning and see if they can arrange for someone to take me around."

"Actually, Maddie insisted that she could get a hire, but I told her with all of us here, why bother anyone else? I didn't think it'd be a problem. I was personally hoping to tag along to spend more time with her," Pippa confessed.

She really was a good person. She didn't deserve to be hurt. They were supposed to have each other's backs. At least one of them understood that. Maddie caught Pippa's eye and cocked her head in a silent thank-you.

"I'd take you myself, but I need to be here for the baby that Kam brought in today. She's still in critical condition," Anna said. "Severely underweight and the snare wound was infected."

Haki scowled when everyone turned to look at him.

"I'm off tomorrow, yes, but I feel like I'm being ambushed. Apparently, everyone at this table knows why Maddie is visiting the

Masai homesteads except me, and my gut is telling me it's not a social call. I get the feeling it's something I don't want to know. Now, why is that?" he asked.

Jack looked at her and splayed his palms. This was her deal. Her battle. Her case. The organized list of defenses Maddie had for why she'd signed on for it rolled through her mind. She'd rehearsed this in her head. It was game time. The lawyer in her geared up for an offense.

"Maddie's law firm is trying to block the proposal you helped put together. They're representing Native Watch Global. She's here on an information-and-evidence-gathering trip," Pippa said.

Maddie's breathing hitched. *Pippa?* And Haki felt ambushed? Truth or not, Pippa sounded like she was ratting on her for doing something wrong. Defending human rights wasn't wrong, but what did Maddie expect if Pippa and Haki were a couple? Pippa was protecting him. It was as it should be. Maddie couldn't help but feel demoted. For all the times she'd come out first in school and at work, she seemed destined to come out second in her personal life. She closed her eyes and raked her long hair behind her ears to gather herself. She needed to focus on what was in reach. Her career. And on what she truly believed was right.

"Is that true? You're trying to stop a law that would discourage the retaliatory killing?" Haki got up from his chair without meeting her eyes. He didn't have to. His mere tone made her stomach tense. He leaned forward, braced his hands flat against the table and stared at the spot where his plate had been. "A law that would protect the intelligent, compassionate and persecuted beings your family has dedicated their lives to helping? You have some nerve coming to dinner."

Maddie, the Trojan horse. She licked her lips and cocked her head toward him. No one at the table spoke, especially not wide-eyed Huru and Noah, who'd either figured out that silence was a form of self-preservation or were starved for entertainment.

"Yes, it's true. Let's talk about why. You make it sound wrong, but hear me out."

"I've heard enough. I can't believe all of you. I won't be taking her anywhere." He left the table and stalked toward the front door.

"Hak-man," Jack called after him. "We have a saying in America. 'Keep your friends close and your enemies closer.' Sorry, Maddie. Don't take that the wrong way. We love you, but you all get the point," he added, addressing everyone including Haki.

Haki turned and, for the first time since he'd freed her from the ladder, he looked directly at her. His lids sank at the corners and the rich brown of his eyes faded. There was something more intense than anger in his eyes—more penetrating, more personal. Something that crushed her core and ripped her heart open.

Disappointment.

CHANGE WASN'T ALWAYS a good thing.

Haki sat on the front stoop peeling a tangerine as the sun scattered its first rays across the eastern slopes of Mount Kilimanjaro in the distance. With death came rebirth, and he'd always loved that sunsets promised sunrises. A new day meant that wrongs could be righted, that mistakes could give rise to better choices, that dreams could awaken progress. Every sunrise was supposed to bring with it the chance to make progress, whether it meant saving a species or a single life or, at least, stopping evil from leaving permanent scars. But this sunrise was different.

He put a section of fruit in his mouth but the fresh tang of citrus failed to energize him. Instead of waking up another day wiser, he'd woken up a fool. A rooster cried out and was answered by the trumpeting of elephants. A door to one of the pens creaked open and Haki could hear singing. Ahron, who had begun working as a keeper at Busara back when it was a mere seedling, always sang to the orphaned babies in the morning, as their bottles of milk were prepared.

Haki couldn't fathom the idea that those same baby elephants they'd put so much effort into saving would someday be free to roam, only to end up getting killed. It was wrong. He thought of Bakhari, one of their first rescues from when Haki was only five, who they'd been tracking ever since. Bakhari was out there now. He could end up a victim once again, only this time, he wouldn't get a second chance at life.

Mosi scampered along the thatched roof of the porch and climbed down one of the hand-hewn wooden columns that held it up. He eyed the tangerine, then wrinkled his brow and gave Haki the most pitiful look. Haki chuckled.

"Mosi, the master manipulator. At least I

know what to expect with you." He tossed the monkey the rest of the tangerine. Mosi caught it, squealed in appreciation and ran off to enjoy his effortless breakfast.

Keep your enemies closer. That was essentially manipulation. The word had such a negative connotation, but what if it harmed none? Mosi got what he wanted by tapping into a human's emotions with one harmless look. Nature was full of lessons, wasn't it? And Jack was right. Spending time with Maddie meant having the chance to sway her. He needed to find the old Maddie, the girl who'd once dreamed of visiting Kenya and going on safari, and had had that dream come true in spades…then abandoned it. He needed to find the Maddie who used to love tagging along with the keepers and begging them to let her bottle-feed the baby elephants. He needed to save her from that high-achieving, put-together, lawyerly facade.

The sun uncovered its full self and cast a blend of shadows and reflections across Busara. He stood and stretched his back. Perhaps progress could happen today after all. He simply needed to appeal to her emotions and conscience. Sure, he'd take her wherever she wanted to go, to get whatever information she needed, but she was going to get a lot more than she bargained for.

The screen door opened and clattered softly shut behind him. He glanced over his shoulder.

"Good morning."

Anna had always been an early riser. She held her mug of coffee to her lips and closed her eyes.

"Mmm. Sorry, I needed that sip too desperately to talk. Good morning." She leaned against the porch banister. "Plans today?"

"Do you need help in the clinic?"

"No, I'm good. And you don't take enough time off. As soon as I guzzle this mug, I'll check on Etana. The baby from yesterday," she explained.

"Interesting name choice. I hope it helps."

"You know Pippa. She insists it can't hurt."

Pippa had been naming the majority of their baby orphans since she was just out of babyhood herself. Etana meant "strong child" in Kiswahili; as weak and malnourished as Anna had said the baby elephant was when they found her, Pippa was no doubt trying to give it hope in her own way. Haki tipped his head to the side.

"No, it can't. Is Mac picking her up?"

"Yes. Very soon. I told her if they get too busy at Camp Jamba Walker, she can always stay overnight to help until he can bring her back."

"I might be able to loop around and get her, depending on how the day goes and if she wants to wait for us."

Anna took her last swig of coffee.

"I was afraid to ask what you'd decided. Are you taking her?"

By "her" he knew she meant Maddie. He inhaled through his nose and let it out with a sigh.

"I'll take her. Jack made a good point last night."

"Ah. So you plan to change her mind about the case?"

He shrugged. Anna smiled as she set down her mug and pulled her hair back into a ponytail.

"And here I thought that all you men in the family learned long ago how hard it is to change the mind of a strong woman."

The image of Maddie stuck to the ladder and looking like her pride would never recover came to mind. Strong woman? If anything, she seemed unsure of herself.

"You're frowning." Anna's voice softened and she put her hand on his arm. "Haki, the ones who've had to overcome the greatest hurdles usually have the greatest inner strength. Having a gentle soul doesn't make a person weak. Take your parents, for example—especially Niara. And Maddie. And you, you've had a good life, but you're so much like your father."

He flinched. His father as in Kamau, not the man who *fathered* him.

"Am I?"

"I helped to raise you, didn't I? Just like Kam. Always the strong, quiet protector."

The back of his neck warmed and he tucked his hands in his pockets.

"Just remember," she continued, "Maddie is not so different."

Anna patted his back and headed to the clinic to check on Etana and the others.

Maddie a protector? Anna was right in a sense. She'd always been the older one, making sure her brothers' or Pippa's feelings weren't hurt growing up. Same for Haki. But now, she was here to defend the villagers and Haki was born to defend the elephants.

The problem was that only one of them could win.

And someone was going to get hurt.

CHAPTER SEVEN

THE JEEP HIT another rut in the dirt trail Haki was navigating and Maddie's ballpoint pen slashed across her notepad yet again. The list of villages the latest crop-destruction complaints had come from, plus her notes on what questions to ask, were beginning to make a modern art statement. Haki picked up speed, though he had to have noticed her failed attempts at writing. She put the pen between her teeth and shoved the notepad between her knees to keep it from blowing away while she tightened the purple scarf she wore as a headband to keep her hair out of her face. He hit another rut and the bounce of the jeep had her grabbing for something to hold on to. She pulled the pen from between her teeth.

"Are you *trying* to hit potholes?" The long stretch of redbrick earth ahead of them didn't look as rough as it felt. She was pretty sure he'd killed his shock absorbers.

"Absolutely."

He snatched the pen from her hand before she realized he was going for it, put it to his side where she couldn't reach and set his hand back on the steering wheel as if he'd done nothing wrong.

"Haki, please give me the pen." She held her hand out but had to clutch the dashboard when he hit another bump. She glared at him and held her hand out again, this time a little closer. "Please."

He took her hand in his, then guided it back to her lap.

"I don't think so," he said. His hand felt warm and calloused and...safe. No, never mind safe.

She swiped the notepad from between her knees and set it out of his reach before he could steal it, too.

"I wasn't going to take it," he said, taking his hand back. "I don't need it. You don't need it, either."

Heaven help her, they definitely didn't need their hands touching. As annoyed as she was with him and despite the hot sun, goose bumps ran up her arms and she had the dangerous urge to weave her fingers through

his and leave them that way for the entire
road trip.

*He's talking about the writing pad, you
dork. And he's off-limits. Stay on the task.*

"You don't know what I need. I'm not on
a safari here. I'm working."

"Who says a person can't enjoy their
work?" he called out over the engine noise.

"I do. This is serious. If something I need
answered comes to mind, I need to jot it
down. And I have where I need to go written down, too. I'm not calling the office and
telling them I lost my information. Do you
want to get me fired?" Lists and notes made
her feel in control. Her attention to detail was
what she had going for her at work. Without that, she'd be the lowest junior lawyer on
the totem pole and her chances at partnership would be nil. In her dad's world, she'd
be outranked by just about everybody. She
wasn't screwing up this assignment. "Come
on, Haki. Swear you won't try to take my papers. It's not funny. We're not kids anymore."

He glanced over at her, not quite smiling,
and in that fraction of a second, their eyes
connected and she knew he remembered. The
way he'd sneak up behind her and run off
with the book she was reading. She never

visited Busara—or went anywhere, for that matter—without a book and she'd always finish whatever she was reading before heading back to the city, so she could leave it for Pippa and Haki to read: stories with animals and adventures in the wild, or stories of life off the grid. Classics like *Watership Down*, *The Swiss Family Robinson*, *The Call of the Wild* and oh, her favorite, *Little House on the Prairie*. Haki claimed it was a series for girls and refused to read it, though he'd snatched *Little House* books from her plenty of times, flipped through and mocked some of the passages. Maddie loved those books. Despite the quintessential American setting, something about the Ingalls' life seemed to parallel life in the savannah. It tied her two worlds together and fueled her daydreams. But as a teenager, it was *My Side of the Mountain* that had really struck a chord with her. She'd felt so much like Sam it scared her at times, though she'd never had the courage to run away and live alone on a mountain.

"Trust me. I know my way around. I don't need your paper." He gave her a mischievous grin. "You think I'll only take you to where the crops look bountiful? Or I'll read it and know your secrets and battle plans?"

She folded her arms and lifted her left brow, the only one she'd ever been able to lift. She used to give her brothers the same look when she knew they were up to something, but they simply began imitating her.

He put on the brakes and came to a stop in the middle of nowhere. Maddie looked behind them out of habit. It wasn't like they were going to cause a traffic jam out here.

"Why'd you stop?"

He crossed his hands behind his head and leaned back, his broad chest and chin raised to the sun. The sleeves of his white shirt were rolled up to his elbows and she could see a few small scars along his forearms. He was definitely not the same young Haki who'd stolen her books. He looked like he'd caught up to or even surpassed her in age, but mischief danced on his lips the same way it had back then, whenever she was around. *He's always so serious. We only see this side of him when you bring Maddie around.* She remembered how special she felt when she'd overheard his parents saying that to hers. She had the power to make him act silly and put a smile on his face. Except she didn't mean to be making him smile right now, and they certainly didn't have time for fun.

"Start the engine. We have several stops to make and not enough hours in the day."

"Mads." His lips flattened and he turned his entire body toward her, resting one arm on the back of his seat. He'd called her Mads. Her dad was the only one who ever called her that. Haki had always called her Maddie-girl and somehow it always sounded endearing and a bit wistful when he said it.

"Look around you. How can you be writing? Take in the scenery. Feel the sun. Breathe the air. *See* the land. I'm not driving until you let yourself get lost in it for just a moment."

"I need to do what I've been assigned to do. There are people counting on me."

"Which people? The Masai? Or the men in suits you're reporting to?"

Reporting to. It was a cut-down. Like he knew her degree held no power. Like she had no voice of her own. Her eyes stung. No voice, like when she was ten and had to use pen and paper to communicate. She cleared her throat and blinked away the burn.

"What I tell those *men in suits* makes all the difference. I may not own a practice yet. I may not even try my own cases yet, but I will. And when I do, I'll give it my all, just like I currently put everything I have into gathering the information needed for my firm to win a case. I believe in what I do."

"If you do, then stop making military-style checklists and let yourself see the big picture. People aren't checklists. The Masai you're defending? This is the land they hold sacred—all of it, from the soil to the plants to the animals that roam it. Look around. How can you understand the situation if you don't?"

"Why should you care? You should want me to fail at this."

He rubbed his lips and stared off for a second.

"I have *never* wanted you to fail at anything. That's not what this is about." He sat back in his seat and rested his elbow on his door frame.

She rubbed nose against her shoulder and looked out onto the dry grassland. A herd of zebras grazed peacefully in the distance. An egret took off from its perch on a lonely tree and landed near a muddy watering hole. A gazelle lay lifeless near the edge. She imagined it had spent its last drops of energy in search of water, only to collapse at the parched bed. Its body gave life to the flies and buzzards that hovered over it. The circle of life. Desperation. Survival of the fittest. A willingness to adapt to change.

All life here adapted to change. The Masai and other native tribal people had been given no choice but to adapt.

"I'll never forget the first time you came from Nairobi to visit Busara—the first time we met," he said. "You were ten and I was almost seven. You'd been promised a safari up in the Masai Mara. We needed three jeeps to fit everyone. You sat next to me in the one my father was driving. I'd never seen anyone's face light up the way yours did. Me, I'd always lived here, but you? I was mesmerized by how mesmerized you were by everything. Even by ridiculous Ambosi."

"Especially by Ambosi. I really loved monkeys." She smiled at the memory. Yes, she'd been out here before. Not for a very long time, though, and not specifically on this trail. She'd never forget the Masai Mara, Kenya's section of the Serengeti ecosystem, which extended from Tanzania's Serengeti National Park across the border. The Masai lived all along that border, and the first clan she and Haki were headed toward was near the Ewaso Ng'iro River, still quite a distance from the Mara and not an area invaded by tourism. However, she knew from her aunts and uncles that the border with Tanzania made the fight against poaching more difficult. Since the Masai knew the land so well, they made convenient bribery targets for poachers crossing the border seeking elephants or rhinos for ivory.

"I thought you and Pippa were the luckiest kids on earth, getting to live out here," Maddie said. "It's the only place I've been that manages to be wild and dangerous, yet so serene and exquisite in its beauty."

"We always looked forward to sharing it with you. When you left Kenya for college, we were—I mean, she was—heartbroken." He started the ignition. "By the way, I read every one of those books, even the ones I said I wouldn't."

She hadn't mentioned the books out loud. Had she?

"Why?" He'd been so dead set against them just because the main character wasn't a boy. She'd never insisted. He had free choice.

He scratched his unshaven jaw and twisted his full lips, but didn't look at her.

"Those books knew how to get your attention and make you light up like the sun or, sometimes, bite your lip and frown like a volcano on the verge of erupting. Just watching you read was captivating entertainment."

"I was entertainment? A funny face?" Boy, she must have had more of an expressive face than people had told her. Haki tipped his head and tapped his thumb against his jeans.

"I wanted to understand you," he said, his voice softening. "To really know you. And I figured that if I had any hope of that, of getting your attention, the secret Maddie-girl would be in those books."

Maddie's chest warmed and her stomach fluttered. He'd wanted her attention? He'd cared that much? Back when he was just a boy to her, he had cared enough to understand her. And if he'd truly read those books with her in mind, then he understood a part of her no one else did. Maybe he'd only taken an interest because he knew she'd suffered and Haki hated suffering. He'd always had a good heart and a precocious sense of responsibility. That had to be all it was. He was reminiscing. But then why did something in his voice make it seem like he was saying more?

Because her ears were playing tricks on her. Because a part of her wanted to hear it.

A part of her *longed* to hear it. She rubbed at the sudden pang in her chest.

"Pippa loves you, Haki. You're meant to be together." She closed her eyes but it only made the burn in her cheeks more intense. She'd blurted that out all wrong. Revealed too much. "What I mean is—"

"I know what you mean. She loves you, too. I was just remembering. A lot has changed since then. We're not the same kids anymore."

He started the jeep and continued westward on the unpaved road.

HAKI UNSCREWED THE CAP on his metal thermos and offered it to Maddie. He needed water. His mouth felt dry despite his efforts to stay hydrated, but he'd seen her drink the last drop from her canister over half an hour ago and the temperature had risen considerably since then. He had another bottle, but they'd need it for the trip back. She accepted his thermos and drank a few sips. She hadn't said a word the rest of the way to the village. It had him worried. He didn't know what had come over him, but he'd said too much. He'd wanted her to remember how much she loved this place and the connection she used to have with animals. Instead, he'd overstepped. Crossed a line.

"Thank you." She handed back his thermos and wiped her mouth with the back of her hand.

He took a long drink, tightened the cap and put it away. He picked up her pen from the door's side pocket. *Native Watch Global* was printed on the side. He handed it to her. She wanted her notes; she could have them.

"Let's get this done," he said. This was the first place on her list, and he knew it well enough. It had been the site of the last crop raid a few days ago.

A young warrior wrapped in scarlet-and-orange garb with a blue-and-orange checked wrap thrown over his shoulder and wooden staff in hand marched his herd of white goats out of the entrance to the *enkang* and off to pasture. The ochre-stained head and red *shuka* of another warrior stood out against the pasture beyond, as he tended to a herd of thin cattle. It wasn't too unusual for warriors of the tribe to help with the herding during a long drought. Everyone needed to help during times like this. The women were often the hardest working of all, building their homes and maintaining life in their tribal village.

The *enkang* was marked by a wall of thorned acacia branches that served to protect the huts within, as well as the flocks, from nighttime predators. Maddie tucked her pen into her pocket and hugged her notepad against her blue camp shirt.

"Do we need permission to enter the compound?"

"They'll recognize me. I was here recently. I'll take you to the father who works the crops—over there." He pointed out the small sorghum field not far from the *enkang*.

They passed the thorny gateway and came to a clearing lined with small huts.

"You were here recently? Because of the same incident I'm investigating? Why didn't you say so? No wonder you weren't checking any maps."

"Makes me a good guide, doesn't it?"

She was trying to establish a boundary between the two of them. He could feel the wall going up.

"I suppose. It also means you're a step ahead of me and you were lying by omission. There wasn't a killing here, though, was there? Not from the information I got, at least." She flipped through her notes to check.

"No, there wasn't. I was in the area and the KWS vet was held up on an emergency. When incidents are first reported, it's not always clear if an injured animal will be found. One in need of emergency veterinary care or possibly one that's dead. If the cause of death isn't immediately apparent then a necropsy is needed. Sometimes there's no mark on them because they've been poisoned. And sometimes, they're not even found near the site. One of the men from the village might go and hunt it down after the fact, so we have to check the entire area."

"I see. So the authorities' only concern is for the elephants?"

"I didn't say that, but, yes, that's a major concern."

"What about those children playing over there? What if they got injured in a stampede or went hungry because of crop-related income loss?"

Haki dug his heels into the hard ground and braced his hands on his waist.

"We don't want anyone hurt. Do you think such cases aren't reported or cared about? Be reasonable, Maddie. You know me. I'm not an extremist. It's about balancing humanity and nature. But man is not in danger of extinction here. We cannot condone the hunting of elephants, be it for a warrior's rite of passage or for retaliation, and especially not for ivory. Do you really think that in any elephant death, the ivory is left to waste? One incident is all it takes to perpetuate the cycle. There are dangerous, conniving men out there—poachers who'll do anything for a sale, including bribery, blackmail and threats. And desperation equals motivation. Unfortunately, a farmer desperate enough, financially, will be motivated to work for poachers. They might even use crop destruction as a defense. We have to have consequences in place that are strong enough to serve as countermotivation. Punishments that will make anyone think twice."

Something shifted in Maddie's face. Something as piercing as the eyes of a lioness who'd spotted her prey and knew exactly what she needed to do to feed her cubs.

"The Masai and other tribes have a unique culture and way of life that has been under constant threat. You want balance? Look at the maps that NWG plotted out showing how much land they've lost. Every time a reserve or national park is formed or some private company manages to get their hands on land that shouldn't be touched, the living boundaries for the native peoples shrinks. These were nomads forced into farming. Balance means you can't protect and provide for elephants and not do so for the people native to the same land. Punishments are not always the answer, Haki."

"You're the lawyer. Your entire career is centered on punishment."

"*Defense* law. I'm defending the rights of these people."

"Is man the only one with rights on this earth?"

Maddie sucked in an audible breath and curled her lips. He'd hit a nerve.

"You see those *inkajijik*?" Maddie asked. She pointed toward the rows of huts built of walls plastered with mud, cow dung and urine and topped with a dried grass roof held up by a meshwork of twigs and *leleshwa* wood poles. "People being forced to change their way of life or forced onto designated areas of land is an injustice that happens all over the world. It's been happening for centuries, yet now you want to punish them for being forced into a corner and trying to survive?"

"How far back do you want to go? I believe the elephants and other native wildlife were here first. And now they, too, are restricted to protected areas—otherwise, people hunt them to *extinction*. The tribes have adapted. The elephants...well, one can't adapt to getting slaughtered. They can't adapt once they don't exist anymore. For them, there's only one solution. To punish the killing," Haki said.

Maddie rubbed the back of her neck, then pushed her silver bangles up her forearm.

"I don't want anyone suffering on either side. That's why your bill needs to be stopped, but I suppose getting through to you will be like trying to claw my way through that thorny *enkang* barrier. I'm here to speak with and *for* the Masai. I'm not here to argue with you about the importance of human life."

"You left Kenya. You left your family and friends behind, but I stayed. I stayed to help care for family and have dedicated my life to helping both the wildlife and people here. So don't go lecturing me on who's important."

She'd abandoned *him*. He had been heartbroken and dejected that year. Everyone blamed it on his age and hormones and no doubt those factors made everything seem like the end of the world. But the main reason was Maddie. That kind of blow was hard to forget for a teenage boy. He pinched the bridge of his nose. That was all in the past. He was over it. Over her. It was just that being around her was bringing back old memories.

Maybe driving her out here hadn't been such a good idea after all. He should have stuck with his initial plan and kept his distance from the start. He wasn't sure there was any of the old Maddie left in her.

Change. Adaptations.

The faster she obtained the information she needed, the faster he could get back to his normal routine…and Pippa. He adjusted the radio on his belt and walked through the entrance. Maddie was at his heels.

"The elephants know," he said. "They don't react the same way when they cross paths with a person from a tribe that's attacked them than from one like the Luo or Kikuyu. They've shown this in behavioral studies. That kind of awareness makes them almost human, doesn't it? Or perhaps it is humans who should be more like them."

A group of women passed them. They smiled at Haki and Maddie and one waved. Maddie waved back. He hoped their argument hadn't carried too far on the breeze. Haki recognized them as the wives of the farmer, Lempiris. One carried a large bundle of firewood and another held several calabashes, likely on her way to fill the gourds with fresh cow's milk. He knew the tallest one, Esiankiki, was pregnant with her first child. She announced their arrival in her native Maa and Lempiris stepped out of one of the *inkajijik* and walked to Haki and Maddie.

"Sopa." Lempiris stood tall and proud, the sinewy muscles of his neck and shoulders framed by stretched and adorned earlobes much like the women had.

"Sopa. Kasserian ingera?" Haki asked. It was considered good manners and a traditional greeting to ask about the children before all else.

Lempiris eyed Maddie before deciding to respond in English. He adjusted the bright red *shuka* draped over his shoulder and his earrings dangled and danced with his movement.

"All the children are well. And your families?"

"All are well, thank you," Haki said.

Lempiris knew he didn't have children. He'd asked him during his last visit and had taken pity on Haki. A man without children was truly poor.

"*Meishoo iyiook Enkai inkishu o-nkera.* May *Enkai* give us cattle and children. Rain would be a blessing, too," he added.

"Yes. May this drought end so your herds and family have plenty," Haki said. He didn't bother explaining. He knew Maddie had learned about their culture when she was a child and per their earlier argument, she clearly remembered her history lessons or she'd refreshed her memory recently. They'd learned about all the Kenyan tribes in their schooling. Like how the Masai believed they were the chosen ones and that their God, *Enkai*, had entrusted them with his most precious gift, cattle. The Masai believed all cattle belonged to them. Their ancestors tended the herds. They didn't farm. *Enkai* had made the Kikuyu farmers and they were supposed to be the ones to deal with loss of crops. And he'd made the Torrobo the hunters and bee-keepers and left them to deal with the dangers of wild animals and stings. Yet, here were the Masai, the noblest tribe in their own eyes, dealing with it all. Times changed. People had to change to survive.

"Lempiris, this is Maddie Corallis. She's here to ask about the crops and the elephant raid."

"Sopa," Maddie said, earning a broad, toothy smile from Lempiris. She caught on quickly, saying hello in Maa. "I'm afraid my Maa is limited, as is my Swahili. May I speak in English, or would you prefer that Mr. Odaba translate?"

"English is okay," he replied in a concerted effort to disguise his accent, but it came out sounding almost drawl-like. "I understand very good. I speak so-so."

"Great. Then stop me if I say something you don't understand. Okay?"

"Yes, yes."

"Do you mind if I take a video recording?"

"It is okay."

Maddie pulled out her phone and started recording.

Haki kept quiet as Maddie explained who she was and what she was hoping to learn from Lempiris. It wasn't the time to argue, though he was impressed. Maddie the lawyer was quick and to-the-point. She was much more sure of her footing than the Maddie who got stuck in trees. She'd also paid attention and didn't miss the importance of including children in her reasoning. As she finished, Lempiris's smile vanished. He tapped the end of his staff against the earth.

"We lose too much. The elephants eat everything. Destroy ground. They have their area and we have our land. They come here and destroy."

"I understand. I want to help. May I see your plot that was destroyed?"

"Yes."

Lempiris motioned for them to follow. From the corner of his eye, Haki caught Maddie looking over at him as they walked to the farmer's small field. She marched ahead by a few steps, camera in hand. She seemed awfully sure of herself. Anna was right. There was a strength simmering inside her. Or maybe it was stubbornness, just like her cousin's. How was a guy supposed to tell the difference?

"See. All gone." Lempiris waved a weathered hand through the air. The trampled rows Haki had seen the day of the raid seemed almost ready for new plantings. It wouldn't be the same crop. The rainy season would come soon and then cooler weather. Lempiris's grain harvest was lost for the season. At least from this particular plot.

"How much loss would you say there was? Will you replant?" Maddie went on with her questions and recorded his answers. Haki had heard it all before. It didn't change anything as far as he was concerned. Lempiris still had his cattle and goats and another field that was holding up in the drought.

"Would you be willing to come to Nairobi for testimony if needed?"

Lempiris shook his head left and right, but then up and down and left again.

"It is a far trip. I am needed here. If I must, I will."

"Understood. Now, I don't see where the elephant came through," Maddie said, scanning the area. The fence was intact.

"Good man," he said, pointing at Haki, who stood at the edge of the first row, behind Maddie. "He helped me to fix the fence. Man of his word."

Maddie's lips parted and a crease appeared on her forehead. She glanced at Haki.

"A man of his word," she repeated.

He gave her a small shrug.

He might have rebuilt the farmer's fence, but he was pretty sure he'd just weakened Maddie's.

CHAPTER EIGHT

EVEN THE SKY seemed confused. Maddie looked up at the cluster of wispy, frail clouds that looked like they'd wandered off their trail and gotten lost. The rest of the sky was a vast canvas of blue nothingness—not even a hint of the promise of rain—and the late-afternoon sun was hot and cranky. Or maybe she was. They'd stopped at two other villages but she hadn't gotten much more information, though she'd confirmed the farmers' willingness to testify if called upon. She was beginning to wonder why she'd been sent out here.

Grasses whirred past the jeep, and between the hypnotic visual and the soft vibrations of the engine, her eyes began to drift shut. A flock of birds taking flight over a herd of zebras had her lifting her chin and stretching her eyes open. This leg of the trip, she hadn't touched her notes. She was tired, her mind was too full and—she pressed a hand to her stomach, hoping the grumble had been drowned out by the engine—she was hungry.

Haki pulled up under the shade of an acacia tree, scanning the area before turning off the engine.

"You need to eat something." Haki hopped out and went around back. He pulled an insulated box out of the jeep and carried it around to the driver's seat.

"I'm sorry. Did I fall asleep?" She stretched and rubbed at her face.

"More like meditation on wheels. Your eyes never closed, but a few more minutes and your head would have hit your lap."

"How much farther?"

"Far enough. We won't make it back today."

That woke her up. She sat up tall and looked around. There wasn't so much as another *enkang* in the distance. Nothing but wilderness surrounded them. What had she expected when Anna warned them about camping? Some kind of lodge with tourists on safari?

"For real?"

He judged the position of the sun in the sky and the corner of his mouth creased.

"The sun sets a little earlier here than

you're used to back home in America. We could make it part of the way to the last stop you have on your list, but we'd have to set up camp either way. Might as well do so here. It's a better spot than what lies ahead. If we head out early in the morning, we'll have plenty of time to pass through the next homestead, then detour slightly through the Mara to pick up Pippa if she's still there and still make it back to Busara before dark. Tomorrow."

She pulled off her scarf and gave her scalp a soothing scratch. When she'd been given this assignment, she'd never imagined that she'd be spending the night in the middle of nowhere with Haki Odaba—friend, enemy and more of a real man than she was used to being around. She pinched the bridge of her nose. He was also the only person she trusted to keep them safe out here, other than perhaps her uncle Mac, or maybe Kam. Haki reached for his radio and leaned on the jeep, watching her as he checked in with Camp Jamba Walker as planned. She let out a sigh, tucked her notebook in her sack and waited for him to end the communication.

"I assume you heard," he said, tucking the radio away. Yes, she had overheard, but she didn't know everyone's radio code names. "Mugi said that Pippa insisted we pass through there. She'll stay an extra night so we can meet up with her."

"Okay, then. Tell me what I can do to help," she said, getting out of the jeep.

"You can eat something."

"I mean in the way of a tent or digging in posts or whatever."

He laughed as he lifted two folding camp chairs out of the back and set them in the shade.

"Tent? Who needs a tent?"

"Are you serious? What about things that slither and crawl? Or mosquitoes? Or lions." She had no problem with camping, so long as it involved a hermetically sealed tent or a cot to keep her off the ground. She shuddered at the idea of something crawling up her shirt or nibbling at her hair. Or having her for a late-night snack.

"You'll be safe and I have insect repellant. I'll keep a campfire going and I'm a light sleeper. I won't let anything happen to you. I've done this many times and I'm always prepared."

He unlocked a long metal case that was

bolted down in the back of the jeep, opened it and waited for her to peer in.

"Oh."

A couple of rifles lay on their sides, one that looked a little different with a box of feathered darts next to it. She assumed it was for tranquilizing, but the other...that was the real thing. A box labeled *bullets* was tucked next to it.

"Only for emergencies," he said, closing the lid.

"I'm glad you keep that locked up."

"Always. Safety is a priority."

"That's what my dad says. He had to be extra careful with his handgun when we were growing up. Especially with Chad."

"You know how to use one?"

"You know my dad. He made us learn how. Just target shooting and gun safety. Guess what my law school acceptance gift was? He said that if I was going to live in a big city alone, I needed a gun. It's locked up in a safe at home. I hate them. They make me uneasy, even if I do know how to use mine if my life was threatened."

"Good to know."

"But I've never shot at anything fast. Especially, not in my sleep."

"I was messing with you. I have a small tent in the back and you're welcome to use it. I have to warn you, though. You'll miss out on sleeping under a spectacular night sky."

Her shoulders relaxed.

"You look at the stars all you want."

He opened the cooler and handed her a sandwich. "There's fruit here, as well. Take your pick. You can stay in the jeep or stretch your legs. I recommend stretching your legs." He took his sandwich, sat in a camp chair and crossed his ankles far in front of him.

Maddie peeked in the cooler. Okay. She really did need to eat. Her stomach was beginning to sound like a hyena in heat.

"Oh, my gosh. This is peanut butter," she said, going around and sitting next to him. "I'm in heaven." She sank her teeth in. Who'd have thought? A good old peanut butter sandwich while surrounded by the wilds of Africa. She felt like she was sitting in one of those giant, domed, surround-sound theaters she'd been to in a museum once.

"My mother packed the food. She remembered about you and peanut butter." Haki chuckled as he took another bite of his.

"I eat everything now, but yes, back then, I was culinarily cautious, if that's a term."

When they'd first moved to Kenya, she hadn't been too keen on trying different foods. Peanut butter sandwiches had been one of the few things she'd eat.

Haki finished his sandwich faster than she ever could and went back to the cooler. He took out two bananas and tossed her one. She fumbled the catch and caught it in her lap.

"Why were you so anxious to leave, Mads?"

There it was again. *Mads*. He remained standing and looked out on the grasses and pockets of trees. Mount Kilimanjaro lifted its snowcap to the sky southwest of where they sat, Mount Kenya rose to the northeast and the echoes of elephant trumpeting seemed to come from all directions. She chewed slowly and took in the surroundings that had once been so much more familiar to her. He looked down when she didn't answer. She wasn't sure if she wanted to or if she should.

"You could have gone to any of the universities here. Or you could have returned more often, or at least have moved back to work after law school."

"Why haven't you left?"

"What do you mean? Why would I leave this?"

She laid her banana peel on the arm of her chair and got up to stand with him. A family of giraffes sauntered along the tree line just over the ridge, then stopped for a taste. Beneath them, a herd of gazelle grazed silently. Only their backs rose above the grass blades, like domes of tumbled citrine. Why *would* anyone leave this?

"I must admit, this is probably one of the most beautiful spots I've seen," she said. Maybe he'd forget his question. "It's as if all of it is right here. Everything people think of when they envision the savannah."

"It is." He squinted at the horizon. His mind was churning. She could tell from the subtle movement of his jaw, the way his temple flinched with every thought. He'd looked the same when he was fifteen and his serious nature had been topped with the usual angst and worries.

"A little louder," she whispered.

"Hmm?" He turned his face toward her.

"You're talking very loudly in your head. A bit louder and I won't feel as if I'm not worth sharing with."

He smiled, then reached up and tucked her hair behind her ear. The way his fingertips skimmed her neck made her hyperaware and seemed to snap the faraway look from his eyes. He put his arm around her.

"Come here."

Oh, she wanted to. A part of her wanted to lean her cheek against his chest and let him tuck her close with his arm. The other part of her kicked and screamed for her to stay in control before damage was done. *He's not for you.* Her pulse skittered and her leg muscles tried to ground her in place.

He didn't pull her in. He pulled her *along*. Guided her to a specific spot a few yards on the other side of the jeep, put both hands on her shoulders, faced her toward a rise surrounded by trees and gunmetal gray boulders, then let go.

"Right there." He pointed before folding his arms.

He didn't have to say any more. She understood. This was it. This was where he felt right. It was as if all the perfect places from all the books they'd read had come together. She couldn't say how, but it was as if she could hear everything he'd been thinking. She could feel an energy coming off of him that was so powerful it made her want to stay there, too. Right in that spot. That special place, no matter how wild, that made a person feel like they'd found home, like their struggles had bonded them to it. An indescribable tie to the land that was rooted in spirit, rather than logic.

A calling.

She watched his face as he gazed at the rise. He looked like he wanted to capture it somehow. Like he wanted to be there always.

"It's amazing. Beautiful. Like in the stories we read," she said. "But how would you make this work? What would you do here?"

"It's not something that will happen. Just a dream I have from time to time. One that's not part of the plan."

The plan. Like the one she felt like she'd be forever chasing. The plan to succeed. To prove herself and have everyone respect her. The plan to show her father that she didn't need to know what she was doing wrong, because she was doing everything right.

"Why can't this be part of your plan?"

"Because…" He glanced at her. "Because even if I felt free to live here, I'd be torn. Enough land has been taken away by those who need it—people and animals. Too many businesses have cropped up, building luxury safari houses or cabins for tourists to escape to. When does it stop? Isn't it enough that the tribes and herds are competing for land?"

"Camp Jamba Walker caters to tourists, too, doesn't it?"

"It's not the same. They cater to a different type. To begin with, it was primarily Mugi and Kesi's home and what they're doing with Mac and Tessa there is more than a photo-op. They're educating. They're making an effort to raise awareness. Ignorance is everyone's worst enemy. Ignorance and greed. They're fighting it. And Mac has spent his life helping track poachers and injured animals or helping behavioral researchers get where they need to be. They're giving back to the land they live on. Not just coming and going, turning a profit."

"I get it. Like Camp Busara and others like it, but you give, too, Haki. Every day. Kenya is your home. You've never lived anywhere but Busara, except during veterinary school."

"True. But I went to school to help save the elephants and rhinos and to help fight poaching. I went so that I could help at Busara. What I'd thought of doing out here is…well, let's just say it would be a disappointment to all. And I can't do that. Not after what my mother went through to raise me and the guidance and faith Kamau put in me as a father. And I need to set an example for Huru. One where family comes first."

She stepped closer to him and put her hand on his arm. Her silver bracelets slid down her wrist and pinged delicately against Haki's skin where it met hers. She knew what disappointing someone was like.

"Haki, I can't imagine anyone ever being disappointed in you. But do you want to leave Busara because you're not happy? Is it that you don't like medicine?" That didn't make sense. He was so passionate about stopping the killing and saving lives.

"No. I do. In my *dream*, I'd go back and get my masters and PhD in vet medicine. I'd specialize in disease vectors and parasitology. And I'd create not just a home base here, but a work base from which I'd not only save wildlife, but also provide veterinary care for the herds of goats, cattle, sheep and even dogs on the farms and *enkangs*. Most of the herdsmen do have guard dogs. Their access to vet care is abysmal."

She knew the college degrees here differed from those offered in America, where becoming a vet required several years of graduate studies. All Haki needed to practice vet medicine here was a bachelor's degree, but if he wanted to specialize, he could go for his masters and even a doctorate, the way his father had because he wanted to be involved in the research aspects of Anna's work at Busara. She was stunned, though. Haki didn't want to restrict his practice to wildlife medicine, the way he was now.

"You want to help the Masai."

"And other tribes. Anyone raising animals out here." His cheeks lifted ever so slightly, as if he was excited but afraid to hope. "There's a need. And I have this idea that if the people are helped, if they don't feel forgotten, if they don't get frustrated or desperate because they've not only lost crops, but they've lost cattle to illness, then maybe the chances of restoring peace between them and the wildlife will increase. Their relationship could be restored because they'd see that the men outside of their tribes were helping. They'd see that we, not the poachers, have their backs. You have to understand, their cattle are of ultimate significance to them and there was a time when the herds were wiped out by rinderpest. Many were forced to make a life in agriculture. I want to not only provide care, but monitor and research the spread of disease. I would still be able to treat wildlife, too, but it would be starting from scratch. More of a head start than Busara had with its first tent, but still. It'd be a big step back, just to move forward."

He wanted to work more closely with the people, those who needed his care for their animals, the way her mom had decided to branch away from the orthopedic sports-medicine practice her parents owned because she'd wanted to reach out to the children in rural Kenya, in places like the Masai Mara, where they needed medical care and vaccinations. It was wonderful, but Haki had caught her off guard. This was so different than the steep fines and jail time he was pursuing for Masai who came into deadly conflict with elephants.

"See." He wiped a hand across his short hair. "I told you it would make no sense. It's nothing but an outlandish theory and one man can't make that kind of difference anyway. Keep it to yourself, Mads. This stays between us. I mean that."

He'd called her Mads again. It came out whenever he was being serious or concerned.

"Of course. I won't say anything. But promise me something. Don't write this off as some dream. It makes so much sense, Haki. It makes more sense than punishment. It gets to the root. And if I ever had to name one man who could make a difference, it would be you."

"That bill still has to pass. I explained why. But, thank you. For listening. For keeping all of this to yourself."

"But this could be what you were meant to do. Your destiny."

Destiny. Heavy word. She wasn't sure she knew what her own was.

"We all have our paths in life. Mine doesn't lead here. Just like yours led you out of Africa once and will again soon."

He made it sound so bittersweet. She looked back at the rise that overlooked the surrounding boulders, trees and mountain in the distance. She longed to kick off her hiking boots and socks and feel the earth against her feet. He was right, though. Both her home and her career were in America. She didn't belong here. But then why did this place tug at her, too?

A family of elephants, likely the ones who'd announced their presence earlier, appeared beyond a dried creek bed in the distance and she watched them wind their way toward the juicy leaves of a thicket for lunch.

"They're the true gardeners of this land. The keepers. The wise ones. They weed and spread seed. They keep things in balance. Even their footprints catch rain so that those smaller than them may drink. And they never forget...not their ancestors, nor those who cause them harm. I still care. I just want to help all animals."

"Haki, I promised I would keep this to myself, but didn't you tell Pippa? She'd back you up. She'd defend you if anyone said it wasn't a good idea. You—both of you—could make this happen."

Haki began collecting dried sticks. A tiny monkey scampered up the tree with the banana peel hanging from his mouth.

"I brought her here. Once. Started to tell her. Not all of it, but enough. She's the one who put some sense in my head. It's too late to go off chasing ideas that could fail. I have to be able to earn an income, and I'd barely scrape by out here, if at all. I have responsibilities to think of, especially if I plan to marry and start a family."

He was sounding just like her father. Trying to use logic to fix something that was already just right. So right that he couldn't see it. He felt it, though. He couldn't hide the faraway look in his eyes or the disappointment that laced his voice. She couldn't believe Pippa didn't share his dream. Pippa, who was all about the outdoors. Pippa, the slightly wild child who threw caution to the wind all the time. Apparently, for herself, but not for Haki.

Because as good-hearted as Pippa was, one of them had to be the responsible one.

And it had always been him.

HAKI REALLY NEEDED to gather enough wood to keep a fire going through the night, but Maddie's reaction made him want to hike up to the rise where he'd imagined having a home.

"Are you up for a short walk? Up there? There's a view of the valley from the other side." He hoped she was because he couldn't very well leave her down here alone.

"Sure. I'd love to see it."

He set down the sticks he'd collected thus far and led the way, stopping at a broad boulder. He leaped on top of it in one move, then held his hands out for Maddie. One look and he could tell she saw the way around it would be longer. She held his wrists as he held hers, and he hoisted her up effortlessly.

"Thanks."

"Stand over here and look. It's even more amazing than the view of the valley from Busara."

She walked to the far side of the small plateau and her lips parted. The breeze lifted her hair, then set it down gently on her shoulders. A glimpse of the old Maddie surfaced, and he wished he had a camera on him so that he could capture her standing there. She looked as dreamy and serene as the landscape that surrounded them. He came up beside her and they both stood quietly, arms grazing every time one of them moved slightly.

The remains of a skeleton, half-sunken in the dirt, sat at the edge of the bank a little ways downstream.

"When the rains come, we rescue elephants and other animals stuck in the mud, which can be like quicksand. Often, with elephants, the herd manages to pull a baby to safety. Then drought hits and some of the very animals we saved meet their deaths anyway. The cycle of life and death. The danger of extremes. But we keep trying. We're all programmed to survive. All life needs water, so most of the danger lurks down there, near the creek bed. Up here—this very spot—is where I imagined building a house. Just far enough removed from the clinic, down where the jeep is."

A cheetah was in hot pursuit of a herd of zebras near a dry creek bed in the distance. They watched quietly as the herd wove its way across the length of the valley below. Up here, they couldn't hear hooves pounding or the hot, panicked breathing as each zebra tried to ditch death. From up here, the herd moved as a single, fluid beast, rushing like a river swollen after a rain. From here, it was all so clear—how even the most subtle change in direction by one was mimicked precisely by the rest. It was hauntingly beautiful.

"How do they do that? Make an escape from death look so elegant?" Maddie asked, though it was more of an observation than a question.

"Each one of them is part of a larger consciousness. No radios, no time to call the one at the end of the line. No time for red tape and paperwork. They haven't lost touch with one another. They still have the ability to *sense* one another, to feel each other's energy and to know they don't stand alone. They are part of something much bigger and greater than any single individual in the herd. By being in sync, in tune, with others around them, their chance for survival is much higher. Working together for the better," Haki said.

He'd witnessed this time and time again in the behavior of animals. People—not so much. Then again, according to his readings, humans tended to be more focused on the self. The vast majority didn't pay attention to or believe in collective energy or, put more simply, intuition.

Was that what made people like the *Laibon* different? Was that what Haki was sensing right now? Was the tug at the pit of his stomach, the swirling feeling in his chest, the warm awareness of every atom in his body, all a result of Maddie being near him?

Was he sensing her?

Was she sensing him?

"Like starlings before a storm," she whispered, as she stared at the flow of the herd below, but he heard so much more in her words. The cheetah lunged and a younger zebra stumbled and fell on its side. Maddie's eyes glistened and her chin barely quivered.

Haki swallowed hard. Yes, starlings before a storm. He wanted desperately to wrap his hand around hers. He needed to pull her close and feel her heart beating against his as if his life depended on it, but whatever energy was flowing between them, it had to be ignored. If not, the damage from the resulting storm would be too high a price to pay. Pippa would end up the victim and he knew neither of them could live with that.

Maybe this was a case where the needs of the individual—Pippa—outweighed those of the herd. Or maybe humans were just too complicated.

CHAPTER NINE

WISPS OF SMOKE rose from the kindling, twisting and twirling like sultry dancers in the spotlight of a Masai moon. Maddie hugged her knees to her chest and watched as the first flame shot up, chasing the dancers higher and higher until they fell apart and faded away. The fire cracked and popped as Haki fed it more wood.

"Your mom packed more food than I keep stocked for a week back in my apartment," Maddie said, picking up her thermos and spoon when Haki finally sat down. He'd urged her to go ahead and eat while he got the fire started, but doing so hadn't felt right. She put a bite of spiced beans, corn and diced potato in her mouth. "Mmm. This *githeri* is so good."

"She does love to cook." He sat down, opened his thermos and set the cover on the cooler they were using as a makeshift table between their camp chairs. "Have some *chapati* with that."

She ripped one of the flatbreads in half, cupped it like a taco and put a spoonful of *githeri* inside. At this rate, she couldn't imagine being hungry in the morning, but there were boiled eggs and fruit packed away in the cooler, too. She washed down her bite with a swig of water.

Dusk settled all around them and cricket song filled the air. Night sounds were mesmerizing, and for the most part the rhythm of grunts, cackles and chirps was calming, but the deep bass of a lion's roar from somewhere in the tall grasses behind her had her jumping to her feet and dropping her spoon.

"Don't worry, Maddie-girl. It's not as close as it sounds." He chuckled and she shot him a look. "I'm not laughing. I swear. I was choking on a bean."

"Yeah, right," she said, picking up her spoon. "For the record, I wasn't scared. It just startled me."

"Noted."

"Although, maybe we should have set up camp where you pictured building a cabin."

"So the invisible walls could protect you?"

"Because it's a little higher up." She

glanced at the one-man pup tent he'd set up. "And because, as far as I'm concerned, a tent with a broken zipper is useless."

"I promise we're fine right here. I'm sorry about the tent. Huru was the last one to borrow it and it was fine before that. He must have broken it and figured I wouldn't notice for a while. He knows I don't use it unless it's raining. If you aren't comfortable sleeping on the ground, with or without the tent, you can curl up in the jeep. You pick. Height or cover."

He had her there. The jeep might work. Anything could crawl into the tent without him noticing. The jeep was in plain view. The memory of that one night as a kid when a snake had gotten cozy at the foot of her sleeping bag made her skin crawl. It had been enough to scare her off sleeping bags and sleeping on the ground for life.

"I hadn't thought of the jeep."

She looked behind her one more time before finishing her food. Neither said much, but the silence didn't bother her. There was a certain comfort to simply being here with him and not arguing about why she was on this trip in the first place.

The fire hissed and he poked at it with a

long stick. Maddie got up to retrieve her note-book and pen from the jeep. She returned, sat down and flipped through the pages.

"I know I'm not the best of company, but I thought you were at least enjoying the fire and relaxing," Haki said.

"Why do you say that?"

He motioned toward her notebook. "Back to work at this hour. You're one of those, huh?"

"You mean someone who doesn't have an off switch when it comes to work? The type who takes her office home with her at the end of a day?"

"Something like that."

She stopped on a blank page, drew a tic-tac-toe board and held the page up for him to see.

"It's not chess, but I thought it would pass some time."

He narrowed his eyes at her and a smile formed on his lips.

"I stand corrected," he said.

She sat back down, set the open page on the cooler between them and handed him the pen. He marked an X and held up the pen without lifting his arm from where it rested on the cooler. She marked an O. Their hands rested there, close enough to pass the pen back and forth without effort. Close enough for their fingers to brush innocently every few moves.

"You're too easy to beat at this," she said. "How is it you're a chess genius, but you can't beat me at a simple game like this? Unless you're letting me win."

"Let you win? I don't play with fire. You'd kill me. The first time I took it easy on you in chess, you got kind of scary."

She laughed and flipped to a new page.

"Yeah, I remember that. Here. Try this for more of a challenge." She drew a hangman's noose and set up blanks for her secret word.

"You always did love word games. I bet you do the crossword puzzles in the newspaper every weekend."

"Totally."

"I remember when Jack and Anna brought back that board game with the loose tiles. You used to beat everyone."

"And you got a little scary when you lost," she said.

He wrote his letter guesses down and she marked them off or filled them in as they chatted. They had a rhythm going with the pen being passed back and forth. She hadn't felt this relaxed in years. This was so much better than playing solitaire in front of late-night TV.

"What do you do in your spare time back home?" he asked.

She wasn't admitting to solitaire and television. It sounded pathetic.

"Read. Jog. I don't know."

He shook his head.

"Admit it. You really do work all the time. Even if it's research on your computer at home."

"I plead the Fifth."

"No dog to walk? No boyfriend to go out with?"

Was he fishing? She felt her neck warm. Maybe she was sitting too close to the fire.

"I have a fish. A really nice one that's the color of a Masai warrior's hair."

He glanced at her but made no comment. She assumed her answer implied no boyfriend. Not that it should make any difference to him.

"Fundamental."

"Correct. And you didn't lose your legs. Pretty good." Maddie flipped the page for him.

"I get it. As in 'fundamental human rights,'" he said.

"I'm not picking a fight. It was the first word that came to mind. Your turn."

He set up his noose and the pen passing resumed. A breeze fluttered the leaves of the tree that had offered them shade earlier. Instinctively, she looked up to make sure it was only wind.

"Why human-rights law and not animal rights?"

"Why veterinary medicine instead of human medicine?"

"Point taken."

"*Annihilation.* As in the annihilation of a species."

"How in the world did you get that on the first guess? You're cheating." He tapped the pen against the pad. Her noose was empty.

"I'd have to be a mind reader to cheat at this. You used a word with three *i*'s, three *n*'s and two *a*'s, and I happened to guess those letters. You have to choose your words carefully, my dear."

She rested her chin in her hand as she set up the next word.

"I must admit," she mused, "I sometimes wish I had someone around who was counting on me. Family or close friends or kids who trust me to help them. Someone I could care for or do something for. I don't mean clients. But then, seeing you and how much you give to the point of neglecting yourself makes me wonder if I should be happy the way things are."

"Dependable." He smiled without making eye contact. "There are three *e*'s in there. Don't go easy on me."

"Fatigue must be making me slip up," she said. He really was a dependable guy.

"You have too much love to give and no one but your fish to give it to on a daily basis. That's why you're craving someone to count on you. You could always move back to Kenya."

"That's not an option."

"Because of work?"

Well, there was that, especially if she ever made partner.

"Because I can't live around my dad."

"I can see how that might not be easy."

"Compassionate." She tucked her hair behind her ear and licked her lips.

"And do you always use your days off for others or do you ever do anything for yourself?" she asked as she took the pen. Their hands touched again.

"Sometimes I come here to be alone. I

might bring a book or magazine or just nap. But a little time to think without anyone around is all I need."

"So I suppose in some ways, we're at the opposite extremes when it comes to our living situations."

"Noble."

He got that one quickly. Her cheeks felt hot.

"I suppose so," he said.

"Deserving." The rims of her eyes burned. She hadn't been told she was worth it by anyone in a long time. She blinked and hoped he'd think her eyes were watery because of the smoke and heat. She set up the next word.

"Kindhearted." He reached out and brushed a fluttering insect from her shoulder before playing his turn.

"Beautiful." Maddie closed her eyes. She needed to pull back. The night, the fire, his presence… It was all too intoxicating.

"Pippa tells me you two are planning to get married soon," she blurted.

Something shifted between them the second the words came out. He set down the pen, reclined and stared long and hard at the canopy of stars.

"It has been mentioned. Discussed in general. Expected. But I haven't actually proposed yet."

"She made it sound pretty definite. Her heart is set on it."

He leaned forward, resting his elbows on his thighs as he studied the embers.

"We should get to sleep." He got up before she could press the issue. He pulled a few blankets from the back of the jeep and handed her one.

"You remembered my hatred of sleeping bags."

The corner of his mouth lifted.

"Jeep or broken tent?"

"Jeep."

She wrapped herself and settled into the front seat, leaning her head against her arm on the door frame. It wasn't exactly comfortable but she wasn't about to complain. She'd live. She could see him moving the chairs back, setting his rifle within reach and laying his cover on the dirt. He stretched out his long body and tucked his hand behind his head. Her lids grew heavy as she watched his chest rise and fall, and her eyes slowly closed...

A shriek akin to someone having their limbs pulled off had her screaming in response and leaping out of the jeep. She ran to the fire, where Haki was already on his feet. Maddie hugged her blanket and tried to catch her breath.

"What was that? Haki, did you hear it?"

"Yes, I heard it. You scared the life out of me, Mads. I thought something had bitten your arm off."

"*I* scared you? It sounded like someone *was* getting their arm bitten off!"

He plopped back down on the ground and resumed his sleeping position.

"That's it? What happened to 'I'll keep you safe, Maddie?'"

"That was a hyrax. Herbivore, if it makes you feel better. Some people think they're cute."

"I know what a hyrax is, and they don't sound cute. I'd forgotten about them."

It shrieked again.

"Tell me it's not going to do that all night."

"I don't make promises I can't keep."

She looked back at the jeep, then at the unzipped tent, which was essentially a giant sleeping bag. She hesitated, then spread her blanket on the ground next to Haki. He didn't comment. She curled up on it and flipped the end over to cover herself. The few inches of invisible boundary between them was going to have to do. They were friends. It was no big deal. Besides, Pippa wasn't the jealous type. And she had no reason to be. But then why was Maddie feeling so hyperaware? His breathing, his scent and the silhouette of his strong features against a fiery backdrop... she tried to block her senses. She reminded herself that he was her opposition. That if he had it his way, she would fail at stopping his proposal and fail at impressing both her boss and her father. That made him the enemy. Only he wasn't, really. Did they qualify as frenemies?

"Do you trust me?" Haki whispered as he gazed at the stars.

"Yes."

"Then try to get some sleep."

HAKI HAD THE CAMPFIRE safely extinguished and all their supplies back in the truck before Maddie woke up. He was a light sleeper, but last night he hadn't even come close to a catnap. For one thing, he'd had no idea she talked in her sleep. Nothing discernible, but her soft mutterings had him mesmerized and intrigued by what was going on behind those dark lashes of hers. And when she'd unknowingly rolled over and nestled against him, his chances of getting any sleep had been destroyed.

Maddie sat up and frowned as she got her bearings. She rubbed her eyes and pushed to her knees.

"How long have you been awake?" Her voice was husky and still laced with sleep.

"Not long." Last night they'd both come too close to saying things that would have had damaging consequences. His shoulders were stiff from keeping his hands safely locked behind his head all night and he stretched and rubbed them in preparation for the drive ahead.

"Um...safe, private—"

"Behind that bush over there. I made coffee before putting out the fire, if you want some," he called out as she disappeared into the shrubbery.

"Definitely," she said, reappearing and picking up the jug of water they'd designated for washing up. "I'm so sorry if I overslept. I don't even sleep in on weekends. I have no idea what came over me."

He handed her a metal mug of coffee.

"No worries. We can still make good time."

Her eyes widened as she glanced around the campfire.

"Where's my notebook?"

"Shredded by jackals."

"Haki."

"On the passenger seat. So is your pen." And so were the words they'd exchanged last night. Dangerous words. She looked at him knowingly, then swiftly broke eye contact.

"We should leave," they both said simultaneously, then hurried to their seats. Haki turned the jeep northwest, toward their next stop. Coming out here for time alone was never going to be the same again.

CHAPTER TEN

THE TWO HOURS it took to reach the next homestead were excruciatingly long. Maddie occupied herself by focusing a bit harder on the scenery, taking a few photographs with her phone camera and doing mindless things like digging out her portable battery pack to recharge her cell and readjusting the scarf on her head.

Haki was obviously avoiding conversation as much as she was. He pointed out a few herds or vistas and she snapped shots of them, but he was otherwise reserved. She was sort of relieved. She felt a little more centered. She needed to keep her emotions detached from him. She needed to stick to facts and reality, the way lawyers did when presenting their cases. Every time she caught a glimpse of him from the corner of her eye, her resolve began to crumble. Haki acting withdrawn meant he was upset. It was like a part of his spirit had drifted off, and she was to blame. She didn't know which part of her heart to follow—whether to protect her cousin or protect the connection and... magic...she was sure Haki was feeling, too. She'd never experienced it with anyone else. She might never experience it again. No matter what she did, she'd be hurting one of them.

You had over a decade of your life to realize there was something special between you. It's too late now. He's off-limits.

"Almost there." Haki pointed to a staggered row of acacia trees. Maddie craned her neck and could make out the uniform pattern of a cultivated field and the thorny border of the *enkang*. She unplugged her phone.

"About how long is the drive from here to Camp Jamba Walker?"

"Another couple of hours."

Great. A few more hours of torturing themselves.

"Have you been to this farm before?"

"No, not this one. It's farther from Busara than I typically go for rescues."

She took a deep breath as he pulled up near the entrance. She didn't have to look at her notes to remind herself why this testimony would be different. There had been an elephant killing on the outskirts of this farmer's cornfield about two weeks ago. According to records, its body was still warm when KWS arrived after a timely and anonymous tip. Roinet, the farmer, claimed he hadn't killed the cow. None of his fields showed signs of damage, and her tusks hadn't been removed. After the *enkang* had been searched by KWS, they released him. He had no motivation and there had been no evidence to link anyone here to the death, other than proximity. It was a classic example of how wrongful accusations could potentially ruin a family's life. Roinet had been lucky.

An older man draped in orange and blue emerged from one of the *inkajijik*. None of the clans they'd visited had known about her arrival ahead of time. She wanted it that way—spur-of-the-moment, natural and unstaged. She wanted to hear the truth in their voices and see it in their eyes.

"Sopa," Haki said, walking up to the man she thought might be Roinet. She repeated the greeting and he confirmed her assumption.

"Sopa. Kasserian ingera?" Roinet asked.

Maddie and Haki glanced at each other and she could have sworn he was blushing even more than she was. She knew that asking how their children were was a traditional greeting, but still. Roinet had no reason not to assume she and Haki were married with kids. Haki simply said they were well and let it go.

Roinet had a bright smile and kind eyes. His hospitality rivaled that of all the other villages they'd been to. He invited them into the compound and one of his sons set some seating out in front of the first mud hut. He spoke very little English, so she had to rely on Swahili and any Maa that Haki could translate for her. Roinet caught on that she knew some Swahili and used a bit of it when speaking directly to her, but it was clear he preferred his tribal language. She hadn't realized how many Swahili words she'd forgotten until this trip. She had no trouble saying "no thank you" when offered a refreshing drink of cow's milk and blood by one of the women, but the term for recording or videotaping escaped her, if she ever knew it at all. There was truth to the expression, "use it or lose it." *Truth*. She had to trust that Haki wasn't adjusting anything to suit his side of the case in his translations.

"For real? He doesn't want me to film? Not even the field or village without him in it?"

she asked. Haki cocked one brow. "I'm not questioning you. It was rhetorical. I left my notebook back in the jeep, but I don't need to get it if I can do notes on my phone, since I'm not recording with it. Is that okay with him?"

She took out her phone and pulled up a "notes" app.

"Hapana, hapana!" Roinet waved his hand back and forth to make his point, but she understood his emphatic "no." A back-and-forth between him and Haki followed. She stood.

"I'll just go get my paper. It's not worth upsetting anyone."

Haki nodded to him in reassurance, then turned to Maddie.

"I explained that you are only typing notes and he's okay with that. He apologized and explained that he had a bad experience when the authorities came to investigate the dead elephant. The accusation shamed him and his family. He is protecting their privacy because he feels it was invaded."

"Pole. I'm sorry," she said. "Haki, he seems comfortable with you, so to make this go faster, can you have him tell you what happened and what would have happened to

his family had he been arrested, imprisoned or fined?"

"Ah. So you do trust me," he teased.

"Yes. Okay?"

He translated her request and Maddie tried to see if she could pick up on any of Roinet's response as she waited to type in notes.

"He says he doesn't know who killed the elephant. His family doesn't use bullets. They hunt on more equal terms with the animal, out of respect, and only for food. The drought has been difficult, but his crops haven't suffered too severely yet. He had no reason to do harm, yet every one of their huts was searched. He doesn't know for what, since the tusks hadn't been taken."

"Ask him what would have happened here if he'd been taken away or fined." She watched Roinet's face as he spoke. He looked around his tiny village and pointed beyond the thorns to the fields and at the huts that had been searched.

"He says that many of the children here are still young. Only a few are old enough to herd or help in the field. The women do much of the work, but he has to go with one of his sons to sell crops and the jewelry they make to tourists. Without that money, they can't afford medicine if needed or to send his son Gathii to school. Also, if the drought kills their crops, they'll have to buy food. He adds that he has heard that in big cities sometimes people go to jail for years before the police find out they have the wrong person. He fears this happening to him."

"See? This is what we're trying to avoid," she told Haki.

"Remember, this is one side of the story. You should interview KWS, too."

She was about to answer when one of the women came and offered her a necklace made with blue glass beads. Maddie held the necklace and admired the way it glistened in the sunlight.

"Tell her it's beautiful. She's a skilled artist," Maddie said.

"Roinet says this is his wife and the necklace is a gift to you for helping to protect them and their way of life."

"Oh, wow. You don't have to give me anything. I'm honored to do my job."

His wife gestured for her to keep the gift. Maddie hesitated. Though it felt good to be valued and appreciated, as a lawyer, she had to be careful. It was a token gift, not a bribe. It wasn't expensive, but relatively speaking, it was significant considering how little the family had. But she didn't want to offend them. She'd definitely let both the law office in Nairobi and Mr. Levy know about it. She smiled at Roinet and his wife.

"*Asante sana.* Thank you so much." She put the necklace on and his wife cocked her head and put her hand to her heart. Maddie touched her fingertips to the beads. "It's lovely. I'll treasure it forever."

They stood up to leave but Haki pointed toward the *kraal* in the center of the *enkang* and asked Roinet about the few goats who were penned at this time of day instead of out in the field. The man looked a little uneasy and shook his head.

"He says a few of his goats are having difficulty birthing. He's letting them rest. I explained that I'm a veterinarian."

He started for the enclosure. Roinet called out his son Gathii's name and, from the corner of her eye, Maddie noticed him making eye contact with an older boy standing in front of one of the huts across from the pen.

"Hang on," she said to Haki and lengthened her stride to catch up to him. "I get the feeling that maybe he doesn't want your help with the goats."

"I'm taking a quick look. It could be something I can help with. The loss of any livestock is a big deal for a clan."

A few more huts down, a woman paced with a crying baby. The cry didn't sound right. Maddie had been old enough to remember when Ryan and Philip were babies. She'd accompanied her mom on enough clinic trips to see and hear sick children. That baby wasn't feeling well and the mother seemed distraught.

Gathii took one step forward, watching them intently. He looked directly at Maddie and there was something in his eyes that made her uneasy. Haki kneeled down and peered through the gaps between the long sticks that formed the walls of the pen. One doe stood next to her stillborn kid, and another was suckling a newborn who appeared weak and frail.

"It's not going to make it," Haki said, keeping his voice low and only speaking to her.

"Poor thing." She felt terrible for them, but the creepy feeling she had took precedence. She glanced over her shoulder at Gathii, attempting nonchalance. The animal skin at the door to the hut behind him fluttered and she could have sworn she saw the glint of

metal and knuckles wrapped around a rifle.
She didn't let her gaze linger long enough to
confirm it, shifting her attention to the crying
baby and pretending not to notice anything
amiss. Haki stood up and Maddie took advantage of their supposed wedlock by moving in for a side hug. She leaned her cheek
against his shoulder and rubbed her hand on
his back. She felt his muscles stiffen.

"Act normal," she whispered. "Trust me.
We need to leave now, but act like nothing is
wrong. And don't look behind us."

He pointed at the goat in the pen and she
nodded, catching on that the action would
make everyone assume he was telling her
about the loss.

"Let's go," he said.

She tucked her thumbs in her front pockets and they made their way toward Roinet,
who was standing closer to the gate. She felt
Haki's hand settle on her shoulder. His touch
was reassuring and his firm hold protective.
Roinet broke eye contact with his son and his
expression switched to that of pleasant host
as they neared. Haki apologized for not being
able to help with the condition the goats were
in and Roinet gave thanks to both of them.
He seemed as anxious for them to leave as

Maddie was to get out of there. She smiled and waved to his wife, calling out her thanks for the gift as they made their way past the entrance.

"Don't say anything until we're on the road." Haki didn't let go of her until they reached the jeep. He didn't drive any faster than he would have under normal circumstances—at least until they were out of eyeshot. Maddie braced her hand against the dash when he floored the pedal. Her pulse was still slamming the base of her throat.

"See their herder in the distance? His flock is too small for a clan this size. Smaller than I would expect for the pen the goats were in, too. Do me a favor and keep an eye out. I want to be sure we're not followed," he called over the engine noise. "Tell me what you saw. I need to radio rangers in the area."

"I didn't get a good look, but I'm sure the son, Gathii, wasn't just standing around. He was standing guard. There was some-one hiding in the hut behind us, and I think he was holding a rifle of some kind. I'm not one-hundred-percent sure, though. It was in the shadows and I didn't want to let on that I'd noticed. Haki, there was most definitely something wrong. It hit me that Roinet specifically said they don't use guns. Plus, the way Gathii was looking at me was, I don't know…piercing and hostile, and I got that feeling a person gets when they're being stalked in a parking lot at night." She glanced behind them again. No other vehicles were in sight. Her heart rate slowed by a couple of beats. "Maybe I'm overreacting and misinterpreted what I think I saw."

"You weren't imagining things. When you said we needed to leave, I noticed that there was someone standing against the side of a hut on the opposite side of the pen. He wore a Masai shawl but he didn't have it on right. There was too much bulk beneath it, and he either wasn't one of the clan or he was of the younger crowd who choose not to adorn themselves in traditional garb. Either way, it didn't seem right."

"Did you notice there weren't as many people going about their day as we've seen in the other villages?"

He nodded and rubbed the few days' worth of stubble on his face.

"Q fever," he said.

"What?"

"It's a bacterial infection in herds that can also be transmitted to people handling them. I think maybe some of the villagers were indoors due to illness. Fever, malaise, headaches and such. That baby could have contracted it from her father or anyone handling her who was sick. I'm only assuming here. Blood work would prove the theory, but it was my first suspicion. Q fever can cause livestock to suffer stillbirths or abortions or very weak, unhealthy offspring. If a herd can't perpetuate itself, it eventually shrinks in size and if the farmer can't afford to buy replacements—"

"Then they get desperate and we have a motive for killing," Maddie added.

"Exactly. They could have been aiding poachers or they could have been after the tusks for money. The elephant still had its tusks, but it was a fresh kill. The rangers were tipped off so quickly that perhaps Roinet and his son or sons didn't have time to harvest their ivory."

She touched her necklace.

"His wife. Do you think she ratted him out? It would have had to be someone there who knew a killing was planned. How else would the tip have gone in so fast?"

"It's possible, but of course we can't be

sure. I think we're far enough. I need to call this in. They'll investigate again."

He slowed down and pulled to a stop near a copse of trees. Maddie leaned forward and held her head in her hands as he radioed details to KWS. Her head spun and chest felt tight.

"Are you okay?"

His hand on her back was soothing and grounding. He stroked her hair and nudged her to sit up.

"Maddie, are you okay? Talk to me."

"I don't know. I was fine. Now I feel like—" A gasp escaped her and she held her breath.

"Come here." He turned her shoulders to face him. "Don't hold it or you'll start hyperventilating. Take slow breaths. You're coming off an adrenaline rush."

He pulled her close and wrapped his arms around her. She buried her face into his chest and the lingering scent of campfire smoke and soap calmed her. Her gasps settled down but she didn't want him to let go. She didn't want him to stop running his hand through her hair.

"What do you need? Tell me what I can do to help."

"Just keep holding me." Her words sounded muffled and sleepy against his chest. He pressed his lips to the top of her head.

"I'm so sorry. This is my fault. I should not have taken you there. I walked you right into a dangerous situation when I should have been protecting you."

She pulled away and he released his hold. She wiped her face with her hands. God, this was embarrassing. She didn't want him thinking she was weak and emotional.

"I'm not crying and this wasn't your fault," she said as she swiped the corner of her eye and swallowed back tears to keep them from spilling. "I don't cry for nothing."

"You can cry. Let it out."

"No."

"It happens. Maddie, you were amazing back there. You saved us. Things could have gone much worse had you not paid attention to detail the way you always do. It paid off. I was suspicious about illness as a motive, but I didn't know what was going on behind me and I might not have looked up and seen the other man had you not alerted me. You literally had my back. When the adrenaline dissipates, you suddenly realize the danger you were in and you get a physical reaction.

That's all that's happening. It's not a sign of weakness." He reached into the back and got a water bottle. "Here. Drink this. It'll help."

She took a long drink and nodded. It did help.

"Thank you. I guess we made a decent team back there." She hated that her voice cracked and she still felt like crying. Her head was pounding and she rubbed her fingers along her brow. There were two sides to everything, and she'd just gotten a firsthand taste of why he wanted stronger punishment.

"We did."

"Maybe we shouldn't say anything about what happened when we get to camp. It would only worry everyone. It might be better for KWS if we stayed mum until their investigation is complete, too."

"I think you're right."

He linked his fingers in hers.

"Maddie, I can't do this." She started to pull her hand away but he didn't let her. "I can't pretend or be dishonest. If something had happened to you back there, I would never forgive myself. The thought of something happening to you is the only thing that scares me. There's something powerful going on between us, and if I'm the only one feeling it, I need to know right now."

Goose bumps trailed from their hands to her shoulder despite the sun beating down on them. She bit her lip and looked down.

"The truth, Maddie-girl. That's all I'm asking for."

"It can't happen. Things are too complicated."

"That's not what I asked. I want to hear it from you. Is something happening here? Do you feel it?"

She'd had courage back at the village. She needed to find it now.

"Yes."

"Do you want it?"

"Yes, desperately, but we can't. Things are too complicated. I have to return to the US. You have a calling here and a dream. You can't abandon that. And then there's Pippa, who's expecting a proposal. There's too much at stake. We can't risk everything when we know there's no way to make it—whatever this is between us—work long-term."

"You're saying we're not worth the risk."

"That's not what I said. Are *you* saying you're willing to destroy Pippa and her trust? We can't be that selfish."

Haki closed his eyes in defeat and his Adam's apple rose and fell.

"No."

She agreed with his answer. She expected it. But it still hurt. It had a finality to it—the death of something that felt right and beautiful and miraculous before it had even had a chance to be.

A stillbirth.

"But what we're feeling is a betrayal of her. Denying it is betraying each other," he said.

"I didn't come here knowing this would happen. We can't always control what we're feeling or where our thoughts wander, but we can control our actions, and we've been fighting this."

"So this is it."

"Yeah. Let's not throw away our friendship, though. Promise me that," she said.

"I'll treasure it forever."

They both looked at the path ahead. Life was about moving forward. There would be no turning back.

"Haki. Would you keep holding my hand until we're almost there? Just this once."

He pressed his lips together and squeezed her hand.

This time she couldn't keep the tears from

escaping. This was life. God knew she'd seen death many times. She was only now realizing how many faces it had.

CHAPTER ELEVEN

MADDIE GOT A second wind as they approached Camp Jamba Walker. It hadn't changed much since she last saw it. It still had its rustic charm and central fire pit encircled by lava rocks. Breezy wood-framed tents lined each side of the camp like clean-lined art pieces leading the way to a riverbank, where guests could sit under a thatched-roof gazebo and watch, photograph or paint the scenery. Two cottages sat on the property, as well—the original one, where Mugi and Kesi Jamba lived, and one built about fifteen years ago, after Mac Walker and Tessa Henning had married and, along with their then thirteen-year-old orphaned nephew, Nick, moved to the camp.

Haki drove past Mac's helicopter, which sat in a clearing a safe distance beyond the main camp quarters, and pulled up to an area near the cottages that had been cleared for a couple of family-sized safari vehicles. They were typically used for taking guests on day trips designed to teach them about the area's geology, plant life and animals, and to show them ways they could be more eco conscious and do their part to save the environment.

She'd kept quiet during their approach and let Haki update her on the changes since she'd last been here, such as the sort of survivor training class Mugi loved to teach, especially to kids. Maddie understood that Haki was just trying to use conversation to regain some normalcy between them. If only he could hear the admiration and longing in his voice as he spoke about the camp. Didn't he realize that Mugi, a lawyer, and his wife Kesi, an architect, had left those careers behind to pursue their dream? Obviously Haki knew that, but apparently he hadn't registered it as a lesson or example for himself. They weren't doing what had been expected of them. They were doing what fulfilled them.

She took a deep breath. His future was up to him and Pippa. She needed to stop thinking about it.

"I always loved the atmosphere here. I can't wait to see everyone," Maddie said, jumping out of the jeep. Between her numb bottom and cramped legs, she nearly lost her footing. She stretched the muscles in her stiff back and slung her backpack over one shoulder.

The place was clearly busy with several guest families. It was getting late in the day and it looked like they'd all just returned from outings and were getting ready to have dinner. A buffet on fold-out tables covered in white linen was already set up. Kesi, dressed in a white shirt, geometrically patterned wrap skirt and sandals, came out of her cottage carrying a large dish of something steamy and no doubt delicious. Maddie was starving and she didn't usually have a big appetite. She couldn't imagine how ravenous Haki must be.

"Auntie Kesi!" Maddie trotted over to give her a hug.

"Maddie, dear! Oh, my goodness, you look so lovely. It's so good to see you." Kesi left the plate on the table and caught Maddie in her arms. She was getting older and had a warm, grandmotherly air about her. Her hair matched her shirt and made her warm skin tone and the vivid green of her malachite necklace stand out beautifully. The artist and architect in her had an eye for aesthetics, down to the array of culinary treats she'd laid on the table.

"And I'm not ignoring you, Haki. Come here and give me a hug, big boy. You both must be hungry."

Haki gave her a tender hug and a kiss on the cheek.

"*Hungry* isn't a strong enough word. Besides, with your food, I'd be hungry even if I'd already eaten. Which we haven't. But feel free to put us to work to earn it."

"Nonsense. We were expecting you. I thought we'd all eat outside today. Mac is fetching some more wood for the pit, Mugi is washing up since he just got back with a group, Tessa is helping me prep and Pippa…" Kesi craned her neck and searched the area. "Pippa is around somewhere. She took five of the kids with her to find different rocks and formations to see if they were listening to the talk she gave them. I think it takes someone with her energy to handle a bunch of kids like that, and she knows it takes hands-on teaching to keep their attention because she was just like them once."

"She's definitely all about experience and exploring. I hope she didn't take them too far," Haki said, glancing down the path Kesi had pointed to. This camp's surroundings were more dense with trees and shrubs than Busara was.

"Oh, no. She's good about that. Not when she's alone, but with the kids, she's careful."

"She probably remembers the stunts she pulled at that age, so she's fully aware of the trouble they can get into. If they don't show up, their parents will find them dangling from trees and squealing like monkeys, like in *The Sound of Music*. Maybe we should nickname her Fräulein Maria," Maddie said.

Kesi laughed and put an arm around her.

"Ah, Maddie, that is so Pippa. I won't be able to get that image out of my head now. Come, let's finish setting up."

"Haki and Maddie?" Tessa came out from behind the cottage with a platter of hot *chapati*. She set it on the table and embraced each of them. "I was hoping that you'd arrived when I heard laughing."

"We are here and that bread smells so good." Maddie said.

"I was just in the back making them over an open flame with Kesi's iron pan, the way she taught me. It's my go-to for a carb craving."

"Let me help you set up," Maddie said.

"I'm going to make sure that Pip—"

"Hey, guys!" Pippa came up the path with a kick in her step and a group of kids ranging from what looked like nine to fourteen. She said something to them that put grins on their faces; then they scattered to find their parents. She hurried up the rest of the path. "That was so much fun. Great kids. Now all experts on lava rock, volcanic soil and, as always, we had a few budding paleontologists in the group, so naturally I told them about the big Kenya dig and the fossil of an ancient croc that was over twenty-seven feet long. They had fun trying to say its name— *Crocodylus thorbjarnarsoni*. That, my dears, is how I keep kids a safe distance from the riverbank. It works every time." She patted Haki on the back and grinned. "You were worried about us, weren't you?" She turned to the rest of them. "He was about to come hunt me down, wasn't he?"

Kesi, Tessa and Maddie chuckled and nudged each other along. Kesi held her palms up.

"I don't know a thing. We were on our way to feed the guests. Take it easy on him, Pippa. He's had Maddie on his hands for two days."

FOR A MOMENT, Haki felt the blood rush from his head. Kesi was ultra observant when it came to people, but, although the feel of Maddie's hand still lingered against his skin, no way could Kesi have picked up on anything between them—they'd barely spoken to each other in front of her. And if she had, she wouldn't have said it out loud. *He's had Maddie on his hands.* He gave his head a quick shake. His blood sugars had probably plummeted and the drive had been long. Kesi thought he was sick of driving Maddie around and dealing with her determination to block the proposal he supported to protect elephants. That's what Kesi meant.

"Come on, I'm not that much trouble," Maddie said. She was going out of her way not to look at him. She went off to help out with dinner.

Pippa wrapped him in a hug.

"So how'd the trip go? Did you convince her to drop the case?" Pippa asked.

"No. I don't think so."

Haki put one arm around her and walked back toward his jeep. He really did love and care for her. There was a certain comfort in their routine and in knowing what was ahead of them each day. There was sentimentality in knowing each other's pasts since birth. But then why didn't he feel anything beyond tenderness and protectiveness whenever they touched? That had been the case even before Maddie's return. Why didn't the touch and scent of her hair when she rested her head against his chest make him burn for more? Why did his chest feel like it was splintering into a thousand jagged pieces?

He and Maddie had agreed that nothing could happen between them. He needed to get over her and make things work with Pippa. Being caught between them like this made him feel like a pile of dung.

"You've only spent one night and a couple of days with her. That's not much time," Pippa said, watching his face carefully. Too carefully.

He swiped a finger under her chin and tugged playfully at one of her curls. She seemed satisfied that everything was okay.

It *had* been only one night, but a very long one. He still had their earlier scare on his mind, too. Pippa had no idea how much "convincing" had happened since they'd left Busara. But if Maddie managed to kill the proposal, it'd be enough to kill any attraction between them. Right? What if she didn't? Pippa elbowed him.

"Don't look so worried. I'm sure if you get the chance to take her to a few more villages and she sees that not all farms get raided and not all farmers hate elephants, she'll come around. I'll make sure she spends time with the babies when we get back home. That might be another way to sway her."

"Sure. Maybe."

They reached the jeep and he proceeded to double-check that all firearms were locked up and secure from guests. With kids running around the camp, even a tranquilizer dart could be dangerous. He needed to clean out the cooler, too, so leftovers wouldn't spoil in it. And check the engine oil. And tire pressure. And—

"Is everything okay?" Pippa began collecting the canteens for him.

"Sure. Why?" He checked the glove compartment.

"You seem more bothered than you should be. You're brooding and not really talking to me. I've known you long enough. You have that look you get when you know someone's close to beating you in a game of chess, but you refuse to accept it. What's the word? Tortured." She lowered her chin and peered at him from under her lashes. "Did Maddie torture you?"

Sweat began trickling down his back. He reached around and scratched his spine. Maddie was torturing him in every way possible. It was the worst kind of torture: to feel comfortable with someone in a way that you weren't with anyone else, not even family. To feel that the timing of your heartbeats was in perfect sync. To be able to open yourself up, mind and soul, and not hold back. To long for more hours in a day because you spent twenty-four with that someone and it wasn't enough. And to close your eyes and see her face, when you were supposed to be seeing someone else's. It was enough torture—and guilt—to kill a man. He held on to the jeep, let his chin fall to his chest and took a deep breath. Too much had gone on in just a few days. He'd let it all get the better of him. He straightened his back and did his best to relax his face.

"How could Maddie possibly torture me? Are we talking about the same person?"

"I'm thinking maybe she already checkmated you on the proposal."

"She has her lists and names, but I don't think it's enough. I'm not worried," he lied.

"Well, you don't look good. I mean you always look *good*, but if this is just you being tired because of all the driving and not having a bed last night, we could stay here tonight. Have a campfire like old times. Then drive to Busara in the morning."

Haki studied the sun's angle over the river on the west side of camp. If they rushed, they'd make it, but by the time they ate and visited, it might be too late to head out. His back really was aching.

"Are you sure you're okay staying here another night?"

"Yes, I'm sure. You need a break and I know if you go home you'll be in the clinic or field within minutes."

"Okay. You might want to let Maddie know."

"Great. She and I can share the tent I stayed in last night. Let's get this stuff of yours inside so we can go eat."

She ran on ahead of him as he continued to gather his stuff from the jeep. Mugi stepped out onto his front porch and waved.

"Hey, old man," Haki called out. He took the few steps up to the porch in one long stride. Mugi greeted him with a wide smile and handshake.

"Who are you calling old? Those aren't gray hairs. They were bleached by the sun. What's left of them, at least. Are you up for a game of chess after dinner? You wouldn't deny an old man, would you?"

"Challenge accepted, if you don't mind another guest or two tonight."

"Mind? You're never a guest here. This way, if I lose, we can play again."

MUGI ENDED UP LOSING, but rather than a second game, he entertained everyone, especially the guests, with stories around the lava-stone fire pit that Mac had made many years ago. Listening to Mugi tell a story was the next best thing to reading a book. He had a gift and Haki still remembered the times Mugi would gather him, Pippa, Maddie, their brothers and Nick around the fire and keep them mesmerized for hours. Tonight was reminiscent of those times, except that Maddie—no doubt trying to keep her distance—sat on the far side of the fire, while Pippa nestled next to him, resting her head against his arm. A part of him felt like one of the logs in the pit getting burned to ash. *Tortured.* He could smell Pippa's mango-scented shampoo and feel the caress of her fingertips up and down his forearm as his hand rested on her knee, but for all her effort to keep her distance, Maddie was right in front of him. Directly in his line of sight. Even when he looked at the wondrous expressions of everyone else in the circle sucked in by Mugi's story, he could still see her in the periphery. He could see her with his eyes closed.

"I believe that's it for tonight," Mugi said, after the unexpected ending that had everyone laughing. Haki must have heard that one a million times, but it never got old. The guests gave their thank-yous and headed to their accommodations. Haki stood, forcing Pippa to lose contact with him. He needed sleep and time alone.

"Do you mind if I leave you to put out the fire, Mac?"

He hated admitting to being tired, but he didn't have to explain. Mac was one of those guys who understood the drive to be strong all the time and the blow to the ego when a limit was reached.

"I've got this covered."

Haki removed himself from the circle and called out good-night to everyone, including Pippa, who kept a straight face, but had a confused, faraway look in her eyes. He cursed himself silently. She'd known him too long to be fooled. He was giving off mixed signals. He rubbed the back of his neck as he retreated to his tent and settled down on the cot.

Twenty minutes passed and he still couldn't sleep. He'd come so close to dozing off…then Maddie and Pippa had entered the tent right next to his. Even with the canvas rolled down for privacy, the tents were far from soundproof and he was beginning to think that the heads of their beds backed up to his. He closed his eyes and tried not to listen, but Pippa's whispers carried.

"Did he give you a bad time? He's always so serious."

"He was fine. I spoke to the people I needed to meet." He could barely hear Maddie.

"He seems out of sorts. I've known him all my life and understand him better than anyone else ever could. I can tell he's stressed out."

"I'm sorry if my job here is causing that, but I have to do what I was sent here for. It's not easy. I'm exhausted myself. I'm sure we'll all feel better in the morning."

"If you're sleepy, I won't keep you up," Pippa said.

"You can talk. But if I don't answer, you'll know I fell asleep."

There was a brief silence before their hushed voices came through the canvas again.

"Do you have a boyfriend?" Pippa asked.

Pause.

"No. Why?"

"I'm just wondering how other women feel when they're in love. How they know."

No one spoke after that.

CHAPTER TWELVE

MADDIE SAT AT the dining table in the Busara house, as everyone called it, and sipped mint tea while she uploaded her video testimonies to a file. She'd woken up much later than everyone else, and Niara had explained that Haki and his father were both out in the field. Pippa was helping Anna with Etana, the baby elephant they were hoping to save.

She took another sip of the sweet tea and began typing up a report to send to the firm in Nairobi. She hoped it would be enough and that she wouldn't have to visit any more villages. Especially not alone with Haki. She copied Mr. Levy on the email, as well, in case Patrick had him believing she wasn't working as hard as he was—on a case she'd already done all the work for, no less. It certainly didn't feel like a regular work schedule, but Patrick would have never lasted that many hours in a dusty jeep with old shock absorbers, surrounded by danger. Haki would have never put up with him. He never could stand anyone he sensed was being under-handed or had no integrity. Haki had always played by the book. He was a firm believer in setting rules because they kept people safe.

Maddie dropped her head in her hands and rubbed her temples. God help her, that sounded just like her father. She lifted her face and blinked at her screen. Honestly, was it really shocking that Haki was coming down so hard on any tribesmen who were in-volved in killing or setting traps? He was so caught up in details and rules, though, that he was missing the big picture. She loaded the files to the email and hit Send…and waited. The internet connection here was super slow and went out often. She took another sip.

"All right," she said out loud when it sent. She closed her laptop and stood.

"Finished?" Niara asked from the other end of the table. She was working on a post for the Busara blog, where they shared pho-tos of the baby elephants with readers and gave updates. It helped tremendously with donations for funding all the food, medicine and other expenses it took to keep Busara running.

"Yep. For now. I might need to get more testimony, but it doesn't have to be today."

She stretched her arms behind her, then held each elbow across her chest to release the stiffness in her upper back.

"What about you?"

"I'm almost done. I promised Tessa I'd send her this. She takes care of the actual formatting and posting. I enjoy the writing, but not the rest."

"I'm the same way. I think a part of me was meant to live centuries ago. No computers. Pencil and paper. Old, simple games like playing jacks or hopscotch. It's probably why I loved all those books either set long ago or that centered around the basics of life. You know?"

"Oh, yes. I know. Haki is also that way. He was always an old soul, ever since he was born. I could see it in his eyes before he could speak. No wonder he took to games like checkers and chess."

An old soul. That was Haki to a T. Mothers really did know their children.

"He beat Uncle Mugi badly the night we stayed at Jamba Walker. It seemed to energize him after the long day he'd had." Maddie grinned.

"Poor Mugi. He loves the challenge." Niara paused, then moved her work aside and linked her hands. Niara's face always had peacefulness about it, even when she was concerned. "Maddie, dear. If you don't mind my asking, did everything go okay when you were gone with Haki? He's been more pensive than usual the past two days. You didn't fight over this case issue, did you?"

The muscle between Maddie's shoulder blades pinched again. How was she supposed to answer that? To his mother, no less. They'd agreed not to bring up the danger they'd been in, not only because they wanted to spare their families worry, but also because the more it was discussed, the more likely someone they didn't know well would overhear. They didn't want anyone potentially tipping off Roinet before their suspicions could be investigated. She was definitely not telling his mother about what had passed between them, either. Maddie struggled to come up with something that wasn't a lie. She couldn't lie to Niara.

"We didn't fight. We shared our opinions and perspectives, but no one drew blood," she said.

"Perhaps he was just tired, then," Niara

offered, but she sounded more polite than convinced.

"All that driving, as captivating as the scenery around here is, did take its toll on us. I'm definitely not used to it."

"Yes…it's just that he was so motivated to write that proposal. Yet I know he's always had a great deal of respect for you. Always—even as children. You might be a little older but he has always been too mature for his age. Not negative, just…mature. As a mother I could see you both shared a serious outlook on life. You both care intensely about what you believe is right. You always have. What I'm trying to say, or advise, is that when two streams merge, the watering hole is less likely to go dry."

Haki had always respected her? Maddie bit her lip.

"Auntie Niara, I don't see where we could compromise on this. It's effectively a document. It either gets passed or it doesn't."

"I didn't say to compromise, necessarily. It's always good to cooperate, but neither of you is the type to compromise what you believe in, and I wouldn't want you to. When two minds are so alike, though, the ideas can flow together and never feel like a sacrifice."

"I understand. But I tried to tell him that punishment isn't always the answer." *Except you just saw how desperation can trump morality. What if Roinet and his sons had pulled their guns out? What if Haki's life had been taken? You wouldn't hesitate to go after maximum punishment if that happened.*

Niara sat forward and cocked her head.

"Maddie. Between you and me, I agree with you. Yes, he's my son and yes, I stand for our mission here, protecting the elephants. That cause is close to my heart. But I'm sure you've heard at least a little about my past. About how Haki was conceived. I won't get into that now, but the point is—I was wronged. I understand what it's like to be a victim of a heartless, evil act. Yet, punishment alone won't stop crime. One has to get to the root of the issue. Problem-solve. The advantage right now is that you're both here. At Busara. You're not in a courtroom. You're both thinkers. Remember that in chess, the queen is powerful, but only when thought goes into the steps she takes." She pushed back her chair, got up and gave Maddie a kiss on her temple. "Now. I've said my piece. I won't meddle beyond that or tell you what to do. I love you too much for that."

"Thank you," Maddie said, putting her hand on Niara's. "I'll do my best."

"*Usijali.* Don't worry—it'll all work out however it's meant to be. For now, if you'd like, you could go over to the pens and see the elephants. Pippa is there."

Pippa. Maddie took a deep breath as her cousin's words came back to her. *I'm just wondering how other women feel when they're in love. How they know.* Didn't Pippa know? Did Maddie?

She slipped her laptop in its case. Their entire family and circle of friends was made up of couples who were madly in love and devoted to each other: Kamau and Niara, Jack and Anna, Ben and Hope, Mac and Tessa, Mugi and Kesi, Simba and Chuki... So why was it so confusing? Why did it feel so messed up? The gap between watching love and experiencing it was as wide as the distance that separated her from life here and her life on the other side of the world. What she felt for Haki was strong and all-encompassing, but she wouldn't be here long enough for them to figure out if it was the real thing. Pippa's life *was* here, and when Maddie returned to America, she needed to know that her little cousin was going to be happy. That was all that mattered.

"Thanks, Auntie. I'll head there now."

Maddie stepped out into the midday sun and had to shade her eyes with her hand. Mosi squealed from a nearby tree at the sight of her. He swung down, scampered along the porch rail carved from a single log and jumped to her feet.

"Hey, buddy, I don't have anything on me."

He poked at her leg, stepping back each time just in case she turned out to be a not-so-nice human.

"Sorry. My pockets are empty." He pouted and ran back up the tree. Maddie stepped down onto the dry earth and started across to the pens and clinic. Something hit her in the back.

"Ow!" She spun around and Mosi screamed at her. He had another shelled nut in his hand. "You little…monkey. Don't do that. If you have nuts to throw at me, then why are you begging for food?" She marched off. He squealed.

"Nope. No treats," she called back without turning around. "That is not the way to treat a girl."

One of the keepers witnessed the exchange

and laughed as he led a baby elephant toward a grassy clearing where several others were playing.

"Our Mosi is in love. He wants your attention," he said.

Maddie laughed and splayed her hands.

"What's a girl to do?"

She approached the baby and it reached out with its trunk to search her pockets.

"That tickles. He's so sweet," she told the keeper, running her hand along the baby's trunk, then rubbing him behind the ears.

"You are good with animals."

"Yeah. I've always loved them." Yet, she'd left them behind and didn't have any pet but a single fish. A pet she could only watch in a glass bubble. No contact. No real bond. Nothing like the undeniable connection she was experiencing with Haki now. But no way could she have a place in his heart after all these years. She'd left Kenya and he had Pippa here—right in front of him. A longing pulsed in her chest. She touched the fuzz on the elephant's head.

"I like you, little guy."

"He likes you, too. His name is Enzi. It means *power*. Between Mosi and Enzi, we'll have to see who wins your heart—*first born* or *power*." His face lit up with pride at his own sense of humor.

"Oooh, hard choice," Maddie said as she let them pass. Hard choice, if she had one, which she didn't. First born or power? She tried to silence the echo in her head. Haki or senior partner? Love or loyalty? Her heart or Pippa's?

Most of the pens had wooden gates on the outside so keepers could get in and out with their charges without causing a traffic jam, but there were two indoor pens in an interior area, closer to the clinic, where emergency patients were taken for treatment, surgery or recovery until they were out of the woods. She figured that Etana would still be there. She let herself through a gate that led down a short, dirt-floored corridor and was drawn by voices to the room on the left.

"Hey there." Dr. Bekker waved for her to join them. Ahron, the keeper assigned to Etana, was crouched next to Pippa in front of the baby. Pippa's cheeks were streaked with tears and her nose was red. She looked over at Maddie as she held the oversized bottle for Etana.

"She's eating. Look at her. Good girl," she

added, giving the elephant a rub and coaxing her to take more.

"She's going to make it. Pip, you have the touch," her mom told her.

"She's the most precious thing I've ever seen." Maddie swallowed back a lump in her throat. The baby had a bandaged wound on her ankle from the snare and the way her leathery skin draped against her bones was heartbreaking. Etana gazed at her with soulful eyes as she sucked hard at the bottle. She'd found her appetite and the will to survive. Dr. Bekker had treated her, but she'd also been given love and hope. It mattered. Life was nothing without love and hope for something better. Maddie rested her shoulder against the wall of the pen and cocked her head as she watched. Etana kept looking at her, ears twitching and fuzzy forehead wrinkling with expression. A sudden awareness and bittersweet ache washed through Maddie. *You know, don't you? That I also lost my mother at a young age.* Etana almost seemed to rear her head in a nod as she took a big gulp. Haki had said that elephants *know.* Was this Maddie's imagination? Was guilt messing with her? It felt unmistakably real.

It's going to be okay. I got a new mother

who cared for me, just like you're getting here. My mother's name is Hope. And you're a strong one, Etana. This is your family now.

Maybe there really was something to a name.

GRINDING HIS TEETH did nothing to quell Haki's anger. A stabbing pain shot through his ear and he rubbed at his jaw and opened his mouth to stretch it. The coppery stench of blood from his clothing and the baby elephant's open wounds filled the jeep. He checked to make sure the needle he'd inserted for the IV was holding despite the rough road. He, Kamau and their team were riding with the baby in the covered truck bed of their medical unit. He double-checked her breathing and heart-beat. She was in critical shape but he refused to lose hope.

His father grabbed the radio.

"Mama Tembo. This is Busara One. Do you read?" He waited for the static to pass.

"Busara One. This is Ahron. Mama Tembo is in surgery."

"We'll be arriving in approximately twenty. Infant. Leg injury. Severe blood loss. Prep medical. Over."

"Copy, Busara One. I'll tell Dr. Bekker now. Over."

"Was she scheduled for surgery today?" Kamau asked, tucking the radio in its holder and checking to see if the bleeding had slowed.

"I saw notes that Sefu was trying to loosen the stitches on his trunk. She's probably restitching," Haki said. Anna would be ready. She always was. Busara was her life's work.

Haki was proud to be part of it all. The surgery and emergency care he did as a vet had been his goal growing up. But Anna was *Dr.* Bekker, a respected researcher and vet with a doctorate of veterinary medicine from the US, and his father was *Dr.* Odaba, who'd studied vet medicine in Kenya but gone beyond that bachelors to earn a PhD, as well, and make a name for himself as a field-rescue vet. Haki had earned his BVM, and although that degree earned him the title of doctor in Kenya, he wanted more. He wanted an actual doctorate degree. He knew he was making a difference as things stood, but he was restless. He wasn't satisfied with following in others' footsteps. He wanted to mark his own path.

But his drive to forge that path bothered

him because going back to school for years would mean leaving Busara and Pippa... and they both needed him right now. Unfortunately, Busara was getting busier. That meant the number of casualties was going up, not down. They needed the extra veterinarian more than ever. He was family. He owed them. That degree wouldn't make a difference in terms of what he could do—was already doing—to help with rescues. It would only make a difference to him. The timing wasn't right. It wasn't meant to be.

The chopper that had helped sight the incident was getting smaller as it flew away. It wasn't Mac's this time. An hour ago, Mac had called in an injured adult he'd spotted from the air while he was flying some people toward the Masai Mara. He was too far out. This baby had been found closer to Tsavo East. KWS had been called in and they had a vet on board who had tried saving the mother. Kamau and Haki's crew had been in the area when the call came over the air. Busara was the nearest rescue prepared to take the calf.

Haki glanced at the time.

"Son, we'll get there. That calf wouldn't even have a chance if it weren't for your quick action back there. No matter what happens to her, I'm proud of you."

Haki swallowed hard and nodded, but he couldn't get past knowing he wasn't able to do more.

When they finally reached Busara, Haki handed the IV bag to one of the techs to hold above the baby. He got out of the jeep and prepared to secure the thick tarps that served as a stretcher for the calf. Kamau and two others grabbed the edges from inside the truck bed. They needed to lift her gently and get her to where they could treat the wounds. They needed to save her.

"Ready, one, two, three—lift," he called out. They hoisted the tarp and set her down on the ground. From the corner of his eye he could see Dr. Bekker running over from the clinic. He barely registered Pippa and Maddie emerging from inside.

"Haki!"

He jerked toward Maddie's panicked voice. She looked pale and had started toward them but Pippa took her arm and said something to her. *The blood.* He was covered in blood.

"I'm okay. It's not me. Tell them to keep the others out of the way," he yelled. Pippa would know he meant the other keepers and babies who were out of their pens. She left Maddie and ran to the open area, where the elephants were playing, and warned the men to keep them from coming to check on the new arrival. He was sure all their residents picked up on the scent and the tension whenever a new patient was brought in. He didn't want to expose them to further trauma.

Dr. Bekker reached them and took a corner of the tarp to help bring the baby at least closer to the clinic, if not inside. If they had to do surgery out in the open, it wouldn't be the first time. They'd treated adults out in the savannah before. Out here, you did what you had to do.

"What happened?" Anna asked as she, Kamau and Haki worked to clean the wounds and stop the bleeding. They kneeled to ground level as the baby lay on the tarp.

"An electric fence was down and several elephants wandered out of the forested area and got to one of the farms. Another Masai farmer heard and set out snares to stop his crops from getting raided. This little one was with her mother and stepped on a snare. The mother didn't want to leave her, which made her an easy target," Haki said.

"KWS found her embedded with arrows in

her leg and side. Dead," Kamau continued. "One of those arrows hit the baby—we're not sure if it was by mistake or not. She was already injured by the snare."

"We think they were there awhile. Possibly days. This is full of pus," Haki said as he cleansed the baby's ankle. It took an iron stomach to handle the stench from the infection. Kamau stuck massive tweezers into the baby's side wound and pulled out an arrow about eight inches long.

"Unbelievable. I don't want her out too long. She's really frail," Anna said.

"It's been an hour since I administered the sedative," Haki told her. "I went ahead and set up the fluids, too. She looks dehydrated."

He finished cleaning the ankle wound, then loaded a syringe with antibiotics and stuck it in her hip. Anna packed the arrow wound while Kamau checked her vitals.

"Wake her up, stat," Kam said.

Haki flipped her ear over and quickly injected the drug to reverse the sedative into one of the veins. Then they stood back. All they could do now was wait and pray that she'd come around.

"Come on, girl," Anna coaxed.

Haki ducked his head to wipe his face

against his shoulder and caught Maddie standing there watching. The color was drained from her face and her eyes and nose were red and swollen. Her lips parted, but she didn't say a word. The baby had yet to come around. They finally met each other's eyes.

This, Mads. This is what happens.

CHAPTER THIRTEEN

MADDIE GRABBED A bag of sugar and a container of tea from the back of the jeep as Pippa unloaded a cloth sack, plus a bag with her water and soil sampling kits she'd held on to since her college geology labs. Maddie's mom had asked Pippa to check a few wells in the area when she could. Apparently, Hope was concerned about some clinical symptoms that had been showing up in the rural villages. This particular village was the closest to Busara, and Busara's water had been fine when Pippa tested it.

"I don't need my fortune told," Maddie said, holding up the sugar and tea gifts. She should have known the water wasn't the only reason why Pippa wanted to visit this place.

"Oh, come on. You need a distraction after yesterday. So do I."

"I guess it's not something anyone can get used to."

"No. You had me worried, though," Pippa

said. "Me? It shreds me to pieces every time. I've learned to stay out of the clinic until I'm told a baby needs a name. I can't handle it when they don't make it. That's why I didn't go to vet school. That takes a certain type of stoic strength I don't have. If I knew you'd followed them, I would have stopped you. I'm sorry."

Maddie didn't respond right away. She was still devastated by what she'd seen. It was burned in her memory. She wasn't good at dealing with death. No, she was downright terrified of it. She'd handled the passing of her fish over the years, but that was the extent of it since her mother's passing. Fear. It was what kept her from adopting a cat or finding a way to include a dog in her busy life. She loved each fish she'd had, but there was something about the glass between them that made her feel sheltered from the pain of loss. Safe from heartbreak.

"I'm okay."

"Then don't resist. This fortune reading will be fun. It'll help clear your mind."

"Are you sure about that? The last time you did it, *Laibon* Leshan told you something like, 'Enemy will make earth break and bleed.' I fail to see your enthusiasm for dire divination. That would have given me night-mares for weeks."

The *Laibon* was the one who everyone turned to for healing and guidance, from is-sues of infertility to where greener pastures lay for the cattle. A medicine man and oracle all in one. And it was traditional to bring him an offering or a gift in return for requesting his help. *Laibon* Leshan loved getting sugar and tea.

"Ah, but we had a small tremor a few days later. Most didn't feel it, but I thought I did and looked it up. Sure enough, it showed up on the Richter scale readings on the geolog-ical website. Get it? Tectonic plates shift-ing. Small earthquake. Cracks deep in the earth are the breaks, and magma—since we didn't have any volcanic eruptions or lava flow above ground—is the blood. He totally saw that coming."

"How can you have studied science and believe all this?"

"First, because you can't grow up here and not have the mysticism of the land and its people touch you. And second, because every scientist knows there's so much we still *don't* know or understand. Think multi-universe theory and space-time dimensions. You can never be sure where psychics like the *Laibon* get their stuff."

"The universe and multiple dimensions. Having studied geology, I'd have thought you'd be more, should I say…grounded? Then again, you always did like climbing trees."

Pippa laughed.

"Maddie. You're funnier than you think you are. Look, don't overanalyze and ruin the fun. Call it a cultural experience for a *Laibon* to throw his stones for you."

"Okay, fine. Just this once, so you'll leave me alone about it."

What could it hurt, really? Maybe he'd tell her she was going to succeed and make partnership at the law firm. Or maybe he could help stop the tension headaches she was starting to get every afternoon. Or predict whether her father would ever have full confidence in her.

Pippa waved as they approached the *enkang*. The women and children waved back and called out her name, some with giggles and some with broad, bright smiles. Due to its proximity to Busara, this particular clan had known Pippa and her parents since she was a baby. Anna and Niara had been invited to special occasions here since Busara's inception. Maddie vaguely remembered coming out to the village once, but she'd been a teenager and didn't stay long. She'd heard about the weddings, though, from Pippa. Ahron, Busara's head elephant keeper, who'd been there from the start, was from this clan. She'd heard that, years ago, one of his cousins had aided poachers. No one blamed Ahron or the rest of the family, but it reminded Maddie of Haki's warning. He was trying to prevent acts of desperation.

Maddie followed Pippa, who seemed to know where to find the group's medicine man, but first Pippa went to the women and handed over the cloth sack she'd brought along.

"Sopa!" Pippa called out to the group. Maddie echoed her. Their voices rang out in greeting as they eyed Maddie curiously. Pippa turned to a young woman holding a baby on her hip. "Sopa, Nashipi. Kasserian ingera?"

"All the children are well, Pippa," Nashipi said in accented but fluent English. "Are you Maddie? You've grown so much. I saw you once, many years ago, but you don't remember me. You were with your mother, Dr. Alwanga, when she set up a day clinic here for the children."

Maddie grappled for any memory of Nashipi's face, but was at a loss.

"*Sopa*. It's good to return. I think I came when I was a teenager. I can't believe you remember me," Maddie said in her friendliest voice. "I hope everyone is well."

"Thank you, yes."

"I brought more books for the children and a few you might enjoy," Pippa said, handing her the sack. "Nashipi is a wonderful reading teacher," Pippa explained to Maddie.

"Well, I owe it to Pippa," Nashipi said.

"Actually, some of the first books I brought you, I had been given by Maddie here."

Maddie hadn't known that. Pippa had been an extremely early reader, *that* she knew, so it made sense that she wanted others to read. It was why Maddie had shared her love of books with her. Knowing that some of those very books had helped Nashipi and the others here made something tender and pure bloom in Maddie's chest.

"Thank you, too, Maddie," Nashipi said.

"Sharing is an honor," Maddie replied.

"We're going to see *Laibon* Leshan. If you need anything else, let me know before we leave. Oh, and I'll check the water well, but if you have any messages for Dr. Alwanga, I'll pass them on," Pippa said. She brushed Maddie along with her free hand.

"By the way, I sometimes speak in Maa here, but sometimes in Swahili. They speak both well, so feel free to greet with *jambo* instead of *sopa*. *Laibon* Leshan doesn't speak English as far as I've been able to tell. Actually, he's a man of so few words, I've rarely heard him speak at all. Sometimes I think he understands everything, regardless of language, but likes to act like he doesn't. More mysterious and wise that way," Pippa said with dramatic flair.

Laibon Leshan sat cross-legged under an *oreti*, or wild fig tree, near the entrance to his *inkajijik*. A wooden staff lay propped across his shoulder and his weathered hands hung loosely in his lap. He looked up at Maddie and Pippa with his sun-soaked face and glassy eyes, and the air seemed to still. *Too late to back out now.* If she walked away, she'd be insulting him. Besides, Pippa would throw a fit. She bit the inside of her lip and steadied her breathing as Pippa presented him with their gifts. Why was she so darn nervous? She'd given her horoscope a cursory read in the newspaper occasionally. But she didn't live by it. Standing before someone who was supposed to *know*, someone who had a striking, mystical presence that couldn't be ignored, made her uneasy.

Life was about cause and effect. A person had control over what they caused, and then they dealt with the consequences. Just like in a court case, results were supposed to be based on facts. Otherwise, judges would rule based on horoscopes and psychics and no one would ever have a fair trial.

As a young teen, she had wondered: if the future could be seen, if danger could be avoided, could Zoe, her birth mother, have been saved? But then, with a twinge of guilt, she'd realized that she loved the people around her and loved her life. To change one part of history would mean changing it all. Or worse, what if she had to live knowing something bad was going to happen but she couldn't do anything about it? How could she live if someone told her that Chad would die in service…not the given possibility, but that he *would*? What if it was divined that elephants would go extinct? Would people stop trying to save them? Was fate unavoidable? Or were divinations warnings that could be used as guides for free will, as motivation for change?

Her hands felt cold, despite the heat. Pippa drew her down to sit next to her in front of the *Laibon*. A goatskin lay on the ground in front of him. He nodded to indicate his readiness.

"Ask him your question or tell him what ails you," Pippa said in a low voice.

"I don't know what to ask. This was your idea."

"Fine, then." Pippa asked him something in Maa.

"What did you ask?"

"Shhhh. Just something about your future. Pay attention."

He studied Maddie's face carefully, then picked up a cow's horn and held it with the hollowed end facing her.

"Spit in it," Pippa whispered.

"Spit?" Maddie hesitated. The old man moved the mouth of the horn closer to her. *This is all for fun. Do it for Pippa's entertainment and move on.* She spat, though it wasn't much considering how dry her mouth had gone.

He rattled the horn, then flicked his wrist, sending a variety of pebbles and river stones tumbling out onto the goatskin. And there it was. Written in the stones.

"I think my future looks at bit…rocky." A snort escaped Maddie's lips and Pippa elbowed her, then covered her own mouth. Maddie couldn't help it. Tension had a way of releasing itself in the worst ways sometimes.

"Don't be disrespectful," Pippa warned as she composed herself.

"*Samahani.*" Maddie hoped he understood her apology in Swahili. She caught an almost imperceptible nod.

His hand shook as he touched several of the pebbles and muttered to himself. The furrows between his brows and the lines across his forehead deepened.

"*Mbaya,*" he mumbled and moved a few stones.

Maddie's stomach sank. *Mbaya* meant *bad* in Swahili. She knew she never should have come here. She never should have let Pippa convince her. Pippa put her hand over Maddie's but kept her eyes on the *Laibon*.

He finally looked up at Maddie.

"You will have broken heart. *Moyo,*" he said, pointing at his chest and shaking his head. "*Uliovunjika moyo.*" He scooped up his stones and returned them to his horn. That was it?

They both sat there. Maddie wasn't sure what had stunned them more: that he'd spoken in English, or the part about her broken heart.

"Sielewi. I don't understand. A literal or figurative broken heart? Am I sick?" The *Laibon* didn't answer.

"Asante." Pippa thanked the old man and, looping her arm around Maddie's, pulled her into the harsh sunlight and practically dragged her toward the supplies she'd left near the jeep. "I really need that water sample. We should get to work."

Maddie pulled her arm out of Pippa's grasp and dug her heels into the dry, red earth that seemed to coat everything from her boots to her lungs. She knew the tightness that spiraled down from her chest to the pit of her stomach had nothing to do with the drought or the sun prickling her skin. Pippa wasn't being upfront about something.

"What exactly did you ask him?" Maddie squared her shoulders and stared right at her as if she was a lawyer facing a witness on the stand.

Pippa side-glanced at the mothers and

children who were perusing the books she'd brought them. No doubt they could hear every word.

"You want everyone to listen or do you want to follow me to the jeep so I can get my supplies?"

Maddie reluctantly followed. A part of her didn't care who heard. She just wanted to know what Pippa was up to right then and there. But then again, her gut told her that there was a good chance whatever Pippa had to say wasn't something Maddie needed floating around Busara because it would no doubt make it to her parents' ears. She had enough to think about when it came to her reputation, both with her family and career-wise. Reputation wasn't something Pippa spent much time worrying about.

"Out with it, Pippa. You talked me into all this. It was my reading. I have a right to know."

Pippa scrunched her face as she picked up her water-sample kit.

"Don't overreact, okay? I asked if you'd find a man to marry soon."

"What? Why in the world would you ask that?"

"It's no big deal. So the next guy you meet

breaks your heart. You'll meet another and marry him instead. Besides, what else would I ask?"

"Hmm, let's see…if I'll win my case? Get a promotion? Or live to be one hundred? Marriage is the last thing on my mind right now."

Was it? She could almost feel Haki's warm, calloused fingertips brushing the back of her hand. She could hear the hope that carried in his words and read the sincerity, kindness and purpose in his deep, brown eyes. She blinked away the thought and pressed a hand to her forehead. What was happening to her? She couldn't think like that. Thinking of Haki wasn't supposed to stir her insides up and make her feel nauseous. He was a friend. Pippa's guy. What was wrong with her? She quickly shifted her hand to make Pippa think she was simply shielding her eyes from the sun.

"Well, if you plan to live a century, you should get married. I read that married people live longer," Pippa said, heading toward the village well. Maddie trailed a few steps behind her.

"And by your logic and my heartbroken future, I guess a long life is out of the question for me. Seriously, Pippa. After all the divorce cases I read about in school, I'm pretty sure marriage only helps if you marry the right person."

The knot in Maddie's stomach tightened even more. The right person. What happened to a person's future if their right person—their soul mate or perfect match—was taken from them? What happened if they suddenly died the way her mama, Zoe, had? Had she been Ben's perfect match? Or had he finally met his soul mate in Maddie's adoptive mother, Hope? She knew Ben and Hope's love and respect for each other was timeless and immeasurable. Maybe both Zoe and Hope were his soul mates...meant to be a part of his life at different times. They'd both been destined to be a part of her father's life and those of his children.

Destiny... Did she believe in it? And if she was destined to get her heart broken, then maybe this ache that welled up in her chest every time she was with Haki—or even thought about him—would fade away after she returned to the States. It had to. He couldn't be the "right man" for her if he was destined to be that man for Pippa. And if somehow he was right for both, then life was just cruel. It wouldn't be the first time her heart had been broken. She'd experienced just how merciless life could be when her mother was killed. If anything was written in her future, it seemed to be loss.

Suddenly the simple, half-empty rooms of her apartment back home seemed sheltered and comforting. Pippa glanced up at her as she retrieved the water sample and gave her a sheepish smile.

"I'm sure you'll find the man you want to spend your life with when you're ready. Look at my Grandma Sue."

Sue was Anna's mother. She was super nice and a lot of fun, but she'd struggled with severe depression most of her life. After Jack and Anna married, Sue had moved to Kenya and worked as Mac's office manager, until she met a kind, handsome and well-to-do Greek widower on vacation with his son and grandkids. She'd finally found her happily-ever-after and was living it in Greece, but she had had her heart crushed long before she reached that fairy-tale ending.

Pippa closed her eyes and sighed.

"Your guy is probably a dashing lawyer in Philly, who'll understand you and your career needs. You'll have things in common

and tons to talk about. Hey, maybe you've
already passed each other in the hallway of
some courthouse or something and you had
no idea that one day he would be a part of
your life. It all sounds so romantic, doesn't it?
I must admit, though, that I'm glad I already
know what my future holds. I'm so lucky to
have Haki."

She had no idea just how lucky. Maddie
rubbed at her chest, but nothing could stop
the unbearable despondence that gnawed at
her. Her mouth suddenly felt as dry as the
dirt beneath her feet. She licked her lips and
swallowed back the lump in her throat.

"You're both lucky. I'm happy you have
each other."

As warm as the days were, it was almost
startling how cool the nights and mornings
could be on the savannah. Maddie pulled on
her thin, dusky purple sweater and eased the
screen door shut so as not to wake up everyone in the house. The sky was still a deep
indigo but for the halo around the moon. Busara's silence was broken only by the occasional breeze rippling through tree branches,
or the distant sound of nocturnal predators
rustling through the dried grasses for their

last kill before dawn. Even Mosi—who she was quite sure didn't have an off switch—was sleeping quietly somewhere in the safety net of camp. She took a deep, cleansing breath. The air was sweet and fresh. The dust and sweat that filled it when the camp was alive and abuzz seemed to have settled back to the earth for a rest. Dust to dust.

Maddie hadn't been able to sleep any longer. The few hours she'd managed to get had been restless and cluttered with nonsensical dreams. Fatigue nipped at her muscles and every cell in her body craved a mug of hot, rich Kenyan coffee, but she didn't dare fix herself anything in the kitchen and risk making too much noise. Waking others up would mean no alone time. God, she needed some alone time. Time to process everything that had gone on. Time to breathe and decompress. She loved her family, she really did, but as lonely as it sometimes felt, she'd gotten used to living by herself, save for her pet fish. She didn't have to search out alone time back home. She had plenty of it, and now she realized how much she took that for granted.

She wrapped her arms around her middle and almost settled into the wicker rocker at the end of the porch. A light flickered across the camp near where the old mess tent and rustic living quarters still stood. She peered into the shadows cast by the moon and felt a spark of energy akin to a first sip of coffee in the morning. She knew that silhouette. The long back and broad shoulders hunched over like Rodin's statue, *The Thinker*. Haki.

The two of them didn't need to sit around together in the dark. It would be too reminiscent of their night in the wilderness. But they'd agreed to preserve their friendship and friends sat around or had coffee together, didn't they? She turned back toward the porch steps, then hesitated again. What if he didn't want company? As a kid, she used to hide in the pages of a book, and she hated getting interrupted. Maybe he did, too. His arm lifted and he moved something on a small table in front of him. Maddie warmed her palms against her jeans and stepped off the porch. If he didn't want her around, he'd let her know. If anything, they were honest with each other. Right?

The ground crunched softly beneath her feet as she made her way toward the light. He looked up and the corner of his mouth curved up in a soft smile.

"Hey." His voice was low and soft and welcoming, like down-filled pillows and crushed velvet. An LED lantern hung from a wooden pole that framed the left side of the mess tent and only seemed to flicker, she realized, because of the overhanging tree branch that had blocked her view from the porch. A chess board was set up on an overturned barrel, and judging by the layout, he was playing against himself. He absentmindedly rubbed his finger across his lips and sat back in his chair.

"Hey, you. Couldn't sleep, either, I take it," she said.

"I guess some nights aren't meant for sleep."

Maddie so wasn't about to read into that.

"Too much on my mind," he explained. "Pull up a chair."

"If you'd rather be—"

"No, I'd like your company."

Maddie gave a nod and pulled up a nearby stool.

"I made coffee," he said, jerking his head toward the mess tent. Maddie knew that, even after the main house was built for Haki and Pippa's families, they kept the old kitchen up and running for the keepers and crew. She'd noticed that Haki, Kamau and Anna often ate lunch with the rest out here, so as not to track dirt into the house. Haki had told her he enjoyed eating with everyone. He considered the keepers extended family and wanted them to feel that, too. The people Maddie worked with didn't even come close to acting like family, let alone friends.

"Bless you. I really do need coffee," Maddie said. She started to get up, but he waved for her to stay seated.

"I'll get you a cup."

She watched him through the screened walls of the framed tent as he poured a cup and headed back out.

"Who's winning? You or yourself?" she asked, as she took the metal mug from his hands and closed her eyes as the first sip warmed her throat and the caffeine coursed through her body.

"That depends on your next move. Do you remember how to play?"

Oh, boy, the last time they'd played games, hangman had taken a wrong turn. *For crying out loud, this is chess. There aren't words involved.* Maddie peered at him from beneath her lashes.

"How could I forget?"

He'd taught her how all those years ago. She'd been about twelve, if she remembered correctly. She'd tried hard to beat him and never could. Except once, but she was sure he had let her win, a fact that had annoyed her enough that she'd called him out on it.

She studied the board. Based on the number of moves made, he hadn't been at it that long.

"It's been years since I've played. You sure about taking me on?"

"Absolutely."

There it was. One word, yet the way he said it was loaded with dangerous possibility. Maddie bit her lower lip. Neither of them said anything, but the way he looked at her said too much. She broke eye contact. *Broken heart. Be careful.* Haki wasn't the cheating type—he was too loyal—but the idea of settling for only getting to be around him as a friend, for being limited to seeing his face and hearing him talk or playing a game of chess, was acutely painful. She looked down again at the checkered board that separated them. Life was complex and it all boiled down to one wrong play. Maddie reached out and moved her wooden queen one space forward.

In chess, the queen is powerful, but only when thought goes into the steps she takes.

"Hmm. Are you sure about that move?" Haki thrummed his fingers while contemplating his next turn.

"Absolutely." *Not really.*

"We could start from scratch if you prefer."

"This is fine. Make your move." As far as she was concerned, it was too late to start from scratch. Pretty soon she'd be out of the picture altogether. *Focus on the actual game, Maddie.* "And don't let me win."

"You still haven't forgiven me for that?" He laughed quietly and Maddie had to smile at the way his eyes relaxed and his face lit up.

"Can you blame me? We're equals. I don't need a free pass, even if you are more experienced at chess. I'm betting Pippa wouldn't want you taking it easy on her, either."

Something shifted in his face.

"Pippa can't stand playing chess. I've even tried bribing her, but it didn't work. However, cards are another story. She plays a mean game of gin rummy when she can get enough of a group playing to make it fun. She thinks chess is too intense to enjoy. Huru is learning to play, though. It's not his favorite, unless he plays against Noah because he can beat him. I usually have a solid game against my father."

Intense? Of course it was. Maddie had always loved it, as well as checkers, and missed having a person to play with. Computerized versions didn't cut it. She even preferred using a real deck of cards to play solitaire. Besides, how could she not love that one-on-one time with Haki, watching his mind churn and sharing in something that brought him joy?

He moved his bishop and took out one of her pawns, leaving her queen exposed.

"I hear you'll be leaving Busara to take care of business in Nairobi. Will you be coming back here?"

The question caught her by surprise. Haki rarely took his mind off a game of chess in progress. She took another sip of coffee. A sliver of pink outlined the horizon and the crow of the camp's only rooster rang through the air.

"Not unless the office asks me to find out more from the villagers. I suspect they'll have me quite busy at the office. I am here for work," she reminded. She moved her queen to the left and out of immediate danger.

"I have something for you. I think you should have it before you leave. Give me a second."

He pulled a small flashlight from his pocket and headed into the tent that had once served as the shared living quarters of Niara, Anna, Pippa and himself, back when Busara was in its infancy and he and Pippa were toddlers. Within a minute, he came out holding a book. Maddie frowned.

"That couldn't be what I think it is. I've always wondered what happened to it."

"Your first copy. My only criminal act. I…liberated it, from your backpack the last time you visited us before leaving for college. I sort of thought I was hanging on to a memento of you."

He handed her the book and their fingers brushed as Maddie took her copy of *Watership Down* and ran her hand over the spine. She loved this book, with all its animals, and she used to read and reread it. It was her go-to story on the trip from Busara to Nairobi and back. She'd looked everywhere for it when she was packing for her overseas trip to college.

"I'm sorry," he said. She shook her head and held the book to her chest.

"Don't be. I'm glad it was safe with you. I hope you had a chance to read it again, too." He'd wanted a keepsake that reminded him of her? Maddie swallowed back the lump in her throat. "As a lawyer, I must say, this was a very touching criminal act."

"Forgiven?"

His hand rested on his knee and she reached out and held it.

"Forgiven. Thank you for returning it. I'll never be able to read this again without thinking of you. I mean, the story does involve a battle and, if you've forgotten, we're playing chess and you're trying to kill my queen. Don't think I'll take it easy on you because I have my book back. It's your move," she teased, letting go of his hand. The sound of footsteps and the flash from a camera had them both turning their heads.

"I'm sorry. I couldn't resist. You two looked so cute holding hands over a game of chess." Pippa walked up and put her hand on Haki's back. She pressed her lips together as if at a loss for words. "Who's winning?"

"No one, yet," Maddie said. "I was just thanking Haki for giving me my book. I'd forgotten it here a long time ago and he just remembered where he'd put it for safe keeping." She hated lying. Even white lies had a way of coming out. Yes, she was protecting Pippa, and the part about thanking Haki was true, but all lawyers knew that lies revealed themselves eventually. Criminals almost always tripped up.

"Cool. I remember you loving that story. And chess, boy, anyone who skips sleep for chess must be...very motivated."

Oh, boy. Whatever Pippa was implying, this had to stop.

"We actually haven't been out here long, although, I do believe I'm winning," Haki said, reaching up and taking Pippa's hand in his. The action seemed to console her and the furrow between her brows softened.

The sky swirled with bloody hues of crimson and rust and the yawning sun stretched its first rays out like arms after a deep slumber. The dream was over. There'd be no more waking up before dawn and sitting around with Haki. They needed to be careful.

The door to one of the pens swung open and Ahron carefully led a baby elephant out toward the grassy area, where the others would soon congregate for their morning bottles. Kamau stepped out of the house and gave them a quick wave as he made his way to the clinic.

"Well, I'm heading out to Hodari Lodge with my dad for one of his lectures," Pippa said. Hodari Lodge was one of the luxury accommodations farther south, near Amboseli National Park, where conferences were sometimes held. As a well-known geneticist, Jack was often called on to give lectures at science conferences held there. The lodge catered to the wealthy and had a safari-resort atmosphere. It had been the original home base of Mac's one-man company, Air Walker Safari, because of access to the airstrip there. Although Mac now lived at Camp Jamba Walker, everyone had connections at the lodge and went there often. "Our moms were asking about you two. They have breakfast on the table. I guess you won't be finishing this game of yours."

Maddie's hands went cold. She knew Pippa well enough to know she wasn't referring to chess. Not with the way her tone changed and eyes narrowed. Pippa was suspicious.

There was no doubt about it. She was giving them a warning.

Checkmate.

CHAPTER FOURTEEN

HAKI TORE OFF his stained shirt and splashed cool water on his face. He'd had long days before, but somehow, today had been worse. He and his team had saved an elephant and her child. The cow had an arrow injury on her back leg that looked infected. They had had to dart her and keep the baby safely close by as they cleaned necrotic tissue from the wound, packed it and treated the mother for infection before administering a sedative reversal. He'd saved a life—two, because the little one wouldn't have survived if the mother had died before they were found— yet he felt like the scum of the earth. Pippa's tone of voice that morning had been eating away at him.

His every breath today had been burdened with guilt. He hadn't done anything overtly wrong, but his feelings for Maddie weren't fair to Pippa. His feelings, though unspoken, were a silent betrayal and he couldn't forgive himself for that. Returning Maddie's book had been an act of closure. It had been meant to help him let go and move on. But that private moment was now caught on camera. Pippa's camera. He pumped more water into the basin, cupped some in his hand and drenched the back of his neck, then grabbed a towel off a nearby supply rack.

"Haki, Pippa isn't answering her radio again." Anna marched out of the clinic with Maddie close behind. He scanned the grasslands beyond camp. "You won't see her. I tried, even from the lookout, with my binoculars. She must have gone beyond the ridge," Anna added.

"It's getting late." Haki muttered a curse. "Why does she do this?"

Maddie stared at her boots. They both knew why she'd done it this time. Anger? Attention?

"I saw her take off in her jeep right after she and Uncle Jack returned from his conference. That was over an hour ago," Maddie said.

He snatched a clean T-shirt off the rack and pulled it over his head. "I'll go. Keep calling her, but I have a feeling I know where she is. If I don't touch base within thirty minutes, send the others out to search."

"That girl is going to make me lose my hair," Anna said.

"You and me both." He took long strides toward his jeep and within minutes was flooring it toward the northern side of the ridge, which was the only way around it.

They still had a little over an hour before dark and there was a good chance Pippa was already on her way home, but given what had happened that morning, he couldn't say what state of mind she was in. It didn't take much to bring out her reckless side and the savannah at dusk or after dark was not the place for a lone person to take risks.

He raised dust as he cleared the ridge and slowed as he maneuvered downhill toward a rocky outcropping that overlooked one of the few watering holes that wasn't completely dried up. He radioed Anna as soon as he spotted Pippa's jeep, then pulled up alongside it.

The air shook with the sound of a gunshot and his blood rushed to his ears.

"Pippa!" He couldn't see her. He ran toward the outcropping. "Pip, answer me!"

She stepped out from behind the rocks and

put her rifle back in safety before slinging it over her shoulder. Haki stopped dead in his tracks.

"It was a black mamba and I had no choice but to take the shot."

"Why would you sit here at this hour? You know it's not safe. And you haven't answered your radio. Pippa, you can't do this."

She glanced back at the dead snake.

"Obviously, I didn't need rescuing. And the shots I captured are priceless," she said, patting her camera. "It's been a great day for taking pictures, don't you think?"

He held on to her arm as she tried to walk past him.

"You misinterpreted what you saw this morning. Neither of us could sleep. We played some chess over coffee. I returned her book. That's it. We're friends. All three of us are."

"You've been spending a lot of time together. Alone."

"Do you hear yourself? Do you even realize how you were acting this morning? You have no idea how much Maddie cares about you." She really didn't. She had no idea how adamant they were about not letting whatever was between them go beyond friendship...

because of Pippa. She had no idea how hard it was to be so in-sync with someone and turn your back on it for the sake of doing what was right. He was putting Pippa first. He always had.

"Please, tell me. How was I acting?" Pippa set the rifle in her jeep. A small reassurance, given the fire in her eyes.

"Just…stop being territorial."

"Territorial? I can't believe you. I have every right to be territorial. This is my home. The land I grew up on. My life. And you're supposed to be—"

"*Supposed* to be what? Don't you see, Pip? That word doesn't belong between us. Whatever we have shouldn't be because of expectations or routine or because we're *supposed* to be together. It should be because we both want it with our every breath. It should be because it just is and we can't explain or define it."

Tears welled in Pippa's eyes and she shook her head.

"I didn't mean it that way."

Haki swiped his hand across his face and stepped up to her.

"I know. Pip, we love and care for each other. We've tried to be true to each other, but have we been true to ourselves? Has either of us escaped the current of this life we've been living long enough to figure out who we are and what we want, as individuals?"

"Of course we have. We lived in Nairobi for college. We haven't always been here."

"We've always been together."

"What's wrong with that? What are you saying, Haki? You don't want to be around me anymore?"

"Heck, no. Don't think that, Pip. I'm asking if you really know what you want in life. You weren't sure what you wanted to major in and you ended up in geology because you were determined to be in Nairobi when I was there, and now you barely do anything with your degree. I'm saying that two people need to be strong and secure apart if they're to be strong together. Don't you want to leave your own footprints on this land you call home? I'm asking if you know what *you want*."

"No, I don't!" Tears streamed down her cheeks and he wiped them with his hands. "I only know that we're meant to be, Haki. I can't lose you. I can't see my life without you. I can't see it." She buried her face in his chest.

He wrapped his arms around her and pressed his lips to her hair.

"I just want you to be happy, Pippa. I don't want you to have regrets."

Her sobs shook him to the core and ripped at his heart. *Can't see it. Blinding sun.* The words hit him like the first thunderbolt after a dry season. No one could tell what the future held. Not even the *Laibon* and his stones. Even Pippa knew that stones weathered the elements and changed over time.

MADDIE READ HER EMAIL twice and scrunched her face. The message was from her office in Nairobi. She'd been afraid of this. They were impressed by the testimonies and information she'd sent, so much so that they wanted her to ask Lempiris if he could meet them in Nairobi for an in-person testimony—a final step to strengthen their position and assure that their efforts to halt the proposal didn't fall short. They also asked that she keep the meeting to herself. Just in case. They didn't want the opposition finding out about it and making arrangements with him first. Just in case. Lempiris didn't have a phone or computer, which was why the firm needed her to revisit his village.

She closed her laptop. This meant she couldn't tell Haki. She wouldn't make the trip with him again anyway. She wouldn't put either of them in that position, and Pippa was acting funny as it was.

She tapped her fingers against the table. The only person she could think of asking for help was Uncle Mac. Would he keep their trip confidential? No one, including him, was on her side in this whole matter. Her family and friends here had respected the line between work and personal relationships, but would it be fair to put him in a position where he might have to lie to family? The other option was asking the office to send someone—a guide or pilot—to take her, but as she'd been told before, bribery was so common in the city and poachers so insidious, that sometimes it was hard to know who to trust.

She would feel safer with Mac, for sure. He had not been available the first time, but if she gave him notice, maybe he could find time in the next few days. The trip would be much faster in his helicopter than it had been in Haki's jeep. She picked at her cuticle. If she made sure the firm contracted Mac's services and paid him, then she could request confidentiality as a customer. The rest would depend on if Lempiris could spare a day or two in Nairobi. She had no idea if he'd ever flown at all.

SOME DAYS WERE just rotten. The morning would feel off; then there'd be a death or some sort of bad news and everything would seem to go wrong from there. Haki sat on the edge of his bed and tried to shake the feeling he'd woken up to. Maybe he'd just gotten up on the wrong side of the bed...or maybe he was getting sick. Stress did weaken one's immune system. *Oh, no way. Not that.* He'd remembered Roinet's goats and the suspected Q fever. He hadn't come in actual contact but he had touched the ground near the pen. The bacterium was known to exist in the soil and dust around infected animals, as well as in their body fluids. He cringed at the memory of being offered the milk and blood. They'd declined, though. He touched his forehead. No fever. Come to think of it, he felt okay physically. Being tired was too nonspecific a symptom. He'd get a blood test done to be sure he wasn't acting as an incubator and leave it at that. He'd recommend the same to Maddie.

He stood and went over to the window. The

energy of Busara was starting to pick up. His dad was on field duty today. They'd agreed that he would do vet rounds with the orphans, since Anna wanted to go check on some of the wild herd positions. He got dressed and left his room.

"Good morning." He took the cup of coffee his mother offered.

"Good morning. You feel better today?"

He shrugged. "Where is everyone?"

"I think Mac took Maddie to visit Tessa and Kesi. Anna and Pippa are in the clinic."

More testimonies. He figured he shouldn't be surprised that she'd left him out of it this time.

Haki skipped breakfast and headed for the pens. He heard an agonizing wail before reaching them.

"No!" Pippa rushed out of the clinic, her eyes red and swollen. She saw him and broke down. Anna stepped out with her hands covering her mouth and tears pooling. She was tougher than Pippa when an orphan didn't make it, but he knew it cut her deep. But he'd never seen Pippa this bad. He rushed to her side.

"Pip, what happened? Who?" he asked Anna. Pippa collapsed in his arms and he held her against his chest, but when her knees gave out, he picked her up and carried her to the porch and cradled her on the step. "Someone tell me what happened. Etana?"

Anna shook her head and sat next to them. She took Pippa's hand in hers.

"KWS called in because they recognized an elephant that was—" Anna started crying and put her face in her hands. He'd never seen her fall apart like this. Niara came running out of the house.

"What's going on?"

Pippa fisted her hands against Haki's shirt.

"They killed Bakhari. Haki," she sobbed. "They killed him."

Niara gasped and put her arms around Anna.

"Oh, God." Haki tried to process the news. He held on to Pippa even tighter. Bakhari... the baby orphan Anna had saved from a snare wound when Pip was only four. Bakhari, who'd become her favorite elephant—like one of the family—and who she'd watched grow into an adolescent and majestic eighteen-year-old bull. A favorite amongst Busara's supporters and subscribers to their online posts. Haki swallowed hard against the lump in his throat. He'd been a little over five when Bakhari was first brought here. He and Pippa had played with him alongside Ahron, who'd been his keeper. They'd known Bakhari all his life.

A horrific image of their beloved bull lying on the ground, a rotting, deflated mass, covered with flies...and faceless...like so many he'd seen before flashed before him. Only this time the atrocity burned a hole through him. It was personal beyond measure. He let go of Pippa and pressed his palms to his eyes, then suddenly his mourning shifted to rage. He nudged Pippa down next to Anna and Niara. He needed to leave.

"Tell me where. He had a tracking device. Bullets or arrows?" He wanted information. He wanted the murderers to rot in jail for eternity.

"Arrows," Anna said. "South of here, not far from that clan you took Maddie to."

Lempiris.

His blood heated and his head pounded. Lempiris wasn't getting off this time. He'd make sure of it. He had his contacts in KWS.

"Anna, you have the clinic. I'm leaving."

"Where?"

"To Bakhari."

"I'm coming." Pippa looked bleary-eyed and limp but tried to get up.

"No. Absolutely not." He couldn't let her see Bakhari in whatever state he was in. It would be too devastating for her. The images would scar her. "Don't let her leave camp."

With that order, he stormed off.

KWS WAS STILL PRESENT at Lempiris's village when Haki arrived many hours later. The families stood in a grouping in one area of the *enkang* and rangers were searching their homes, the fields and even the nearby streams. First and foremost, they needed to find Bakhari's tusks. They couldn't let them reach the black market.

Something pinched in Haki's chest, as if Bakhari's spirit was calling on him to save one shred of his dignity, to make sure his ivory was burned so that he wouldn't be a part of the evil cycle and so his ashes could feed the earth. A wave of cold washed over him when he marched through flattened crops and spotted his old friend's body. He gritted his teeth and went to pay his respects by laying his hand against Bakhari's leathery skin. He only stayed a moment. Action was needed more than anything else right now. He stepped away and went to speak to one of the rangers he knew well.

"Where is he? Lempiris."

"Missing."

That was a sign of guilt. Between the crops raids he was suffering and now being MIA with the tusks still missing, it was hard to believe he wasn't responsible.

"Are you sure?"

"His wife says he went to the city, but we're still trying to confirm that. There were some tracks leading north of the body, but they disappear at the creek. I have some men searching the water and we're combing the ground for any sign of burial."

Tusks were often wrapped and hidden until it was safe to collect them.

"I want him arrested. I will help search every tree and field, but we can't let him walk."

"We're following protocol and doing our best."

Haki scrubbed his jaw. "I know, I know."

The whir of a helicopter indicated an aerial search. He prayed that they'd be able to pick up a trail or spot clues from above. He shielded his eyes and looked up. *Air Walker Safaris*. Mac still kept his old business name on his bird, even if Camp Jamba Walker was his home base now. Mac had known Bakhari as long as the rest of them. He had to be as livid and determined to seek justice as Haki was.

The chopper landed and he waited for the all-clear. Mac got out, adjusted his cap and put his hands on his hips, waiting a moment before walking around the chopper and opening the passenger doors. Lempiris appeared and several armed rangers hurried toward the chopper.

Lempiris carefully gathered his garments before stepping onto the ground. He spread his hands to his side and teetered for a moment. Then Maddie appeared behind him, offering assistance.

"What on earth are you doing here?" Haki yelled as he marched over. For a second, he thought maybe Mac had picked her up from Busara and they'd been on their way to his camp when he'd heard news of Bakhari over his radio. But Mac wouldn't have apprehended someone involved in a killing, let alone endangered Maddie in the process. He would have left that part to KWS.

"Haki. We heard. I'm sorry," Maddie said, leaving Lempiris's side and meeting Haki halfway.

He glared at her.

"What do you think you're doing?" He heard how harsh he sounded. He didn't care. Her eyes widened and she took a step back before noticing the rangers surrounding Lempiris and Mac trying to intervene.

"Leave him alone!" she insisted, then turned to help the man, but Haki stopped her.

"Do you mind explaining?"

"He didn't do this. He was with us in Nairobi offering testimony in person."

"But you have no proof he or his family weren't involved! Him not being here doesn't mean he didn't give the order or condone it. You're still fighting me on this after all you've witnessed? Now Bakhari is lying over there dead and as far as I'm concerned, unless someone with bloody hands is dragged out of the bushes right now, Lempiris and his clan are the prime suspects."

"Innocent until proven guilty," Maddie said, matching his tone.

"Arrested if there's enough evidence, unless bail is posted."

"Hey, back off, Hak. This is getting out of hand," Mac said, stepping in. "Everyone is upset. I get that. But we stick to facts and defer to the authorities." He looked directly at Haki. "That's how we've always done things."

Haki couldn't meet her eyes. She'd gone behind his back. She'd lied to him.

He felt his soul crumbling to his feet. His world turning gray and white and bleak.

He took one last look at Bakhari's remains and headed toward his jeep.

If the law let his death go unavenged, Haki would never forgive her.

MADDIE WAS GONE.

She'd stayed at Camp Jamba Walker the night of the raid, then by the time Haki returned to Busara from rounds the next afternoon, Mac had already flown her there to gather her things before dropping her off at the closest airport in the Mara so she could catch a flight back to Nairobi.

He studied the report Kam had just given him. It normally took much longer to track down poachers, but they'd lucked out. They'd found the ivory buried under a pepper tree in haste and left it there as bait. Among the men who returned for it, they identified Gathii, Roinet's son.

Maddie had been right. Lempiris wasn't guilty. Haki lowered his head and sat there for what seemed like forever. He'd messed up. Haki Odaba, the composed, methodical and loyal guy he'd always striven to be, had lost his temper and prejudged an innocent man. Even worse, he'd lashed out at Maddie.

Maddie was gone and the ache felt as raw as the first time she'd left years ago. Only now, he deserved it and worse.

MADDIE THREW HER backpack into Jamal's sedan and closed the door behind her. She was grateful that Uncle Mac had helped her catch a charter to Nairobi. The change in scenery and assault on her senses helped to wash out everything that had happened. Blaring horns and acrid traffic fumes gave her relief in the same way bad-tasting medicine treated symptoms. It was a distraction. A temporary fix until she could get back to the US, hole up in her apartment for a few days, then bury herself in work.

"How was your trip, Maddie?" Jamal asked as he inched past the cars waiting in line for passenger pickup. He finally merged onto the road for home.

"Tiring."

"Good tiring or bad tiring?"

Maddie caught his eye in the rearview mirror.

"Let's just leave it as tiring for now."

"Whatever you say. You're reminding me of your mother when I used to pick her up after rounds in the hospital when she was an intern. You look wiped out, as they say."

Maddie rested her head back against the seat. Her mom had been saving lives. Maddie wasn't sure anymore if she was helping or hurting.

"Is she home?"

"She just returned from a Luo village."

Hope was half Luo, from her mother's side. It was sort of cool that she got to visit and experience the culture firsthand, while helping with vaccines and any medical care needed. She was amazing, keeping up with her cause while running a pediatric clinic in Nairobi and raising her kids.

"How does she do it all?" Maddie didn't realize she'd asked the question out loud.

"Love."

Maddie straightened her neck and narrowed her eyes at Jamal. He sliced the air with his finger.

"If you love what you're doing—if you're passionate about it—the energy comes to you. The walls crumble and become bridges you can cross. Hope loves medicine and healing, but even more she loves children—all children, but, of course, especially hers and her family. Ben is the light of her life, as are you, Chad, Ryan and Philip. I knew her before you all came into her life, and let me tell you, there's no comparison. Love helped her find her way."

Maddie looked out the window, letting his words sink in. She could see Nairobi National Park, where giraffes strolled against a backdrop of high-rise buildings instead of mountains. People taking land and absolving themselves of guilt by granting pockets of it to displaced wildlife. She wiped her face with her hands.

When two streams merge, the watering hole is less likely to go dry.

Niara's tender voice echoed in her mind.

"Maddie, you know, before Hope met you, when she used to finish with her hospital rounds, the first thing she did when she got in this car was to tear off her shoes and put sandals on. Every single time. It wasn't really the shoes that bothered her. It was that she was wearing them for someone else. When she finally found her own path, I noticed she'd forgotten about her sandals. She no longer felt suffocated or bound. As for you, don't worry yourself with how or why others do what they do. The only shoes you have to fill, Maddie, are your own."

"Jamal, you're the best. I get what you're saying. My only problem is shopping for the right pair."

"Ah, I can't help you there." He laughed, but quieted when her cell phone buzzed.

Maddie took one look at the screen and opened the full message from her senior at the Nairobi office. Her eyes stung and all the emotions she'd bottled up flooded through her. She gasped and covered her mouth. Everything she'd worked so hard for and hoped for had boiled down to a single text.

Jamal pulled up to their driveway and parked. She closed her eyes and tried to take it all in. The message. All that had happened.

"Go on. I'll take your bags in," Jamal said. "Are you okay?"

"Thanks. I'm fine," she reassured him. She walked through the iron gate and straight into the villa's garden. The white-washed plaster walls that enclosed it were brought to life with climbing passion fruit vines, jasmine and giant urns filled with vibrant yellow flowering hibiscus. Hope was sitting at a rattan patio set with a stack of patient files in front of her and a bottle of her favorite ginger soda in her hand. She looked up from the paperwork she was filling in and set her drink on the table.

"Maddie!" Her mother held out her arms as Maddie approached.

"Hey, Mom." Maddie gave her a tight hug. Hope held Maddie's cheeks in her hands.

"How are you? You look exhausted. And tense. We weren't expecting you back for another week, but Jamal told me you'd called for a ride. Are you getting sick?"

"No. I'm fine." Maddie took off her shoes, and instead of sitting in the other chair, she lay down on her back in the grass with her knees raised. She scrunched the cool blades with her toes.

"I just found out we won the case. The proposal was thrown out. It's done."

"Honey, that's good news for you, isn't it? I thought it would all take longer. You must have gathered exactly what they needed and left quite an impression." Hope frowned. "You don't sound excited, though. Is everything okay? "

"No. Yes. Mom, I honestly don't know. I

don't know what's wrong with me. I don't know what to think anymore." She covered her face and lay there. The ground felt real and solid and secure, and the green, earthy scent of fig leaves from the overhanging tree seeped into her lungs and steadied her breathing.

"You're overwhelmed."

"I'm overwhelmed." She nodded without uncovering her face. "I should be happy about it, but I'm so confused."

She could hear Hope getting up and coming over. Maddie let her arms fall back to the grass just as Hope lay down next to her.

"This feels good," Hope said, wiggling her toes. She took Maddie's hand and gave it a squeeze. They peered up into the tree canopy, bits of blue sky sprinkled throughout it. "I have a feeling this isn't just about the proposal. Do you want to talk about it?"

"I don't think it'll help. Lying here feels good, though."

"It does. Nature is good medicine."

"You would know." Maddie turned her cheek to the cool grass. "How are your patients doing? The children at that one village you said were having respiratory issues? Did the water sample show anything?"

"I'm not entirely sure yet. There were elevated levels of a few contaminants, but then some of their problems have been nonspecific, so it's hard to say what caused them. Respiratory issues, rashes, neurological symptoms and two newborns with birth defects. What bothers me is that I found out that a company was testing an area just north of the village for oil. They were fracking. If they end up taking over that land for oil production, I don't know what the villagers will do. My gut tells me it's a groundwater contamination issue. If I find out it is, I'll fight. Maybe I'll ask your law office for help. If you lived here, I'd ask for you specifically."

So much for changing subjects. They were right back at law.

"Mom, I have a feeling you'll be playing interference when Dad finds out my side won."

Hope crinkled her nose and shrugged.

"Maybe, but honestly, Maddie, I don't think you need me stepping in. Don't ever let anyone—not even your father or myself, or the lawyers you work for—intimidate you. There's a big difference between showing respect and cowering under authority. Everyone starts at the beginning. Just because someone is older or has one title or another, doesn't necessarily mean they're wiser than you. Why do you think you were sent here?"

"Because of my experience in Kenya, my language skills...and because the higher-ups have more important things to do."

"*Because* you're exceptional at what you do. *Because* you're valued. *Because* you have a passion for helping people. I've always seen it in you and I wasn't surprised when you decided to go to law school."

"Really?"

"Yes. Always a bookworm. Always standing up for the underdog. Even when I first met you, I recognized your reserved, inner strength. You knew what you wanted and nobody was going to get in your way. I'll never forget the time you snuck the first of those silver bangles I gave you to school in your backpack and ended up getting in trouble with another student over it."

Maddie grinned.

"School had too many rules."

"You never did like being put in a box. I once told your father not to worry, that when you found your voice again, you'd put every word to good use."

She didn't like being put in a box. Why

did the image of her apartment back home come to mind?

"So, my dear, you need to hold your chin up and not let anyone make you feel less than what you are. Own yourself. Own your style, even if it's different. Own your beliefs, even if others disagree. Carry yourself with dignity because you have nothing to be ashamed of."

What about shame in letting herself fall for the same man her cousin and best friend had staked her claim on? Her mom had no idea how much guilt she packed.

"Some people are confident enough to take someone like you under their wing and nurture them, give them opportunities, because they know that life is about giving back," Hope continued. "I have a feeling your boss is like that. But you'll always come across individuals who feel threatened or who are competitive to the point of destroying those around them. Usually, they want what you have, be it a job, family, money...even talent and passion. They're insecure and jealous and feel the need to put you down in order to climb higher. They step on heads left and right and surround themselves with people they believe to be weaker than they are because it makes them feel good. Those are the ones to watch out for and sometimes they're hard to spot. You're smart, but you're also trusting."

"Bullies." She thought of her junior colleagues back at the firm.

"Exactly."

"You're calling Dad a bully?"

"Oh, gosh, no." Hope chuckled and sat up on the grass.

"He treats me differently than my brothers. He thinks I'm less capable because I'm a woman."

"I disagree. It has nothing to do with you being a woman. I've never felt anything other than love, respect and adoration from him, and the last time I checked, I was a woman, too. Part of what makes us work is that we both stand up for what we believe, neither of us hesitates to speak our mind and—most important—we both listen to what the other is saying. If necessary, we have a sense of humor about it. I've even been told that your uncle Jack didn't joke around as much before he married Anna. Love loosened him up. It puts things in perspective. We come from a family of strong men and women. And a man who can accept and admire a woman's strength is a real man. Maddie, you have to know that your father is so extremely proud of you." Hope reached for her bottle of soda, took a swig and offered it to Maddie. "The man can be rough on the surface," she continued, "but his heart is in the right place. My point is that you were bullied in school, back when you struggled with speaking. Your father and I have both dealt with people like that in our lives, mostly when we were older, in the workforce. When he saw it happening to you, it ate away at him like gangrene. That's why he's so protective of you. So try not to take everything he says the wrong way."

Maddie nibbled at her lip to keep it from quivering.

"We'll see." She needed time to process what her mom was saying. Her view of her dad was so different. She took a sip of the ginger drink; then they both lay back down in the grass.

"How was everyone at Busara? How's Haki doing?"

It took a minute to formulate an answer. The mere mention of his name made her mind spin.

"I'm not sure."

"Mmm." They were silent for a moment.

"What about Noah and Huru?"

"They seem fine."

"And Pippa?"

Maddie knew where this was leading. Hope was a master of misdirection, circling back to the subject at hand once the door was open.

"She's still mourning Bakhari."

"I heard. They must all be devastated."

"More than you know. I think it's better that I left. They need time alone."

"Maddie, sweetheart, are you running away from something?"

She closed her eyes and tried to take in the fresh air, but it didn't help this time. Was she running away?

"What's there to run from?" She and Haki had agreed there wasn't anything they could do about their feelings. She was gone and he could get back to life with Pippa and that was that.

"You tell me."

"I'm just tired, Mom. I mean, it does bother me that, although the proposal won't pass, the problem with the farmers and the elephants still isn't solved. There are two sides to every issue and every case, right? And I saw why Haki felt so strongly about that proposal. I saw Bakhari's body." A tear escaped the corner of her eye and trailed down her temple. "It was awful. And here I am, case won…and I'm supposed to walk away. The rest isn't up to me to fix. It's not part of the mission they sent me out here on. We won, so why do I feel like a failure?"

"Perhaps because those who work the hardest and achieve the most are often the ones who are the hardest on themselves. You're not a failure. You never have been. But the girl I know doesn't do things halfway. She goes above and beyond. Sees things through. I think that's what's bothering you."

"I don't have a choice. It's not part of my job description. Haki is on his own now. He'll have to find a way to solve things by himself."

"That doesn't sound like two people on opposing sides of a case."

Maddie wiped the corner of her eye and swallowed the tears at the back of her throat.

"Well, he's the one who took me to the villages. I guess you could say we understand each other." She quickly turned toward Hope. "I mean, regarding the case. We came to appreciate both sides of the issue and neither of us wants the other side to suffer." Not the Masai, or the elephants…or Pippa.

"Maddie, I get the feeling that there's something you're not saying. I know it's none of my business and I won't press you, but if something is going on, running away never solves it. Trust me, I know."

"Nothing is going on."

"Okay. If you say so. But I still think you'll feel better if you take a few days to look into solutions on your own and then at least share them with Haki before you leave. That way he can decide whether to act on them after you leave Kenya and you'll feel like you did your best. And it would give you some time to spend with Ryan and Philip, too."

Maddie took a deep breath. How could she possibly return to Busara with Pippa on the defensive? Hope was right, though. She was running away to protect them all, including herself. But she was also turning her back on the wonderful people she'd met in the villages, and on the elephants her family at Busara was trying desperately to protect. If anything, her role in all of this made her a traitor. Weren't traitors banished?

"I can probably stay here a few more days, even with the case over early. I'll see what I come up with, but promise me you won't tell Dad about our talk?"

"Why would I do that? As far as I'm concerned, girl time is girl time."

"Thanks, Mom. I know you said he means well, but he still does things his way, and the last thing I need right now is him jumping in. Could you imagine how he'd react if he thought my seniors were limiting me at work? He'd probably march over to the firm here and have a talk with my bosses to 'straighten things out.' He'd do all the interrogating, too, about why I'm not being given cases to try in court or why I did all the behind-the-scenes work on this one, but got no other recognition. It would be career death for me. If I didn't die of embarrassment first."

"He does hover and worry. Ben is a bit like a marine general crossed with a little grandmother."

That image made them both laugh. Some of Maddie's tension left her body and sank into the ground beneath her. She and Hope stretched out their arms and legs and stared up at the branches.

"This is meditation at its best," Maddie said.

"Yes. I should write it on prescriptions for

patients. Lie down barefoot in the grass, fifteen minutes, twice a day. They'd think I'd lost it. Hmm I could take a nap right now."

"Me, too," Maddie said, closing her eyes.

She heard the screen door to the house open and close.

"You two could have put a sign up saying that you're just *playing* dead. Kind of a scary scene for a man to come home to."

They opened their eyes. Ben was grinning. He held out a hand for Hope. She took it, and he pulled her up into his arms and kissed her like she was the best thing he'd seen all day. Maddie loved seeing them like that. That's what she wanted in life. The *Laibon's* warning rang in her head and she sat up and pushed her hair back.

"Hi, Dad." He held a hand out for her, too, then wrapped her in a hug.

"How's it going, Mads?" He kissed her on the head.

"Great."

"Let me grab these files. I can finish them later. We should get some dinner started. I told Delila to take the rest of the day off with Jamal," Hope said.

"I'm hungry enough to eat leftovers, if you

need to get work done. Where are the boys?"
Ben asked.

"Babysitting for Simba and Chuki."

Maddie cocked an eyebrow. "Together?
Isn't that asking for trouble?"

"Chuki's sister, Ita, will also be there."

"That's worse. She's pretty." Ben chuckled
and put his arm around Hope as they headed
inside.

"So, did you drop the case yet?" he asked,
peeling a banana as an appetizer.

Maddie and Hope glanced at each other.

He finished off the banana in two bites.
"Did I miss something?"

"The proposal won't be making it to the
cabinet for review. It was dropped on humanitarian grounds," Maddie said.

"That fast?" Ben frowned. "But you just
got back from Busara. Don't you have to ap-
pear in court?"

The muscle between Maddie's shoulder
blades cramped. So much for relaxing in the
grass. Hope had encouraged her to show her
strength and to be confident. She needed to
own her beliefs, even if her dad didn't agree
with them.

"I emailed them the information and video

testimonies they needed. The partners here took care of the rest."

"But that sounds like something a secretary or assistant could do. You're supposed to be a top-of-your-class lawyer."

"Wow." It was the only word Maddie could get out.

"Ben, that wasn't nice," Hope added.

"Sorry, but I'm just saying. They're using you. Are they paying you enough to make up for that?"

"I don't technically practice law in Kenya, Dad. I'm not in a position to act as barrister in a court here." She could have left it at that. A part of her wanted to let him read between the lines and assume she tried cases in Philly. This was why she wanted partnership so badly. To prove herself to her father.

The only shoes you have to fill, Maddie, are your own. Jamal's voice echoed in her mind. Her own comfortable shoes. Not red high heels or combat boots. *Own yourself.* Her mom was right. If Maddie wanted partnership, it needed to be because *she* wanted it, because she could use the position to do more for the causes she believed in, not because she needed it to prove something to someone else.

She gripped the edge of the countertop. "Do you know what? I haven't presented my own case before a judge back home yet, either. Not because I'm being used, but because that's the way things work. I'm a new graduate. A junior lawyer. It's not the only profession out there where responsibility and privilege are earned. Or where rank is earned. I thought, as a marine, you'd understand that."

Her dad flinched. Hope, who was looking in the refrigerator behind him, gave Maddie a quick thumbs-up.

"Okay. I get that. I just don't want you being taken advantage of."

"I appreciate that, but trust me, I can take care of myself."

He didn't look convinced, but at least he didn't argue the point.

"That doesn't change the fact that they had you fighting against a bill that your family was behind. One that could have saved lives."

"We were representing Native Watch Global! Don't you think they save lives and protect quality of life? Not everything you stand for is right, Dad."

"I stand behind my family. Is that wrong in your book?"

"Of course not." She pressed her fingers to her eyes, then splayed her hands in frustration. What would it take to get through to him? "I have my own mind and my own voice. You know I care about animals. All living things are sacred. I was out there and I saw firsthand what poachers do. It's sick and unfathomable, and I do care. But sometimes we have to make tough choices."

"This one seemed like a no-brainer to me. Like a case where NWG would get your firm a lot of publicity."

"Really? That's what you think? For the record, when I make a decision, it's mine. My burden to carry, not yours. If a little boy and a baby elephant were caught in quicksand and I could only save one, I would save the little boy. Do you think the other life lost wouldn't haunt me? If all of your children were in a burning house and you could only save one, which of us would it be?"

Something in his face shifted and his skin paled. Hope shook her head at Maddie. She'd gone too far.

"Don't answer that, Dad. I don't want to know. I'm just making the point that my choices and mistakes are mine to make."

Ben pressed his lips together and stared

at the kitchen table. Hope put her hand on his shoulder and offered him a glass of cold water.

"Honey, maybe you should go relax in front of the television for a bit. I think you've both made your points for the day."

Ben took the glass and moved toward the arched doorway that joined the kitchen and family room. He stopped next to Maddie and finally looked at her.

"That scenario with the burning house you asked me about? I was faced with that choice during my first marine deployment. They weren't my kids, but their faces haunt me to this day. I hope you never, ever have to make a decision like that in your life."

PHILIP'S BEDROOM DOOR was ajar and Maddie could see him hunched over a textbook. She knocked before pushing the door open.

"Hey, you're back. Mind if I come in?"

"No, I'm on my last problem and then I'll be done with homework."

"How was babysitting?"

"Meh. Ryan's still over there."

She was pretty sure babysitting wasn't the reason he was still there. She sat up against Philip's headboard and pulled her knees to her chest. His pewter-gray walls were filled with wooden floating shelves that displayed various collections. Most of the items looked antique—inkwells and fountain pens, WWII airplane models and bins of comic books.

"There. Done," he said, stuffing his books into his backpack and setting it aside.

"You like math?"

"Not really. It's probably my worst subject."

"If it makes you feel better, I never liked it, either. What subject's your favorite now? I noticed your World War II stuff on that shelf. Planning to follow in Dad and Chad's footsteps?"

Boy, that really was a terrible expression. How was one was supposed to fill their own shoes and leave their own footprints in this life if they were always trying to fill someone else's? Her brother's eyes lost the spark they'd held when she entered the room.

"No, I hope not. I like studying war, but wouldn't want to fight in one. I like history. All sorts. It's easy for me because most of the things we learn in school, I already know about from books and documentaries. Language is a close second."

"Taking after your big sis, huh?" She gave

him a wink, and a goofy smile that could only be Philip's took over his face.

"You mean you're passing on the title of Family Geek? Sweet. It'll make it so much easier to please Dad."

"I'm so not a geek. Which one of you gave me that title?" She grabbed the pillow out from behind her back and threw it at him.

"You assume it's only one of us? You have three brothers. Wake up."

"Fine. I surrender and you can have my title. For the record, though, Dad told me he thought you were smart. You have nothing to worry about."

"I'm not worried about grades. I just hate that, whenever the subject of what I want to be or what I want to study in college comes up, he always lists careers he thinks I should pursue. One time I mustered up the nerve to mention that I kind of like the idea of teaching history and you should have seen the expression on his face. He launched into this explanation of why all his suggestions were better."

And here she thought she was the only one who had to deal with their dad's constant disapproval.

"I'm sorry about that, Philip. Don't let it

get to you. Do what makes you happy." Her dad's reaction earlier pinched at her chest. He'd never shared the details of what he'd gone through as a marine. Probably because he wanted to protect them from it all. Or maybe because the memories were painful enough without having to describe them. She felt awful for saying the wrong thing to him and triggering that reaction earlier.

Maddie cocked her head and tucked her hair behind her ear.

"You know, Philip, I'm only now realizing that the way he is sometimes…it isn't about me—or us. It's about him. It really helps to know that."

"I wish you didn't live so far away."

She hated that he felt lonely, despite being surrounded by family. But she understood the hollow feeling wasn't about having everyone around. It was about being understood and accepted. That made it tough on a teen with a dad like theirs.

"Come visit me. The last time you all came to the States was to see Grandpa Eric and Grandma Nina. And last time we all went sightseeing in Philly as a family, you couldn't have been more than nine or ten and I wasn't even living there. You'd be in history heaven. I'd take you on a personal tour."

"That would be kind of cool."

"If you ever need to talk or vent or whatever, you know where I am. We could hang out via computer pixels. Just not at three in the morning my time."

"Sounds good."

She got up and demanded a hug. Fourteen had to be one of the toughest ages. Not quite a kid but not yet a grown man—and mood swings to boot. She really wished Ryan wouldn't tease him so much, but Ryan was going through his cocky stage. Even worse, he'd be off to college soon and poor Philip wouldn't have any siblings around. No buffer when it came to their parents. Her brain went into rapid-fire mode. He needed a friend. Someone to boost his confidence.

"I have an idea." It was perfect. Exactly what Philip needed, but it would be great for all of them and she was sure Hope would be on board. Her mom would recall how, before the family moved to Kenya, a less permanent but similar arrangement had helped them all heal. "Let's go."

"Where?"

"I'm getting you a present." There would

be less resistance from her dad if it was a gift. At least there would be if his heart really was in the right place, as her mom insisted. This would be good for Ben, too.

"But Jamal is off tonight and he took his car. Mom always needs hers available in case there's a medical emergency and Dad never lets anyone take his. He thinks drivers around here are nuts."

"We don't need a car. We can walk."

"We're in a neighborhood. There aren't any stores around here. Look, you really don't have to buy me anything."

"I want to, and it's just down the street. I saw a sign up at that pink house and it said 'free.' I'm *getting* you a gift, not buying one."

His eyes widened and lips parted. He'd seen the sign, too. Maddie felt like she'd swallowed a jar of jumping beans. This was perfect. She knew first hand just how much this would help him. And who knew…maybe it would help soften her dad's rough edges a bit. She did a crazy dance and put her finger to her mouth to shush him.

"If we run into anyone on the way out, we're simply going for a walk. Got it?"

"Got it." His voice squeaked and there was

more color in his cheeks than she'd seen in a long time.

"This, little brother, is how we geeks put the word *special* in *special ops*. Mission Furball starts now. We are getting you a puppy."

CHAPTER FIFTEEN

HAKI LOADED THE half-empty box of supplies onto his jeep. Ten goats dewormed and one treated for mastitis and he felt like he'd moved a mountain. It wasn't much in the grand scheme of things, but it meant something to him. He felt good. He felt free, even if he was using his day off to help the herdsman. It was only a small part of his dream, but it was something. The rest—the house and clinic on the hill—wasn't going to happen. Not because Pippa had never been behind it. He simply didn't have it in him anymore.

After sharing that spot with Maddie, the idea of living there alone or with anyone else was ruined. That tree, the rocks he'd helped her climb and every drop of rain that filled the river below would remind him of her and the few minutes they'd spent there together. But he'd still try to help out as many farmers as he could, whenever he could. This was his project, not Busara's, so he needed to use his spare time and cover the cost of supplies himself.

"Ashe oleng." The herdsman held his staff in one hand and put his other hand to his chest in gratitude.

"Meti inya mali," Haki replied. He was being honest. It really was no problem to do something that felt right. Something he knew to *be* right.

He finished loading his jeep and began the drive back to Busara. It was the longest hour of his day. His mind kept wandering, like a parched animal in search of water. He needed to shut Maddie out. They weren't meant to be. That was the bottom line, and it was no longer just about putting Pippa first. Maddie wasn't meant for life off the grid; she'd invested too much of herself into becoming a lawyer and advancing her career, which would wither out here. She'd made her priorities clear. She'd achieved what she'd come out here to do and then she'd left without a word. She'd won. Whatever had passed between them had been nothing more than a vacation fling...without the fling. It was over. He needed to move on.

He rounded the bend for Busara and could

already see Pippa's hair. She was in the grassy area on the outskirts of camp, playing with the orphans as they frolicked in the brush under supervision of their keepers. She looked in his direction and waved.

He pulled up and jumped out just as Mosi swung down from his favorite tree and scurried toward him. The little guy chattered and held out his hand.

"No treats, my friend. My pockets are empty." Haki patted his khakis to make his point clear.

"Hey. Where've you been all morning?" There was a bounce in Pippa's step and her face lit up the way it used to. It bothered him that she seemed relieved that Maddie was gone.

"About an hour from here. The Ngoro homestead."

"Oh. Okay."

He knew she'd figure out sooner or later that he was going to spend more of his free time helping the tribal farmers with their veterinary needs. It wasn't nearly as much as he'd dreamed of doing, but at least it was something. And yes, it would take away from the time he usually spent with Pippa—maybe he was avoiding her a little—but he needed to do this. He'd always put her first. He didn't regret that, but honestly, he was tired of putting this idea of serving the farmers on the backburner. He needed to stop worrying so much about pleasing her.

Maybe he was bitter or had lost his sense of honor and selflessness, but darn it, she was right. She'd said she could take care of herself and that he didn't have to rescue her or hunt her down all the time. Fine. If they were destined to get married, as the *Laibon* predicted, then Haki sure as heck wasn't going to spend the rest of his life walking on eggshells around her. She fell in step with him as he headed toward the house to wash up.

"I sort of thought we could spend your day off together like we always used to. Maybe splurge and go eat at Hodari Lodge or visit Mugi, Kesi and Tessa," Pippa said. He knew she'd only left Mac out because he flew his chopper to Busara pretty often.

"I don't think we have enough of the day left, and I promised Huru and Noah a long hike. You know…a guy thing," he added before she could invite herself.

She looked away and stuffed her hands in her back pockets. The guys had never left her out before. Well, maybe once or twice, but only when she was under the weather or had other plans. Taking kids on hikes was Pippa's thing. She loved doing it. That was why she volunteered to help out at Camp Jamba Walker so much. But Haki really needed to spend more time alone or at least not with women. Not forever...just long enough to straighten his head out and regain perspective.

"They're fifteen and sixteen now. Boys that age aren't kids anymore. They need time with their peers. Guy talk." He hoped that would soften the blow.

"Haki. Are we okay? Just answer me that. Because you don't seem okay, and I'm not sure what to make of it."

"We're fine."

"*Fine* is a bad word. *Fine* is just adequate. Mediocre. We were more than that before. Weren't we? We were planning to get married, for goodness sake."

He stopped in his tracks and hung his head. Had they been only fine all along? Or did it seem that way now that he could compare their relationship to his connection with Maddie? Did this mean he'd be making that comparison forever? That wouldn't be fair to either Pippa or himself. He scrubbed his face with both hands.

"I don't mean to worry you. If you start analyzing my every word and movement, we'll both go nuts. We'll be okay." Oh, man. That sounded worse than fine. He took a deep breath. "But I don't think we should rush a wedding. The time needs to be right. We need to agree on where we want to live. Our future plans. I mean, we've never even discussed how many children we'd have."

"Six. I really want a big family."

"Whoa. Apparently, you want a *really* big family. I was only giving examples of how unprepared we are. I know you love children, but I think I feel a heart attack coming on. Are you planning to turn this place into a city?" He swiped the sweat at the back of his neck.

"I don't see why we have to wait. Vows aren't about timing. They're about the couple."

He looked down at his worn boots.

Vows aren't about timing. They're about the couple.

A lump caught in his throat.

"Haki, are you ready?" Huru called out from the porch. Saved from answering by a question that was almost too on-the-nose. Noah was right behind him. Both carried stuffed backpacks and Huru set a third one down for Haki. His mom must have packed them enough food for three days, rather than three hours.

"I'm ready if you are." He jogged up the steps and picked up his rations. "We'll see you later," he called to Pippa, pushing Noah and Huru along a little faster than necessary. He sure hoped neither one planned to ask his advice on girls.

Pippa stood there with her arms limp at her sides. The fire in her eyes had dimmed and even her hair darkened as a wispy, rogue cloud passed between her and the sun. She was hurt. Disappointed. She'd never forgive him.

She lifted her hand and blew him a kiss.

A kiss he didn't deserve.

MADDIE REMOVED HER HEADSET and waited for the blades of Mac's helicopter to stop spinning, though the butterflies in her stomach kept fluttering in circles. A part of her couldn't believe she was at Busara again. She wouldn't overstay her welcome this time, but she needed to see Haki and share the research she'd uncovered. She needed to see things through.

In chess, the queen is powerful.

Adrenaline coursed through her. A queen ruling her hive. The sting of a bee. It was incredible. The study was amazing. The results, more than promising.

"Thanks so much, Uncle Mac. I'm sorry that I called you so late in the day. I plan on having the firm reimburse you for every flight. Just email me the invoices and consider it done."

"No worries. I don't usually charge family."

"This is work-related, and trust me, they can afford to pay you. Don't forget to include tonight. You're having to stay over because of me." The sun was about to set and the winds were supposed to pick up after dark. It was safer for him to fly out in the morning. Technically, the case was over, but it wouldn't hurt to try. As far as she was concerned, her job wasn't done. If Mr. Levy didn't want her to go above and beyond, then maybe he was better off working with someone like Patrick.

"Okay. I won't argue," Mac said, as they walked down the path that led from the grassy clearing where he tended to "park" his chopper.

The baby elephants were already getting

put to bed and the general buzz of camp had hushed to the rhythmic chirp of cicadas in search of mates.

Noah emerged from behind the old mess tent, where a chicken coop kept the camp's flock safe from night prowlers. He carried a woven basket full of eggs and picked up his pace when he saw them.

"Cool. I didn't know you guys were coming over."

"Last-minute plans. I ran into Jack at Hodari Lodge and gave him a heads-up, but you know how great your dad is with messages," Mac said.

"No big deal. We didn't think we'd be seeing you again, Maddie. Come on in. Everyone will be excited."

She wasn't so sure Pippa or Haki would be happy she was here, but that didn't matter. She'd come back for one reason only. Tomorrow, she'd return to Nairobi, spend several more days with her brothers and the new pup, then leave for the US.

"Where is everyone?" Maddie asked. "It's not usually this quiet until after dark."

"We took a hike today and just got back thirty minutes ago. Pippa is in the shower. She was walking backward to get a photo of Etana before Ahron tucked her in for the night and she tripped and landed on her rump in a pile of dung. Huru's in the other bathroom. Everyone else is in the kitchen except for Haki. I saw him go that way." He pointed toward the lookout platform.

Maddie set her bag on the porch and took out her laptop. This was it.

"I'll be right back. I have some information I need to show him that could help the Masai and elephants, both."

"If you find him, tell him dinner is almost ready. First come, first serve. If we finish all the stew, he'll be stuck eating eggs."

"I'll be sure to warn him, though fresh eggs sound good to me."

She hurried down the path to the lookout. Every branch, shrub and pebble threatened her with the memory of Haki's hands against her skin when she'd gotten stuck on the ladder. She tightened her hold on the computer as a reminder of why she was here. *Stick to business.* She could see him sitting on the platform gazing westward. Pools of creamy gold and rusty orange bled across the sky as the sun fell and cracked against the horizon. The death of a day. But with every death came the birth of something new. Tomorrow would be a fresh start for all of them.

He turned abruptly before she called out his name.

"Maddie? What are you doing here? I thought you were in Nairobi. What happened?"

He started to get up but she held up a finger as she trotted to the ladder.

"Stay where you are. I have something you need to see."

She noticed that the broken rung had been fixed.

"Take this." She held up her laptop. He reached down and took it from her.

"Are you sure you want to climb up here again? You got into a bit of trouble last time."

"The view is worth it. So is the research I need to show you."

She cleared the top of the ladder and settled down next to him, trying to ignore the warmth of his presence and the brush of his arm. She was here to make things right, not complicate them more. The last glimmer of light transformed the sky into strands of banded agate. She angled her laptop screen to avoid the reflection and pulled up the bookmarked page. The title alone said it all, but he reached over and scrolled through the article.

"Here's another." She opened a site with similar information and studied his face as he read it. He was close enough for her to press her lips to the corner of his mouth and trail her fingertips along his brow. He smelled of citrus and wind and something warm and sedating. She wished with all her soul that she could nestle her face against his shoulder and sit here with him until dawn.

She squeezed her eyes and cleared her throat. *This wasn't meant to be, Maddie. You need to let it go. Be strong.*

"Beehives," she said, grasping for reality. "I—I was researching solutions. We could possibly solve the problem with a beehive fence. Haki, it's worth a try. It makes so much sense. I also have a pdf on here that goes into more detail regarding the actual research. This zoologist at Oxford, a Dr. King, first came up with the idea to help save elephants. Pachyderms are afraid of having the tips of their trunks or the softer skin around their eyes stung by bees. They can sense—or hear—when bees are around, and they avoid them like the plague. So, what this scientist proposed and what seems to be working is erecting fence posts with hives attached to them. Not only do they deter elephants who might otherwise invade the crops, but the Masai can also be trained in beekeeping, and the honey can become a source of income. Everyone benefits."

Haki didn't respond right away, but she could tell his mind was churning. She bit the inside of her lip and waited.

"I've heard about them," he said. "I skimmed some information once about the organization that's working to help set them up, but I wasn't convinced. How effective will these hives be in the long run? And there's so much training involved. Supplies. Think of how many farms there are and how many hives it would take. There's probably a waiting list of farmers wanting those groups to help them set up. The process is slow to spread. What happens in the meantime? How many elephants might be killed or injured before then?"

Maddie's insides caved in.

"So we get help. We find a way to support the efforts. Talk to those organizations, and to the villagers. We could even help build fences. We have a saying in America. Fences make good neighbors. Can't you see that this could be the answer? Isn't it worth a try?"

Haki scratched his neck and looked over at her. His eyes settled on hers seconds too long and they both turned their focus back on the screen.

"You keep saying *we*."

She fiddled with the cuff of her sock and twirled the laces on her sneakers.

"I meant *you*. I mean, obviously, I won't be here. But if you're willing to follow through or at least look into it, I'll ask Native Watch Global if they can help. Given my ties to them with the case, maybe they'll be up for it. They might supply funding, come on board as a sponsor. It doesn't hurt to ask."

"You did get the proposal thrown out, so maybe they'll grant you a favor."

Maddie didn't respond. She'd wondered when that would come up. He was bitter that her side had won. She closed her laptop and started to unfold her legs. She should never have bothered coming here.

"Wait." He put his hand on her wrist and she was afraid he'd feel her scattering pulse. "I'm sorry. That was uncalled for. I wasn't expecting you to go to all this effort to make things right for both sides. I appreciate it more than you'll ever know. If you really think NWG might consider lending a hand, that would help. Either way, I'll follow through on this idea."

She took a breath, relieved that he didn't seem angry.

"I'll ask them, and I don't think they'll say no," she said, placing her hand on top of his. He felt strong and good and wonderful, but she wasn't going to let this be about her feelings for him. This was about the elephants and farmers—and him and Pippa. This wasn't about her. It couldn't be. She wanted him to be happy. To have a future he could look forward to.

"Haki, just imagine. If you go back to school and build the home on the hill you've dreamed of and work more closely with the Masai farmers and herdsmen...the hives could be a huge part of it. Maybe NWG will help you get started because you'd be helping bring balance back to life here."

He turned his hand so that their palms touched, then wove his fingers through hers.

"I want that. I want to go after that life, but you don't understand." He lifted her hand to his chest and the movement—or maybe it was static in the air between them—drew them even closer. She could feel his heart racing against her skin. Haki touched his forehead to hers. There was an intensity she couldn't pull away from. She wanted him like she wanted life to be only good, for evil to go extinct. She needed him like she needed her next breath. He rubbed the pad of his thumb against her hand.

"I know what we agreed on and that neither of us wants to hurt anyone, but Maddie-girl, I want that life more than anything, and I want it to be with you. I want to share it with *you*."

She couldn't breathe. She couldn't think. Her lips touched his, gently at first, careful, desperate...then he cupped her face in his hands and they looked at each other. They were playing with fire, but for Maddie, all sense of self-preservation had already burned to ashes. She wrapped her hands around him and they kissed again, this time taking everything and giving even more.

"Maddie." Haki's voice was a hoarse whisper laced with the bittersweet realization that this had to be goodbye.

She didn't want him to stop. She wanted this to be forever. In that moment, there were no casualties, no dangers, no world around them. Nothing else existed.

"Maddie? Haki? Oh, my God."

Maddie jerked away from Haki, almost tipping off the lookout's edge. Her laptop clattered against the wood as Haki shot to his feet.

Pippa covered her mouth and started back toward home with shaky steps.

"Oh, God, no. Pippa, wait!" Maddie pleaded.

She stumbled down the ladder and caught her footing before falling against the thorny trunk. She ignored the pain and deliberately kept her distance from Haki after he jumped down.

"Pippa! Hang on. It's—it's not what you think," Haki said.

This wasn't happening. Maddie was going to throw up. She never should have returned from Nairobi. She never should have come.

Pippa swung around. Everything had turned to shades of gray and the trees cast dark shadows across her tear-streaked face. She shook her head and her chest rose and fell as if the rains and floods had finally come and she'd been caught in the undertow, gasping for air...for life.

"Pip, I'm leaving. I'm going away. I didn't mean for this to happen. We were excited about something I researched and we got confused and—" She grasped for the right words but didn't know what to say. She tried to approach her. She needed to hold her and calm her down and fix everything.

"Get away from me." Pippa pointed her finger at Maddie. Her eyes reminded Maddie of a lioness who was cornered and dangerous. Maddie held up her hands.

"Pippa, don't read into this. Please let me explain. I would never hurt you on purpose."

"Really? I never want to see your face again. Go back to America and don't come back. Ever."

Her words pierced Maddie like a million poisoned arrows. If they killed her it would be a blessing.

"Pip," Haki said. He turned to Maddie and his face was stricken with regret. He looked at the ground as if he'd lost his way, then straightened his shoulders and tightened his face as he always did when he took control, needing to protect everyone and do what was right. "What you saw was nothing. It has never happened before and it won't happen again. I'm not leaving your side, okay? We're supposed to be together. Get married. Have kids. Six, if that's what you want. Nothing has changed."

Pippa shook her head.

"No. I don't believe you. You're a liar. I know what I saw. Oh, my God." She covered her head with her hands. "I knew this was happening. I thought with her gone, it was over. I've been so stupid. I trusted you. Both of you."

She turned and fled before Haki could stop her. He braced his hands on his knees and lowered his head a few seconds before starting to pace.

"I can't do this, Mads. This never should have happened. I'm sorry. This was my fault. I never should have let myself think that—"

"Don't. Just don't say anything else. You're right. This was a mistake. It was nothing. It meant nothing."

They were back to square one. Neither of them had wanted Pippa hurt; now all three of them were in pain. But Maddie was supposed to be the one destined for heartbreak, wasn't she? Pippa had been sitting next to her. Pippa had asked the question. Maybe the stones had answered for both of them.

A sob escaped her and she covered her mouth. She wasn't sure if her cousin would ever forgive Haki, so they could go on with their lives as planned. The only thing she was sure of was that she'd lost the two most important friends she had in her life. And if there was any chance that Pip and Haki could find a way back to each other, it could only happen if Maddie left and never returned. She owed them both that much.

She looked at Haki, knowing it would be the last time she'd ever see him. Everything around her—the trees, the path—rippled through her tears like it had all been one big mirage. Fool's water in an endless desert. She choked back another sob.

"Make her happy, Haki. Do that for me. I need to know she'll be okay."

The path Pippa had taken had grown even darker, but Maddie ran as fast as she could, stumbling once over a fallen branch and catching herself.

"Mads!"

She could hear his footsteps behind her, but she never looked back.

MADDIE TAPPED AT Pippa's locked room door again but the only answer she got was the muffled sound of sobs. The hopeless cries of a broken soul. Maddie squeezed her eyes and held her breath but nothing could stop the gouging pain of heartbreak, regret and shame. She made a futile effort to dry her cheeks and steady her voice.

"Pippa, please let me in. Let me explain. I swear I'll leave Busara and never come back again, but I have to talk to you first. Please."

Still no answer. Maddie braced her palms and forehead against the door.

"Pip. You mean the world to me. I love you. You're my best friend. I never wanted to hurt you. I swear what you saw was the first and only kiss. I'm so sorry. I don't know what came over me."

Still nothing. Maddie slid down and sat there with her knees tucked in and cheek to the door.

"It was all my fault, okay? A mistake. Don't blame Haki. You heard him. He loves you. He's ready to start a family with you. The two of you were meant to be. I'll never stop regretting hurting you and I don't expect you to ever forgive me, but please forgive him. That's what love's about, right? You two have a whole future together. I won't ruin it. I'm leaving for good. I just want you to know how sorry I am and that you'll never stop being important to me. I'll miss you. Be happy, Pippa."

Maddie waited a moment, listening.

Silence.

A punishment she deserved, along with losing her two most cherished friends…and the love of her life.

CHAPTER SIXTEEN

MADDIE SPLASHED COLD WATER on her face, but she still felt like her legs had grown roots and her brain was floating in dense fog. Coffee at four o'clock in the afternoon was not the best idea, but this post-nap grogginess was killing her. Everything was catching up to her and she had simply shut down—head on pillow for a fifteen-minute break and she was gone. Catnaps were supposed to be refreshing, but two hours? That was a lion nap, and she was feeling like she'd been mauled. She rubbed at the kink in her neck, dragged her feet down the stairs and headed straight for the kitchen.

Someone had already boiled water and left their mug and tea bag waiting on the counter. Maddie scooped coffee into a single serving French press and used some of the water, making sure to leave enough for tea.

Laughter carried from outside along with an occasional bark. Philip had to be on cloud nine. That pup was the best gift she'd ever given anyone. Free, yet the joy on her brother's face when he'd picked out his new friend had been priceless. Maybe he'd settled on a name while she was napping.

Maddie took a desperate sip of coffee as she crossed the tiled floor to the back patio. White sheers flitted and swayed as a breeze came through the French doors, along with her parents' voices. She split the curtains with her free hand but stopped short of stepping outside when she heard her name. She didn't mean to eavesdrop. She wasn't exactly hiding, but their backs were to her as they watched Philip teaching his puppy to play fetch.

"Our Maddie has always been sensitive. She wants everyone around her to be happy," Hope said.

"Philip definitely looks happy right now."

"I'm not only referring to him."

"I know." He paused, then deflected. "But I shouldn't have been so hard-nosed about him getting a dog all these years. You know how it is, though. Kid gets pet. Parents end up caring for pet. Neither of us has time or a predictable schedule and the boys are in school all day. I don't believe in leaving a dog alone too long."

He hadn't argued when Maddie had insisted it was a gift, but he did have her write up an unofficial but official-sounding contract regarding dog care that he'd made Philip sign.

"I don't either, but he's older now and very responsible. And the house is never empty for long. Besides, with obedience training, he could tag along with you sometimes."

Ben gave a subtle shake of his head.

"Hope, you saw how long it took for Coop to recover after his dog was killed in the line of duty."

Something melted inside Maddie. She had first met Cooper, her dad's friend and fellow marine, back when she was a little girl. He'd been struggling to overcome physical and emotional trauma at the time. Some of the physical ones remained, but he was doing well...living with his wife Brie, not far from Maddie's grandparents in their Pennsylvania hometown.

Was that why her dad had resisted getting a dog all these years? He was afraid that if he bonded with it and it died, he'd spiral out of control like Coop had? Maddie had always thought it was because her mama had planned to surprise Ben with a puppy—Wolf—right before she was killed.

"But he and Brie have always had a dog and they still raise service puppies."

Ben cranked his neck.

"I guess. Okay, I'll admit Mads did the right thing getting Philip a dog." He scrubbed his hands over his military short hair. "She always seems to know what's right."

Was she actually hearing this? Tears welled and her nose tingled.

"She does. The same sense that drove her to win her case. She wasn't trying to act against you, Ben—you know she loves elephants, too. She wasn't against anything so much as she was *for* something."

"That girl has a strong sense of morality," he agreed. "One that I wish more people in this world had. Then maybe I wouldn't have witnessed some of the atrocities etched in my mind."

Hope rubbed her hand between Ben's shoulders and, in that moment, seemed to sense Maddie's presence. She glanced back and Maddie creased her forehead in apology. She knew she shouldn't have been listening to their private conversation, but Hope just smiled softly.

"I'm going to go fix my tea. You sure you don't want some?" she asked Ben, as she rose.

"Nah, I'm good. Thanks. For everything." He held on to her hand and tugged her in for a kiss before letting her go.

Hope slipped past Maddie, pausing only to give her shoulder a squeeze.

Ben still had his gaze on Philip, as he rolled a tennis ball across the grass and his pup bounded after it.

Maddie took a long sip of coffee before walking over and sitting down next to him. His back straightened slightly the second he registered that she wasn't Hope returning with her drink.

"Hey. Feeling rested?" he asked.

Maddie twisted her lips and shrugged.

"Where's Ryan?" she asked.

"Babysitting again."

Interesting.

"Did Philip decide on a name yet?" She really didn't want to be the topic of conversation.

"Roosevelt."

Maddie smiled and took a sip of coffee. That Philip really was a history buff.

"Good old FDR, huh?"

"The one and only," Ben said. "Do you remember Wolf? He kind of reminds me of him with that coat color."

"You're right. He does. I'm guessing he might have some lab or golden retriever in the mix."

Ben tapped a red, rubber bone against his palm. Had he actually succumbed to puppy charm and played fetch while she was upstairs? He knocked his knee gently against hers.

"Philip said he picked the name because Roosevelt was a good man, well-loved, and mostly, because he gave people hope and helped them get through rough times like the Great Depression and World War II. He cared about people...like you do."

The fluttering in her chest had nothing to do with the caffeine. Had her brother really made that observation? Or was her dad only referring to the fact that she'd defended the Masai in the case because her mom had just made that point? Could it truly be Ben's opinion of her?

"He's a good kid, Dad. I think he worries too much about what others think of him, though." *Especially you.*

"He's a great kid. I'm proud of him. Of all of you."

Maddie ran her thumb over the abstract design on her mug.

"I'll be honest with you, Dad. I think you're just saying that because it's the right thing to say. I've never felt it. I'm not sure any of us does, except maybe Chad. I realize that I disappointed you by taking on a case that opposed—well, you and Haki and the whole family, but I have to follow my own path. I'm not you. All I've ever wanted was to please you and get your approval. I mean, that's all any child wants from their parents, isn't it? To not disappoint? All I do is disappoint you. Dad, I give up on trying to figure out what it'll take to get you to be proud of anything I accomplish, short of joining the marines."

"What?" He shifted, facing her head on. "Mads, of course I'm proud of you. How could you not know that?"

Did he want her to list the evidence? The lawyer in her itched to let him have it, but it wouldn't get them anywhere. It would start another battle. *Patience. Hear him out.*

"I don't know that, actually. I'm not sure Philip does, either."

"You think I care about the career you've chosen? That any of you has chosen?" He took a deep breath and tossed the bone out into the yard. "Mads, you could change your career a million times over and I'd still be proud, so long as you were giving it your all. That's all I ever expect of my kids. Of anyone, for that matter. If you're going to do something, pull out all the stops and do it well. And in my opinion you've always excelled at anything you put your mind to. I'm proud of you for that. Not just proud, but amazed by the kind, caring, focused, unselfish and nurturing person you are in the process. I'm proud that you stick to your guns and stand up for what you believe. I know I can be opinionated, but I would never challenge you if I didn't know how strong you are or think you could handle it. Mads, for the record, I'm the luckiest man alive for having you as a daughter. I know your mom feels the same way because she says it all the time."

Maddie set her mug down and wiped her face with the hem of her shirt.

"Why don't you ever say it? Why is it so

easy for you to criticize and question me instead?"

"I've never been good with words the way you are. That's a gift you inherited from Zoe. And trust me, I'm better now than I was before I met Hope, but sometimes I just forget to change the way I talk when I'm with family. As a marine I learned to go above and beyond and to expect no less from anyone else. The thing is, Mads, you set the bar high. I'm sorry if I've spoken too harshly or hurt you in any way."

She wanted to completely fall apart. All the stress and fatigue and heartbreak threatened to breach the dam she'd built, but she needed to hold it together. Maybe that was something she'd inherited from her dad. Staying in control…at least until she reached the privacy of her apartment in Philly. She'd already let one too many tears fall. She didn't want Philip to see her upset. She didn't want to ruin his day. And she didn't want to further upset her parents. Not on her last night here.

She leaned against his shoulder and he put his arm around her.

"Thanks, Dad. I'm sorry that I didn't see things from your perspective."

"Two sides to everything, right?"

"Yeah." Boy was there. Two sides or more. She couldn't help but think of all that had happened with Haki and Pippa.

Roosevelt came running up to Ben and propped his paws on his lap. He dropped a wet tennis ball in his lap and wagged his tail. Philip dropped to the grass and sat there catching his breath.

"He was supposed to bring that to me. The traitor."

Ben scratched Roosevelt behind the ears, then held up the ball.

"Mutiny!" Philip called out. Roosevelt barked and Ben threw the ball.

"Looks like you have a new friend, too," Maddie said. She had a feeling Roosevelt was going to be as good for her dad as he'd be for Philip. "I'm gonna miss you guys when I leave."

"You still have some time, don't you?"

She picked up her mug and cradled it.

"In some ways, you were right to worry about me not being careful. I made a mistake. I'm not comfortable getting into it right now," she quickly added. "Trust me on this. I did what I could to make things right and I think things will get back to normal a lot faster if I'm not here."

"But—"

"Dad. I've got this. Trust me."

He pressed his lips together and looked her in the eyes, then finally nodded.

"I do."

CHAPTER SEVENTEEN

HE SHOULD HAVE KNOWN he'd find her here.

Haki had scoured the area and all Pippa's favorite places for spying on wildlife and capturing them with her camera, but there'd been no sign of her. And here she was, much closer to home than he'd expected, parked under the same grove of trees that had marked so many changes in her life. Pippa once told him that this was the spot where Anna and Jack had taken her when she was only four to explain that Jack was her father. It was where Pippa had first told Haki that her love for him went beyond friendship. It was where they'd shared their first kiss. And now, he hoped it would be the place where she'd agree to give him a chance to regain her trust. To make things right.

Changes. Turning points.

He parked his jeep right behind hers but she didn't even spare him a glance. She couldn't ignore him forever. Not unless one of them left Busara. He closed his eyes and rubbed at his brow, trying to erase all that had happened since Maddie's arrival. Trying to wipe away all that had changed between him and Pippa...and Maddie. He was destined to be with Pippa. That's all there was to it. God, he hoped he hadn't completely destroyed that innocent, open-hearted love of life and people that made Pippa so special—the spark that lifted everyone's spirits whenever she entered a room. Maybe things between them would never be quite the same again, but he'd do whatever he had to do to make their life together better.

She looked away from him when he climbed onto the passenger seat next to her. At least she hadn't driven off. That was something.

"You've avoided me for three days now, Pip. We need to talk. If you still don't want to talk to me, at least hear me out."

He tucked her hair back with his fingers and gently lifted her chin. Her eyes were puffy from crying and she brushed his hand away.

"Hear what, Haki? You muddling through damage control? You saying that you're sorry? You think a simple apology will make things right again?"

She sounded drained and defeated. He took a deep breath and shook his head.

"No, I don't. I know it's not enough. It doesn't even come close, but I don't know where else to start. Pippa, I don't deserve your forgiveness. I don't deserve you. I've betrayed you and I'll never forgive myself for that. The fact that I hurt you keeps me up at night, and all I can think about is trying to earn your trust back. Even if it takes the rest of our lives."

"The rest of our lives?" Her brow furrowed and she turned her gaze beyond the horizon.

"I shouldn't assume. I'm just saying that—" he said.

"You're right. You shouldn't assume. I figured you'd find me here. It took everything in me not to drive away when you showed up. But the thing is, I've been going through every memory I have of us over and over and I keep coming to the same conclusion. That if things were right between us, this wouldn't have happened. We wouldn't be falling apart right now."

"We don't have to fall apart. I take full responsibility for what happened. Maddie loves you. She'd never intentionally hurt you. You don't have to forgive me, but I hope you eventually forgive her. She's your family. Your friend. What happened at the lookout between Maddie and me was nothing more than a mistake."

"No." Her voice broke and she covered her mouth as she finally looked at him. "That's the thing. I don't think it was. I think it was inevitable. Deep down, in a very selfish part of me that I'm feeling really ashamed of right now, I've always known there was something special between you two."

"You're one of the least selfish people I know and you're the last person on earth who should be feeling ashamed right now. Leave that to me."

"You don't understand. Even growing up, I could tell you had a thing for her. The way you'd look at her. The things you'd do to get her attention, even if I was standing right in front of you. And she was clueless. She didn't care back then. But I did. Her last year here before college, I realized that if I didn't let you know how I felt, I'd lose you. You'd tell her how you felt before she left. I couldn't let it happen. I didn't want this inexplicable thing between you to be real. I loved you. I still do. We were supposed to be together, always. I've never pictured any other future than one with you, continuing our lives here at Busara surrounded by loved ones. I did everything I could to be right for you. And everything was fine after Maddie went back to the States. We finally became a couple. Except a part of you kept holding back, whether you were conscious of it or not. I sensed it, though I tried to ignore it. You talked about marriage whenever I brought it up, but always put off that next step. I just wasn't good enough."

Her words speared him. Killed him. He shifted closer and took her in his arms, holding her until her breathing steadied and she stopped trembling. He couldn't remember the last time he'd cried. Even with Bakhari's death he'd channeled his emotions into anger and purpose. He'd stayed in control and tried to make things right. But this…this death of what he and Pippa had, seeing her in pain and knowing that he'd caused it…this was more than he could handle. He was worthless. Evil. A criminal, just like the man who'd attacked his mother had been. That man whose blood coursed through him.

Haki held her tight against his chest and let

his own tears fall against her hair. He pressed his lips to the top of her head and breathed in the scent of mango and morning dew and everything that was Pippa.

"Please don't say that, Pip. The worst punishment you could inflict on me would be to think you're not good enough. There isn't a word that describes just how amazing you are. Not even all the power, beauty and abundance of the Serengeti is enough to capture how loving and incredible you are. I do love you, Pip. I don't think there's ever been a day where you haven't inspired me by simply being you."

She pulled away and got out of the jeep, slamming the door behind her. What just happened? What had he said wrong? Haki hurried after her as she stormed past his vehicle.

"Wait. Where are you going?" She was headed into the middle of nowhere. Busara was in the opposite direction. She turned on her heel and glared at him like a buffalo ready to charge.

"You're saying all of that out of guilt. More lies!" she yelled.

"I was being sincere!"

"Why can't you just be honest with me?" she pressed.

"Pippa, I *am* being honest. What I said was the truth."

"The truth is that I'm the 'let's just be friends' girl. The truth is your love for Maddie is greater!"

"The truth is my love for Maddie is different!"

The air stilled.

He took a step back and ran his hands over his face. He hadn't meant to say that. The words were out before he could stop them. This was supposed to be an apology. He was supposed to be getting their lives back on track and instead everything was spiraling downward.

Pippa stared at him, her face suddenly void of emotion. He didn't dare step closer.

"I'm sorry." Haki's jaw ached and his head pounded. He couldn't think straight. He had no strategy, no common sense, no direction. She'd checkmated him. Forced him to admit that he loved Maddie.

"I'm sorry, too. I so wanted Maddie to already have someone in her life when I heard she was returning to Kenya. I shouldn't have had to feel like our relationship needed a buffer. I deserved to feel confident in what we had, and part of me did. The one thing I never doubted—the one thing that reassured me— was that I could trust you. Both of you. The minute Maddie and I stepped off the helicopter when she first arrived at Busara, I knew she still had a way of stirring something in your soul that I'd never quite reached. And this time I could see it all over her face. She was feeling it, too. But I told myself it was okay. That it was nothing more than nostalgia or cold feet on your part. That she'd eventually return home and our lives would get back to normal. That you loved me enough. And I reminded myself that, no matter what, I could trust you."

Haki didn't say anything. He had no defense. He'd let her down in the worst way possible. He couldn't take back what had happened. Pippa had every right to tear into him, and if he had any shred of honor left, he'd stand there and let her.

"You, Haki. The one person who knows me better than anyone else in this world. The one person I'd trust with my life. The one person I can truly be myself around. I could teeter at the edge of the earth and you'd never let me fall. I trusted you." Her last words were barely a whisper, as if meant for herself alone, but they bored through him just the same.

He had let her fall. He'd failed her.

She walked over to her jeep and leaned against the side with her arms folded. He hesitated, then followed.

They stood there, silent, tortured by the everyday sounds of bird calls, branches rustling and the distant, pleading cry of an elephant separated from its family. This was home to both of them. They were born and raised here. Their families lived here. What Haki had done didn't just affect the two of them. It affected everyone. Their everyday lives would never be the same again.

"What can I do, Pip? What do you want?"

"I don't know anymore. I'm feeling a little lost."

He nodded.

"Me, too."

Haki scanned the area. They knew every bush, boulder and tree. Either of them could walk back to the house blindfolded. Busara wasn't only a sanctuary for elephants. It had become theirs, too. Maybe too much of one. A cocoon. He'd confided to Maddie the urge to branch out and start his own clinic. Didn't

Pippa feel the need to break free and spread her wings? Being comfortable wasn't always a good thing.

"Our life here is important," Pippa said, as if she'd heard his thoughts. "What our families have accomplished here is phenomenal. The spirit of Busara is nothing short of magical. All those orphaned animals…they're as much a part of us as they are of Kenya. This place has been my purpose in life. Our purpose."

That was the problem. She hadn't made that choice. She was born into it, yet it was how she defined herself. He rubbed the back of his neck. There had to be a way of getting her to see that without making her defensive.

"Busara is more than that," he started. "It's an all-encompassing family commitment. One that I back and support with my life. You know I share your passion for the animals we save. But sometimes I feel like our lives have become so entwined in the big picture that our individual dreams and goals have gotten lost in it all. And maybe it's the wrong thing to say right now, but I think we've gotten lost in it all, too—going with the flow, falling into step with the expectations set out for us. Making everyone happy. Pip, I see that now. This isn't just about Maddie. You and I, we've been hanging on to comfort…to the familiar. We've been each other's crutch instead of facing ourselves and trying to figure out our path in life. Who we'd be if none of this existed."

"Don't assume that I don't know what I want in life."

Hadn't she just said that she didn't know what she wanted? That she felt lost? Haki pinched the bridge of his nose.

"I'm not trying to presume anything or offend you. I just mean that I've always wondered if us being together was holding you back. You've been breaking rules and challenging boundaries since the day you were born. I've always loved and admired that about you. You'll pull out all the stops when it comes to helping others, but I never see you doing that for yourself. When it comes to you, you hold back. I don't think you realize just how strong you are, even without all this. You have more fire in you than any of us. I just wish you'd let some of it burn for yourself."

A tear escaped the corner of her eye and she quickly dried it, then climbed back into her driver's seat. Haki stood next to her door.

"Are we ever going to be okay, you and me?" he asked.

Pippa kept her eyes on a kettle of vultures circling the tall grasses in the distance.

"I can't fault you for loving Maddie or for following your heart. What I'm not sure I'll be able to get past is the fact that you weren't honest with me. You made a fool out of me, and I'm having a really hard time with that. And I've always truly loved Maddie. But the betrayal… I just feel numb right now. I'm not ready to hear her out and, honestly, I need you to give me some space, too. You and Maddie are the last two people on earth I want to be around right now."

Could he blame her? At least she let him speak his piece. It hadn't fixed things, but it had to be enough for now.

"I'll leave Busara," he said. "I've been wanting to go back to vet school to specialize. I'll be in Nairobi and you can stay here. I won't be in the way. And maybe I'll build that clinic afterward and you won't have to worry about seeing me every day…or at all."

She started her engine and rested her hands on the wheel.

"What about Maddie?"

"Maddie has a life in America. A future

with her here just isn't realistic or possible. Especially after all that's happened. I don't deserve her forgiveness any more than yours. I've cost her something she considered priceless. Your friendship. I wish I had the power to give that back to the two of you, but all I can do is get out of your way. I've hurt you both. I've hurt our families. Just please believe that I never meant to hurt you, Pip. I've always cherished our bond. You're an important part of my life and always will be. That's not going to change."

The corners of her mouth creased in a sorrowful smile.

"It already has," she said, before shifting gears and driving away.

Haki watched her trail of dust get smaller.

She was right. Nothing would ever be the same again. Not with Pippa, nor Maddie.

Some wounds were just too deep to recover from.

HAKI STOOD AS tall as possible under the weight of their dark stares. All four men, like a firing squad. The sweat trickling down his back had nothing to do with the sun burning down on Busara. The leaves on trees were ominously still and even Mosi had the sense to keep away.

"I know what you all are thinking," he said, looking at his father, Ben, Jack and Mac. *Kill him*, for one thing. He deserved it. Jack cocked a brow as if he could hear Haki's thoughts.

"Do you?" Ben's eyes narrowed in a dare. Maddie's father had every right to want to kill him. Haki had let things get too far. He should have held back his feelings for her. He should have somehow drawn up a shield or cut the invisible rope that seemed to bind them together across space and time and all planes of existence. He should have been strong enough to stop what seemed inevitable and impossible. He scrubbed a hand across his face and tried to clear the hoarseness from his voice.

"You know how much I respect you, Mr. Corallis, sir. And I respect Maddie more than you know." He turned to Jack. "And I respect Pippa and care about her more than I care for my own life. I never meant to hurt anyone. This wasn't planned. Father…" He looked at Kamau. "You taught me to honor mothers and daughters. I'm who I am today because of your guidance and because of the unconditional love you gave Mom and me.

I would never intentionally do anything to disappoint you...or any of you," he added, for Jack and Ben.

Kamau's lips flattened. He didn't say a word, but Haki could tell from the way the creases around his eyes deepened and his chest rose that he still loved him back. That he felt proud and trusted him. That he knew Haki had never meant harm, much in the same way that Kamau had once kept his feelings for Haki's mother to himself, fearful of rousing the pain from her past.

Jack sat down on a stool fashioned from a tree stump and leaned his elbows on his knees in a less threatening position.

"I think that deep down, we all know that," Jack said. "But then explain to me why my little girl, who has always had enough joy in her face to light up an entire country, looks like someone—*you*—drained her of life. She's not even eating at the table with us anymore. No spirit. No spunk. Her eyes look empty. You did that to her."

The crack in Jack's voice made Haki's eyes sting. He clamped his teeth to keep his emotions in check. Emotions had gotten him in this mess. He'd always protected Pippa and here he'd turned out to be her biggest threat.

Ben folded his arms.

"And Maddie isn't doing any better. She wants to fly out this afternoon. She's a mess and wants to be alone. I don't want her alone. You know about her past. You know what happened after her mother died. Do you have any idea just how sca—" He stopped and swiped his nose with the back of his hand. "Just how scared I've been every year—every minute—of her life since, worried that someday she'd face the kind of emotional pain that would make her retreat into her shell again? The fear that, if that happened, she might not ever come out of it? That my Maddie would stop speaking for good? You've crushed her. Broken her. If she never—"

"Stop! Please, just stop." Haki's pulse surged and everything in him seemed to lodge in his throat. Maddie…a bird with broken wings. He needed to leave Busara. He needed to run through the desiccated grassland graveyards until he collapsed and was put out of his misery by wild dogs.

He paced and grasped his head, then let his hands fall to his sides. He knew Maddie. He knew her better than anyone here. And Ben wanted to accuse him of hurting her? Of all people, Ben wanted to accuse *him* of making her run and hide? His neck heated uncomfortably and his temples throbbed.

Maddie, hear me. Please, hear me. Sense me. I'm with you. I love you. What happened between us was real. Don't forget that. Please believe it. I hope someday you'll find someone who'll make you happy and never hurt you like I have. Please be okay.

"I messed up. I can't explain why. I grew up here enveloped by love and selflessness and loyalty. Those things are a part of me. They've always been part of my moral code, and I don't know what happened in the past few weeks. Ever since I found out Maddie was coming back to Kenya, it was like a switch tripped in me. And I should have ignored it all. I tried to, but I couldn't. I couldn't keep my head straight. I couldn't focus."

"Give the guy some slack." Mac lifted his old Air Walker Safaris cap, scratched his head and set the cap back in place. "He admitted that he messed up. I'd say he *was* messed up. Women will do that to a man."

"Careful," Kamau said. "We can't blame the women. This is not a safe place to sound sexist."

"Lower your voice. If Anna so much as

hears you imply we're sexist, we'll find ourselves living in the brush with hyenas," Jack said.

"We're not sexist. We all married strong women whom we respect." Ben raised his voice a notch and glanced toward the house. "They're our equals, if not better than us." He suddenly lowered his chin, wiped his forehead and cupped his hands over his face. "Our daughters are women, too—oh, man. They're not our little girls anymore."

"You're freaking me out," Jack said.

"Blame it on love," Kamau said. "Think about it. It's love that causes a parent to stress and worry. Then it tears them apart inside when their children leave home. Love is the drug that draws us to one another, causes the pain of a broken heart and then heals all."

"He's right," Mac said. "Love messes with us. It's like having the home you've always known gutted, remodeled and rewired...and finding yourself there, not knowing where the front or back doors are until someone turns on a light."

Everyone looked at Mac like he was nuts.

"Do we want to know where that came from?" Jack asked. Mac shuffled and shrugged.

"Tess and I are putting an addition on our cabin. That's all."

"You guys have at it. This is between Pippa and me." Haki started for his jeep. This was nonsense. Fathers or not, he couldn't stand having his dirty laundry hanging out for them to toss around and laugh at. If he had one crumb of dignity left, he was saving it.

"Whoa. We're not done with you," Ben said, pointing to the spot Haki had been standing in.

"Excuse me?" Haki curled his lips and pointed at the same spot. "I'm not a soldier or a child and I don't take orders from anyone. I've had enough of all this. The only people I need to answer to here are Maddie, Pippa and myself. Pippa and I, we spoke in private," he said, eyeing them pointedly. "You may not see me as the man that you are, Mr. Corallis, but we're not so different, you and I. We both care so much that sometimes it's taken the wrong way. I didn't see that in myself until now. I know I did something stupid, but I'm far from being a stupid man. I can think for myself and I'll figure out how to fix this. If there's one thing I'm beyond grateful for, it's that Kam has always taught me to fight my own battles." His father gave him a silent nod. He was sitting back and letting Haki fight out this one, too. Knowing he had faith in him was empowering beyond words. Haki cleared his throat and tempered his frustration.

"You may be a smart man, I'll give you that, but you'll never, ever catch up to the years of experience we all have on you. You cut those two girls off at the knees and you think you can fix them?" Ben asked.

"Women. They're not girls. They're intelligent, strong women. Maybe when you get that in your head, Maddie will stop hiding from you."

Ben lunged but Mac and Kamau had him sitting down in a flash. Haki stood his ground and glared at the men. This was it. The moment of truth.

"Maddie is stronger than you've ever given her credit for," he growled.

"Don't you—"

"No," Haki said. "I won't be intimidated or blamed by any of you. With all due respect, sir, you've caused her pain, too. You've smothered her with your fears. All she's ever wanted was your approval. She's smart. She doesn't need you trying to micromanage her life. Why do you think she decided to live on the other side of the world?"

"Are you out of your mind? I've never once thought of her as a failure. I made that clear to her myself, not that my relationship with my daughter is any of your business. And, for the record, I don't micromanage."

The other guys grimaced.

Jack shook his head. "We love you, man, but you're not the easiest guy to live with. Pippa once told me that, when she stayed at your place during college, she couldn't brew a cup of tea without you telling her she was doing it all wrong. Personally, I didn't know tea was your thing. I mean, military experience, machine guns and...tea time? Really?"

Haki ignored Jack's poke at Ben. Everyone had gotten used to their brother-in-law banter over the years. He looked squarely at Pippa's father.

"Pippa and I aren't getting married anymore...ever. That was her decision. I swear I was willing to devote the rest of my life to making her happy, but no matter what I do, I don't think I'll ever be able to make her as happy as she deserves to be."

A shadow fell across Jack's face and the dark circles under his eyes deepened. He shoved his hands in his pockets and looked over at the guys. None of them spoke at first. There wasn't much they could say to wipe away Jack's disappointment.

"So, you've hurt both and ended up with none," Ben finally said. "What happens to Maddie now?"

"Maddie's never coming back here. I doubt she'll ever speak to me again. And even if she did, she wants to stay in America and my life is here. I can't leave my work. You all understand that."

Kamau walked over and put his hand on Haki's shoulder. He paused and looked at the others before putting his free hand to his chest.

"Son. Love, even the purest kind between mother and child, is never easy. If it were, it wouldn't be so precious. And every one of us standing here believes that the kind of love that happens between kindred spirits, true soul mates, is priceless. We can all attest to the fact that nothing will keep two people apart if they are destined for one another. Nothing stands in the way of true love—not pain, history, mountains...or oceans." He glanced at Ben and Jack, who looked as wistful as angry fathers could look. "Not even death, Haki, will stop soul mates from finding a way to one another, whether in this lifetime or another. Unfortunately, sometimes the journey results in casualties. It can turn what we thought we knew upside down. You are a man who has never been less than true to yourself, so I have only one question for you. Why Maddie?"

Why Maddie?

The words echoed through him. All that Maddie made him feel swirled in his chest and tangled in his throat. Why torture himself more? Why sharpen the agony of losing her with every word of explanation? He glanced at Kamau, who backed away. A signal that Haki didn't owe anyone anything but truth and sincerity. He needed to heal the pain he'd caused, and Jack and Ben deserved to hear his reasons. He needed to give everyone closure, even if he suffered for it. Ben deserved to hear why his daughter was worth every bit of that pain.

Why Maddie?

"Because—because Maddie's my blinding sun."

All three men looked at him as if he'd sprouted goat horns and an elephant trunk.

The *Laibon's* voice rang through his head

again. *A wife who would light up his days like the Serengeti's blinding sun.* He pictured them living at the spot he'd shared with her, the place where he wanted to start his own veterinary camp. They would indeed be surrounded by elephants and goats, just as it had been written in the stones. Or had it? Could the *Laibon* really sense and channel energy the way the birds, antelope and all life around him did? Or was Haki simply grasping? After all, he'd previously thought Pippa had to be the blinding sun because of her hair. But maybe he had been guilty of the same crime they'd all been guilty of—not looking deep enough into his soul.

He didn't want anyone thinking he was mocking the situation, but he couldn't keep the smile from forming on his lips. The lead-like weight on his brow seemed to lighten with every thought of Maddie.

"Maddie's my blinding sun," he repeated. "She challenged me to see myself and to be myself. There's no life without the sun, and she's given me the courage to mold my life the way I feel is right. But she also tried to protect herself, to keep everyone at a distance, just like the sun does. But don't you see? I didn't care. I was willing to get burned.

Why Maddie? Because she makes me want to be a better man. We may have started out her visit with opposing views, but we quickly realized it wasn't about winning or fighting. The two of us make each other stronger and we're even stronger together. We're on the same wavelength. We *get* each other. Maddie, because she is my soul mate. *Maddie*, because it was written—"

No. It had nothing to do with how the stones had fallen. He didn't care what the stones said. He was in control of his own destiny. Everyone was. Perhaps their love was fated, but life gave him free will—the freedom to choose to be with her. To take that path. He loved Maddie and that's all there was to it. He wanted his future to be with her. He needed her to be his queen. His partner.

"Well, Kam," Jack said, "I think your knack for romance and poetic prose has rubbed off on our Hak-man, here."

"He's getting there." Kamau chuckled. "So, guys, what are we going to do about this?"

Ben stood up, scratched his knuckles, then flexed his hands. He looked right at Haki.

"I take it you love her?"

"Yes…*sir*," he quickly added. It couldn't hurt and might save his nose.

"And you'd throw yourself into the jaws of a lion for her?"

"Absolutely."

"Would you convince her to live here, in Kenya, so that she'll be near her family?"

Was that a trick question? Maddie wasn't even speaking to him.

"No. I'm sorry, but no. Maddie gets to decide where she lives and what would make her happy."

"Would you promise me that you'll always—*always*—be this honest with me and that, whether I want to hear it or not, you'll let me know if there's ever anything I'm doing that's causing her pain, without my realizing it?"

Haki swallowed hard. That was as close to an admission of fault or weakness as he'd ever heard come out of Ben. The man was as stoic as they came.

"You have my word, but with all due respect, sir, if you ask her directly and give her a chance, she'll tell you herself."

Ben hesitated, then spread his arms out.

"And I," Jack interjected, "promise you that there's a dangerous surge in the levels of estrogen in our midst and, since clearly none of us is vaccinated against, um, estrogenitis, the first symptom has reared its ugly head—watery eyes—and if we don't break this up, the second will take hold. I already see it coming. Hugging."

"I wasn't asking for a hug," Ben said.

"You stretched your arms out, man," Jack said.

"I was about to say something. Some people use hand expressions, like—"

"Okay, guys." Kamau stepped between them. "None of us is hugging. Especially not with Niara and Anna watching from behind the curtains."

"Yeah, old men," Jack said. "Beat your chest like silverbacks. Release some testosterone in the air. Make a show of it." Jack puffed his chest out and slapped his hands against it.

Kamau and Ben broke down. Haki smiled but wasn't sure where their laughing left him. Forgiven? Alone? Still without Maddie.

Ben sobered and looked over at Haki, then back at Jack.

"You thinking what I'm thinking?"

"Yeah," Jack said. "I'm okay with it. Pippa won't be alone. She has Anna and Niara with her in the house. I think she needs them more than she needs me at the moment. All men are the worst things on earth, right now. I heard her say it."

"She needs time," Kam said.

"True, and you all know I don't want her hurting, but we can at least try to reduce the number of casualties. We don't have any time to waste," Ben said. "We need to get this kid to Nairobi before Maddie leaves."

CHAPTER EIGHTEEN

MADDIE PICKED UP the carved box on her dresser. She ran her fingertips across the elephant that stood with its trunk raised overhead. A magnificent creature: massive, stable and physically powerful, yet so vulnerable. So easily heartbroken. How could she expect herself to be any less vulnerable than it?

The midday sun bounced off her silver bracelets as they clinked together against the box. She opened it. Her mama's necklace, Zoe's, had tarnished. She lifted it out, closed her fingers around it and held her fist to her lips. *I miss you, Mama.* Her eyes stung, reminding her of the bees and the arrows and pain that lingered in her heart. She set down the necklace and picked up a piece of ruled paper folded enough times to shrink it to a thick square inch. She opened it and read the poem she'd written as a teen. Man, she'd forgotten all about this. A poem laced with the hope and angst most teens harbored to the point of confusion. It was about a cat. She couldn't quite recall why she'd written about a cat. She'd never owned one. The closest she'd ever come to a four-legged pet was that puppy—Wolf—they were supposed to get before her mother died. She folded the paper back up. Maybe she'd adopt one. Or a dozen. She'd become the neighborhood cat lady and live alone until her skin wrinkled and hands shook like the Masai medicine man who'd given her fair warning about her future.

She sniffed and swiped the corner of her eye. There were so many little trinkets. A miniature purple pony with a golden mane, a figurine from a show she loved as a little girl. A lucky penny carefully set at the bottom of the box with the head side up. Her favorite marbles. Rubber miniatures of an elephant, giraffe, turtle and whale. And… She picked up a small cloth drawstring bag. The memories flooded back before she opened it. A single carving of a pair of doves. It was whittled from wood and lacked much detail. The work of a young boy…if Haki had ever been just a boy. The way the heads touched almost formed a heart. Maddie hadn't noticed that until now. A gift he'd given her before she left for college. Not really given, so much as left her. She'd found it in her bag after returning from her last visit to Busara. She closed her eyes. He'd put the carving in her bag when he'd taken out her book. He'd traded keepsakes without her realizing it at the time. She'd thought it had been a peace offering because of an argument they'd had. Maybe it had meant more, though, and she'd been so set on getting away and being independent that the message had flown right past her. Doves mated for life. She pulled out the tiny note he'd slipped in the bag with it.

It's not perfect. I've never made anything like this for anyone else before. Only you, Maddie-girl.
Love, Haki.

Maddie fought back tears and put the carving back in the box, along with everything else.

Pippa had stayed in Maddie's room during college. Had she looked through her things? Had she seen the doves and the note? Had she been keeping an eye out from the start to make sure no old feelings rekindled between them? Maddie tried to remember everything Pippa had said in the past few weeks. The fact that she'd ousted her at the dinner table her first night at Busara. The fortune reading. The questions in the tent at Camp Jamba Walker. *I've known him all my life and understand him better than anyone else ever could.* Had that been a warning long before the one when Haki had returned Maddie's book? Had Pippa been staking her claim all along? Did it matter now? Maddie had chosen to leave Kenya long ago. Maybe if she hadn't, things would be different. But they weren't and they couldn't go back.

The corner of her notebook stuck out from the soft satchel she used for her laptop and carry-on items. She pulled it out and flipped past her notes to the games she'd played with Haki during their campout. Page after page of hangmen in various stages. *Loyal, deserving, beautiful...*

A tap at her door had her wiping her face. She stuffed the notebook back in the satchel and set the box down near her purse. She needed to pack it and take it back with her this time. Hope cracked the door open.

"May I come in?"

"Of course." Maddie wrapped the box in an old T-shirt, unzipped her satchel and put it safely inside. She couldn't risk losing it if her luggage got lost in transit.

"Won't you change your mind about leaving so soon? Stay at least one more day."

"It's done, Mom. The tickets are bought. I just can't be here right now. In Kenya, I mean. I need to put this all behind me," Maddie said, slipping her laptop into its case and zipping it up.

Mr. Levy had actually sent her an email congratulating her on helping them win their case, and he'd given her the option of spending some extra time with family rather than changing her return-ticket date. She hadn't turned down his offer, but she'd changed her ticket regardless. Technically, family included grandparents, and a little time at their house back in Pennsylvania would be good for her. At least she'd be with family. She needed to get away from here, but she dreaded the loneliness that awaited her in her apartment. The one place that used to be her escape. For all that had happened, the past few days with her brothers and mom…even her dad…had felt warm and loving. She wished she didn't have to leave it all behind. But facing everyone after what had happened? She couldn't do it. She couldn't risk facing Haki or Pippa, either. They were a part of the entire circle of family and friends. It was her duty to leave them all in peace.

"Honey, if it was time to go, I'd understand, but you still have a week before you have to be back at work. You're running away when being alone is the last thing you need," Hope said.

"You don't know what I need." Maddie scrunched her forehead. "I'm sorry. I shouldn't have said that. I'm not myself right now. You're the best and you're always there for me. And whatever you said to dad yesterday, before I intruded, really helped. I can't thank you enough. But I need to focus on work. I need to go back and pray my efforts here will pay off at the law firm."

"You're going to bury yourself in work?"

"No. Yes. I am. What do you expect? I should never have let myself have those feelings for Haki. I knew it was wrong."

"You mean that you let yourself fall in love? It tears me up that you found it at the wrong place and wrong time, but true love is not a crime, Maddie. It's not something you can control."

"It is a crime if it causes someone harm.

It hurt Pippa, and I'll never forgive myself for that."

Hope guided her to the edge of the bed and nudged her down. She sat next to her and stroked her hair.

"Maddie, you were old enough back when we first met to remember things. You remember how I stayed with your family and fell in love with all of you. I'm betting that you remember when I left, too, and how painful it was. I know every situation is a little different, but I do understand how you're feeling. I do know what it's like to love with all your heart only to have it torn apart. Here, turn around and pass me your comb."

Maddie sighed and reached for the comb at the end of the bed. Her silver bracelets chimed delicately. Hope took the comb and smiled.

"My grandmother's bracelets. It means a lot to me that you still wear them."

Maddie ran her fingers around them.

"I never take them off."

"Do you remember what I told you the day I left America? You were upset and I was worried about leaving you feeling so vulnerable. But I knew how strong you were inside. I told you then that, 'When you wear one, good things come your way. When you wear two, happy memories will stay. And the magic of three is, it sets your heart free.'"

"I don't think it applies to this situation. Pippa, Haki and I...we were three friends. And now, none of our hearts is free. I know mine isn't."

"Isn't it? Maddie, sweetheart, it takes a free heart to fall in love, and I think you did. And Pippa and Haki, no matter what happens, you freed their hearts of the expectations everyone had put on them. I had heavy expectations put on me when I was your age. It took me a while to figure out that carving my own path in life wasn't a sin. My heart became truly free when I fell in love with your father."

Hope began combing Maddie's hair. She turned slightly so that Hope could braid it the way she had when Maddie was a little girl and every time she'd visited since college. Maddie closed her eyes and let the sensation soothe her. She loved Hope and missed her enormously when she wasn't here. Hope had always been the voice of reason. The family glue.

Hope began braiding three locks of hair. Maddie closed her eyes even tighter, trying to keep the tears behind her lids. Three locks. Three hearts. Three lives braided together, only now, she'd effectively taken sharp scissors and cut the braid off at her nape.

"How will I ever face Uncle Jack and Auntie Anna again?" The fear of someone visiting and asking her about what happened was part of the reason she needed to leave. "They probably hate me more than Pippa does. And Haki... he lives there. This whole mess has put him in an unimaginable position. I've messed up his life in every way. Dad denied it yesterday, but maybe he was right to worry and question me all these years. He must have known that someday I'd screw up again."

Hope stopped braiding.

"Don't you dare talk like that."

Maddie knew she'd struck a nerve. She'd crossed a line. If there was one thing Hope had been adamant about since Maddie first broke her silence after her birth mother's death all those years ago, it was that Maddie not blame herself for what happened. Nonetheless, Maddie had always thought that it was why her dad didn't have confidence in her. And every so often, when her emotions got the best of her, she could feel herself turn to the past and fall into old thought patterns.

"Your father is hard on himself," Hope said, as she resumed braiding. "He's had to be tough in his life. It's how he survived war, the violent images burned in his mind...and personal loss. But he loves just as deeply. For him, to worry and protect *is* to love, and he loves you. He loves all of his children."

"I know. I do. He loves you, too. You're both incredible parents. I mean that."

"Well, you're pretty incredible yourself."

Hope wrapped a band at the end of the French braid and gave Maddie a kiss on the cheek.

"There you go. Beautiful as ever," she said.

"Thank you." Maddie reached back and ran her fingertips along the perfect braid. "For everything." She turned, wrapped her arms around Hope and gave her a hug. "I miss you already."

"I won't stand in your way because I do respect your choices. But always remember, this is your second home. You don't have to leave. Stay as long as you feel comfortable. And give things time. I know 'time heals' sounds like a cliché, but it became a saying for a reason. Pippa will come around, too. I have no doubt."

Maddie swiped at a stray tear. If time

healed, then maybe leaving was indeed the answer. Maybe given time—and her absence—whatever Pippa and Haki once had between them would heal. It was the only way to make things right again and maybe, just maybe, someday she'd earn their forgiveness.

THE PLAN HAD BEEN for Uncle Mac to fly Ben and Haki to an airstrip in his choppe; then the two of them would get on a charter plane to Nairobi. Just Ben and Haki. Talk about plans changing.

Haki turned around in the front seat of Dr. Alwanga's minivan. None of the guys had been able to resist coming along. His entourage gave him four thumbs-ups and an equal number of grins. He turned back around and wiped the side of his face.

His father, Ben, Jack, Mac and now, even Maddie's uncle Simba—aka Dr. Alwanga—whom they had called in need of a ride since Jamal was scheduled to pick up Philip and Ryan from school, were all packed in the van. Haki had already been worried about rejection, and now he had an audience. God help him.

"I hope you all know that I really appreciate this, but I can't talk to her with all of you watching," Haki said.

"Why not?" Ben asked.

Haki looked back at Ben, then gave Kamau a wide-eyed plead for help. His father slapped Ben on the knee and laughed.

"He's just giving you a hard time, Haki."

"Am I?" Ben asked. He seemed disconcertingly serious.

"Down, boy," Jack said. Ben shot him a don't-mess-with-me look. Jack shook his head. "What can I say? You can be scary even when you don't mean to be. You're like a giant bullmastiff standing in front of his human family and daring anyone to come near."

Ben's shoulders sagged a bit.

"I am not. Besides, I like bullmastiffs. Good dogs. I should get one."

"I hear they're teddy bears at heart," Mac called from the third row. He flipped his cap backward and nestled it in place. "Don't worry, Haki. We're all just here for moral support. We'll keep old Ben here on a leash and give you some privacy. Say...two minutes? Not sure we can hold on to him longer than that."

Haki was absolutely not getting in the middle of the dog analogy.

"Try calling Hope again," Kamau suggested. She hadn't picked up when Ben called from the airport. Ben pulled out his cell and tried again.

"Nope," he said.

"Try texting," Jack said. "Sometimes they go through when calls don't."

He texted and there was a welcome few minutes of silence as Simba tried to maneuver through the heavy traffic.

"We're almost at the house anyway," Simba called out.

"Wait. She texted. She was on the phone with a patient earlier. Oh, no. She says she's picking up the boys at school and that Maddie already left with Jamal for the airport." Ben held his cell at arm's length so he could focus on the words.

"Are you serious? We could have waited there. We'll never make it back in time," Haki said.

"Not in this traffic," Simba added. "Unless maybe they get stuck in it, too." He stepped on the gas and slipped ahead of the car on his right, then made a sharp U-turn.

"Ask her what time they left," Kamau said.

"Hold your horses, everyone. I already asked," Ben said. Haki glanced back impatiently when the cell beeped. Ben had his arm stretched in front of him again—he really needed to give in and get reading glasses. The others were craning their necks to try to see the screen.

"Do you mind?" Ben glared over his shoulder. They all sat back. "Okay. She said they left about fifteen minutes ago."

"That would put them just ahead of us on the route back to the airport. We might be able to catch up, since I'm driving," Simba said.

"The idea is for me to reach her alive," Haki added.

Simba stepped on the gas.

"I have to agree with him there. You mind driving a little more carefully?" Ben gripped the back of the driver's seat when Simba had to brake hard for denser traffic ahead. Haki had seen Ben handle a jeep like a stunt driver when he went through KWS training in the field. But grassland wasn't the same as populated Nairobi, and everyone in the van knew that Ben's first wife had been killed in a car accident.

Simba slowed down a little.

"Is that them? Right there, just beyond the silver Peugeot." Jack leaned forward and pointed at a black sedan. Haki didn't see Jamal's car often enough to recognize the license plate, but the make and model looked right. But Ben would know for sure.

"That's them," Ben confirmed. "Can you get behind him, or next to him? Safely?"

"Just call Jamal's cell phone, for crying out loud," Mac suggested.

"Wait. He shouldn't talk on his cell while driving. Especially in this traffic and with Maddie in the car," Haki said.

Ben gave him a nod of approval. "It's okay, Haki. He has an earpiece. Hands-free," he said, as he dialed. "Hey, Jamal. Listen, we're a few cars behind you. I have Haki here and he needs to speak to Mads. If we lose you, just don't let her through security until we get to the airport. Or wait, can she just get on the phone? Or put it on speaker?"

Haki's palms began to sweat. She was right there...so close that he could see the back of her head. But the idea of apologizing to her over a speaker was enough to twist his brain in knots. He saw her flip around and look through the back window of the sedan. Her eyes widened when she spotted them.

She spun back around and shook her head at Jamal.

There was a pause.

"She doesn't want to talk. I think the best we can do is just follow them," Ben said. "Worst case, she flies out and you end up having to book a ticket to America."

"That would take months. I don't have any paperwork ready."

"Hang in there, Hak-man," Jack said. "We'll get you to the airport."

Haki's stomach suddenly felt like he'd eaten rocks. He glanced back, but the looks of regret and pity the guys gave him didn't help. She didn't want to speak to him. He rubbed at his chest and stared straight ahead. What difference would it make if he caught her at the airport? She had her mind set.

He caught her glimpsing over her shoulder again, only this time, there was something he couldn't put his finger on. A feeling. A sense that she was trying to tell him something. That—

"That's it. I should have known." Haki opened the glove compartment, then the side console. Nothing. "I need something to write on. Something big if you have it. And can you try to get around the guy in front of us so we're right behind them?"

Simba furrowed his brow, but seemed to catch on.

"Hey, Jack. Check the pocket behind my seat. Chuki keeps drawing pads and car games there for the kids. Is there something he can use?"

Jack reached in.

"This should work." He handed a pad and a red crayon up to Haki.

"He's a smart kid. I trained him," Ben said, thumbing toward Haki.

"I raised him," Kamau countered.

"Yeah, but we're his uncles," Jack said.

"And everyone knows kids listen to their aunts and uncles over their parents," Mac added.

"I think that's right. I can't get my kids to listen to their parents," Simba acknowledged.

Haki ignored them and tried to clear his head. He should have known that seeing everyone in the car, including her father, would freak Maddie out. It freaked *him* out. He needed to get through to her, but doing so in front of both of their dads and a full-blown audience was a bit…uncomfortable. He flipped to a clean sheet, tilted the pad for privacy, wrote what he hoped would make a difference…then pressed the paper against the windshield and waited.

MADDIE YANKED A tissue out of her purse and dried her eyes.

"Are you sure you're okay?" Jamal asked, eyeing her in the rearview mirror.

"I'm fine, thank you. I just don't understand. Why would he bring an entire village with him if he wants to talk? My father. He has my father and uncles back there. Jamal, that's embarrassing."

"But you can't be embarrassed if you don't even know what he wants to say. Why don't you hear the poor guy out?"

"Given what happened and how we left things—trust me, there's nothing we need to say to each other let alone in front of… *everyone*."

"When I was a young man, I wanted the world to hear how much I loved Delila. I wanted to shout it from the rooftops."

"This is different. He's not professing anything. He already professed his love for Pippa. He probably just wants to make things okay between us. He needs closure so he can move on." *With Pippa.*

"You don't know that."

"Did you end up shouting from the rooftops?"

"Me? No. I was much too afraid of her father." Jamal laughed, then motioned with his head. "We're almost at the terminal, but I *think* perhaps you should look behind you."

Maddie frowned, but turned slowly. Simba's minivan was keeping pace through the slow traffic. And Haki had a big, white piece of paper pressed to the windshield with three words on it.

You're my world

Maddie swallowed hard and tears stung her eyes. Why was he doing this? What about Pippa? He took it down, flipped a sheet and quickly put it back up for her to see.

my sunshine and rain

Her pulse beat at the base of her throat and her insides jumped like Masai dancers to the rhythm of their drums. She unbuckled, pulled her knees up and turned to fully face the back window. She didn't care about anyone else. As far as she was concerned, the only passenger in the van was Haki. He pressed the next sheet to the windshield for her to read.

Don't leave

She wiped her eyes and blinked to clear her vision.

Marry me.

HAKI COULDN'T BREATHE. No response whatsoever. She wasn't smiling. She wasn't moving. Panic rose in his chest. Sweat trickled down his temple. He couldn't lose her. He couldn't let her answer with nothing but silence. He flipped a sheet and wrote, then slapped it to the windshield.

Honk for yes.

"What in the heck is going on?" Ben asked. All the cars ahead of them, to the right and left of Jamal's sedan and just beyond, were honking repeatedly. Passengers were hanging their heads out their windows and clapping. A bunch of men riding in an open back truck were hooting and wolf-whistling.

"Haki, what were you writing? Everyone out there seems to know but us," Kamau said.

Haki kept his eyes on Maddie. She cocked her head at him and cracked a smile. That smile was enough to keep him alive for an eternity.

Simba pulled up behind them along the passenger drop-off curb at Jomo Kenyatta International Airport. Haki jumped out without answering the guys heckling him in the van. The only person he wanted to talk to was Maddie. She rushed out of her car and he stopped only inches from her. They stood there, taking each other in. He wanting to hold her, kiss her and never let go.

"I'm sorry for what I put you through," Haki said.

"I'm sorry, too."

"What you heard me say that night... I was trying to do what was right, but it was so wrong. Not being honest was wrong. You have to know that what happened between us and what I said to you on the lookout when we kissed...that was the truth."

She bit her lower lip and a tear spilled from the corner of her eye.

"I want to believe that. I want to feel that way again."

"Believe it. You're my life, Maddie-girl. I've always loved you."

"I love you, too. So much that it aches, but I thought—"

"I know. Neither of us wanted to hurt Pip, but we can't turn back and we can't turn our backs on each other. On what we have. Pippa is hurting, but she does understand that part of it. She deserves someone who can love her the way I love you."

Maddie pressed her hand to her chest.

"Is this really happening? Can we make this work?"

"I adore you. I'll cherish you the rest of my life if you'll let me. We have their blessing," he added, jerking his head toward the guys.

"I kind of gathered," she said with a chuckle. "Don't turn around, but they're all hanging out of the van. A little embarrassing, but so worth this moment."

He stepped closer and took her hands in his.

"No matter what happened or what we have to deal with in the future, this is right. We're right. We don't need words to know that, whatever lies ahead, we're worth fighting for. I know I had that dream of the place on the hill, but your life is overseas, and if you want me to—"

"No, Haki. I don't want you to give that up. I love that dream. I want you to make it come true. I want to be here. To move back and be surrounded by family. I want us to have our own someday."

"I want that more than anything. And I promise to always be there for you and to nurture your dreams, too, if you'll do one more thing."

He dropped to one knee and took her hands in his.

"Maddie Corallis, I want to spend every sunset for the rest of my life with you. Will you marry me?"

"Yes. Absolutely, yes."

She pulled him up and he took her face in his hands and kissed her.

The cheering from the airport crowds faded into the background.

All that mattered was his Maddie-girl, and that every sunrise for the rest of his life would bring the promise of another day with her. Soul mates. Forever.

EPILOGUE

Dear Maddie and Haki,

I know it's been a while since you've heard from me. I've enjoyed spending time touring Spain and am settling in for classes. I even had the chance to catch up with Nick in Mallorca for a day. He and his girlfriend flew up from a project he was working on in Morocco. He said to pass on his congratulations and to say hello to his uncle Mac and aunt Tessa for him.

Believe it or not, I miss you both. I'm sorry I wasn't in Kenya for the wedding. I regret not being there, though at the time I didn't want to make anyone uncomfortable. I wasn't ready. I'm sincerely happy for you both. I now realize that this is how everything was meant to be. You're both important to me and I love you both dearly. I want you happy.

Change is never easy and for me it

was so unexpected that I reacted badly.
I'm sorry if I hurt you. But I don't want
either of you to feel sorry…not for me
or for what happened. No one should
have to apologize for finding the love
they were meant to have.

And I'm grateful that life gave me a
chance to spread my wings, so to speak.
I'm fine. Actually, I'm better than I've
ever been. I want you to know that.

I'll be back as soon as I finish the program here. Kenya is too much a part of
me for me to leave it for too long. When
I'm done here, I want to come home and
carve out my place there.

Maddie, my mom told me you decided
to practice law at your firm's sister office in Nairobi. I'm so glad. This way,
when you two bless us all with mini
Hak-mans and mini Maddies—hint,
hint—Auntie Pippa can babysit. I promise I won't teach them to hang upside
down from trees. Well, no promises, but
I'll guard them like a mama elephant
when they're in my care. Promise.

Sending hugs. Spread them around
to everyone. Tell my brother to stay out

of trouble. See you when I find time to get away.
Love always,
Pippa

* * * * *

Catch up on previous titles in
Rula Sinara's
FROM KENYA, WITH LOVE *series with*
THE PROMISE OF RAIN,
AFTER THE SILENCE
and THROUGH THE STORM.

Get 2 Free Books,
Plus 2 Free Gifts—
just for trying the
Reader Service!

Love Inspired

Get 2 Free Books,
Plus 2 Free Gifts—
just for trying the Reader Service!

READERSERVICE.COM

Manage your account online!

- Review your order history
- Manage your payments
- Update your address

> ### We've designed the Reader Service website just for you.

Enjoy all the features!

- Discover new series available to you, and read excerpts from any series.
- Respond to mailings and special monthly offers.
- Browse the Bonus Bucks catalog and online-only exculsives.
- Share your feedback.

Visit us at:

ReaderService.com